FLAME

www.chellebliss.com
CHELLE BLISS
USA TODAY BESTSELLING AUTHOR

Publisher © Chelle Bliss September 17th 2019
Edited by Lisa A. Hollett
Proofread by iScream Proofread, Deaton Author Services, and Read By Rose
Cover Design © Chelle Bliss & Lori Jackson Designs
Formatted by Chelle Bliss
Cover Model: Dylan Horsch
Cover Photo © Aaron Rogers & Dylan Horsch

1

GIGI

"He wants you." Tamara, my cousin, elbows me in the ribs while she gawks at a guy across the bar. "And he's hot, bitch."

I glance in his direction and look away quickly when our eyes meet.

Holy shit.

The guy isn't just hot, he's Freaking Fine with capital Fs.

But the last thing I need is more complication in my life, especially after what happened with Erik.

I tear my gaze away from him and roll my eyes at my cousin. "I'm not here for a hookup, Tam. I'm here to be with my girls, not some…"

"Hot piece of ass?" She finishes my statement and shoots me a smug grin.

"He's not *that* hot." I throw the thin red straw from my drink in her direction, hoping she'll change the subject.

I'm completely lying, of course.

This guy is hot as fuck. He's not a pretty boy... although he is handsome. He's a little rough around the edges and probably couldn't pull off the corporate look to save his life, but that doesn't make him any less hot. There's no way a guy like him rides his bike on the weekends and sits in a cubicle all day to pay the bills.

He lives *the life.*

He's all in.

Balls deep in the biker world by the looks of him. This isn't a getaway weekend to let his shit hang out and cut loose for a few days. Nope. This life—the drinkin' and ridin'—is part of his core.

On a hotness scale of one to ten, he's totally a twenty. But Jesus, he's a little scary too.

I've known plenty of bikers in my short twenty years walking this earth. Growing up with a biker dad who had biker friends, I've been around guys like the hottie my entire life. Since I worked at Inked during my summers, my circle of bikers grew, but they were all good guys...at least in their own fucked-up ways.

Mallory lifts the shot glass in front of her lips and stares over the rim at me. "You know how to get over a douche like Erik?"

I shake my head. "Don't say it," I warn her.

She slams back the shot and winces before the liquid has even slid down her throat. "Fuck, tequila is no joke," she grits out and coughs into her hand until tears are in her eyes.

"I told you," Mary, her identical twin sister, says and shakes her head in judgment. "You never listen."

"I'm fine. Anyway, what was I saying?" Mallory

pauses as she slides the empty glass across the table. "Ah. I was telling you how to get over Erik." Her lips tip up. "Get under someone else."

Ugh.

That's totally Mallory, but not Mary. They are like night and day. Yin and yang. I'm not sure the world could take two Mallorys anyway, so it is a good thing they're so opposite. One's a wild child, and the other is a bookworm.

Tamara nudges another shot of tequila in my direction. "Have a drink. Maybe you just need a little liquid courage to go talk to Flame."

I raise an eyebrow, glaring at my not-so-innocent cousin. "Flame?"

"Well..." She glances in his direction again and shrugs. "He's hot as fuck, so Flame works. Like, he's so hot, you'll get burned." She laughs, finding herself funny even if no one else at the table does.

I tap my finger against the table, staring at her in disbelief. "You know what happens when I drink tequila, Tamara?"

Her smug smirk grows bigger. "I do, and I'm counting on it." She waggles her eyebrows.

Oh boy. Tamara is supposed to be my voice of reason on this trip. We lied our asses off to our parents about spring break. We told them we were staying on campus to catch up on homework and to study for final exams. They would literally shit a brick if they knew we were here, especially during Bike Week.

"Was Erik even a good lay?" Mallory asks out of the

clear blue because her mind always seems to be thinking about sex, even if it isn't her own.

"He was good." I grab the tequila because if my mouth is full or I'm coughing from the burn, I can't talk about having sex with Erik.

I don't know if he was good or not. He was good for me, but he was also the only person I'd ever gone all the way with. Sure, I fooled around with other guys, but my experience wasn't as impressive as some people's.

My answer to Mallory's question isn't a complete lie, but hell if I know if anyone else would say he was good or not.

I wince before the tequila even touches my tongue.

"Good or great?" Mallory asks.

I tip my head back, letting the liquid slide to the back of my mouth before it makes its way down my throat. My eyes tear up immediately, and I almost regret choosing the liquor over talking about my lack of sexual experience with my best friends.

"Does Erik look like he'd be great?" Tamara asks Mallory, saving me from answering.

Tamara knows all about my sex life and everything that happened with my exes. We've always been open and honest with each other. I know she's been with a few more guys than me, but she doesn't judge me. But Mallory doesn't have a clue because she'd totally judge me. She judges everyone.

"He looks like he'd be a lame lay," Mallory says, totally judging Erik.

"Oh, stop, Mal. He does not," Mary replies and

pushes a chunk of her long red hair behind her shoulder.

"I've been with enough guys to be able to spot a bad, good, and great fuck a mile away." Mallory turns her attention toward the hot guy who was staring at me. "And he—" she tips her head in his direction "—would be a great fucking lay."

Mallory has no problem putting herself out there with men. She's unapologetic about her sexuality and goes after what she wants. I envy her, but only a little bit. Not the part where she sleeps with any guy who is even mildly good-looking and wants to get in her pants. But the part where she's so self-assured and gives no fucks what anyone thinks about her or her activities.

Mary purses her lips and looks at her sister in disgust. "You can't tell by looking at someone. Stop with your bullshit, Mallory. Just because you're easy doesn't mean you're better than the rest of us."

Mallory sits up straighter and tilts her head, turning her attention toward her sister. "Sweetie, I'm not easy. Trust me. I make men work for this." She waves her hand in front of her chest. "I don't give it away to just anyone."

Mary, Tamara, and I laugh, but Mallory is shooting daggers at us, looking like she's ready to lunge across the table and wrap her skinny fingers around our necks.

"You guys can kiss my ass," Mallory snaps. "We're talking about Gigi and the sexy beast over there making goo-goo eyes at her. Is Miss Priss too good for a biker guy like that? Or maybe you're too much of a prude to even talk to a hot-ass guy like him."

I grind my teeth and glare at Mallory. Sometimes, I hate her. She can be such a bitch. If it weren't for the fact that she is Mary's sister, she wouldn't hang around us. But wherever Mary goes, Mallory's right there with her. They're a package deal.

"I am not a prude," I hiss and return her glare.

"Mal, by your standards, everyone around this table is a prude," Tamara says, coming to my defense.

Mallory tips her head back and cackles. "Tam, I know you're not a prude. My sister might as well be a nun, and sweet little Gigi over here—" she waves her hand in my direction, and I do my best not to slap it away "—is well on her way to sexual boredom."

The two shots of tequila I've already downed along with the beer I've been nursing are starting to work their magic. Between Mallory's annoying words, the hot guy across the bar, and the alcohol running through my veins, I'm ready to blow.

I curl my fingers around another shot glass, and I know I'm going to regret everything about tonight when I open my eyes tomorrow. But right now, I don't give a shit. I'm over the conversation, and I'm so totally over Mallory, I'll do anything to shut her up.

"Fuck you, Mal. I've been around men like him my entire life. I didn't grow up like you, in a mansion surrounded by overprivileged assholes. A badass biker guy like that doesn't scare me."

"Put up or shut up, sweetie." Mallory grins, thinking she's proved her point because she's always the unpredictable one in the group, while Mary and I play shit safe.

The chair scrapes against the floor and my knees wobble as I stand, but I can't stop now. If I falter in any way, I'll never hear the end of it from Mallory. The last thing I want to give her is more ammunition.

I lift the tequila to my lips, pouring it down my throat and barely wincing this time because it's already working its magic. "Don't wait up for me tonight."

Tamara's hand is on my wrist before I have a chance to storm away in dramatic fashion. "Do you think this is smart?" She stares up at me with wide eyes. "Don't listen to her. You know she's a bitch, Gigi, and she's just trying to piss you off."

I pull my arm away, feeling surer than ever that this is, in fact, the right thing to do. I'm going to prove them all wrong.

I can be wild.

I can be reckless.

I know how to have fun, and I can most certainly talk to a hot, badass biker guy without turning into a mumbling idiot.

"I'll be fine, Tam. I won't be back at the hotel room before the sun rises."

"Gigi, don't do this," Tamara begs, reaching for my hand again and missing.

"One second." I take another step backward.

Mallory's face is covered in a shit-eating grin, and Tamara and Mary both look horrified before I turn my back to them and make my way through the crowded bar.

Goddamn Mallory and her self-righteous bitchiness, making me do crazy shit. Well, it's not entirely her fault.

A man named Patrón is just as much to blame as the bitchy redhead sitting at my table.

My eyes lock with the handsome stranger's, and all rational thought and any reason to stop what's about to happen go right out the window. God, he's beautiful. He has the sexy bed-head thing nailed with his light-brown locks going all different directions, begging to be touched and smoothed. The way his lips curve at the side, exposing just a hint of white teeth renders me a little stupid, and I almost trip over my own two feet, but I somehow stay upright.

Reaching into my back pocket, I grab my phone and unlock the screen as I take the final steps to the guy who's freaking hot.

This man isn't a college boy, looking to guzzle beer and make out at a frat party. Nope. Not this guy. He looks like the type who would have a different chick on the back of his bike every night of the week and make zero fucking apologies for it, offering nothing but a good time.

"Hey." I try to sound upbeat and excited instead of terrified and pissed off. "What's your number, handsome?" I lift my phone, moving my gaze from his face to the phone and back to him.

The corner of his mouth ticks, and I ready myself for a barrage of questions, but they don't come. "Hey, darlin'," he says smoothly.

Oh my God.

His voice is like velvet sliding over my skin, deep and gravelly. I stand there, unable to move, staring at his mouth, surrounded by that killer beard.

I've never kissed a guy with facial hair. I wonder what it would feel like to press my lips to his. Would the beard tickle? *Get ahold of yourself, girl.*

"Name's Pike." He tips his head back, tilting it a little to the side as his gaze sweeps over me.

I open my mouth and close it because, for a moment, I can't think of a damn thing to say. I can't stop staring at him and all thoughts, rational or not, just seem to vanish. I don't know how many seconds I stand like this, staring at him while he stares at me, but it's more than a few and entirely too long.

"Gigi," I finally mutter like I'm a complete and total imbecile, unable to say more than a few syllables. I can't seem to stop staring in his eyes. They're beautiful, but I can't tell if they're blue or green in the shitty lighting of the bar.

"Still want my number?" he asks, moving his hand across his face and partially covering his mouth to hide the smile he's sporting.

I nod because somehow, I'm still mute. *Way to go, Gigi.* In this moment, standing in front of this hot biker, who I now know is named Pike, I am indeed everything Mallory said I am.

Pike gives me a chin lift, and I raise my phone before he rattles off a set of numbers.

"Be right back." I smile, or at least, I think I do. With the tequila, it could very well be a grimace.

Thankfully, Pike doesn't ask me anything else. He just dips his head, those beautiful lips still quirked before I turn my back to him and hustle away as quickly as possible.

My eyes are wide as I stalk back toward the table where Tamara, Mary, and Mallory are all sitting, staring at me in complete disbelief.

"Tam, take down his number. If I die, you know where to start."

"Don't do this," she pleads and covers her face with her hands.

"Just take down his number."

"Don't listen to Mallory, Gigi," Mary tells me, but I shake my head.

"You want his number or not?" I stare at my cousin, ignoring the other two. "This is happening, so you can either have my back or not, Tam."

"If you fucking die," Tamara says as she fishes her phone out of her purse, "I might as well die too, because my daddy and your daddy will kill me. They'll find out about our fake IDs, underage drinking, and me letting you walk out of here with a scary as fuck biker."

I tap my foot. "Just open your contacts and type, Tam. I don't need a lecture."

She snaps her mouth shut and nods. Her fingers move fast as I read his number off the screen.

"His name is Pike."

"Of course it is," she mutters into her phone screen. "I still think—"

"Don't," I snap as I jam my phone into my jeans pocket while she stares at me with her mouth hanging open. "I'll be fine. You have his name and number. He's not going to murder me. I mean, look at him." I look over my shoulder, catching those beautiful eyes again.

"I'm looking, and he's fine," Mallory adds like any of us give two shits about her commentary or opinion.

I swallow hard, suddenly feeling like I haven't had a drop of liquid in my mouth for days. "Don't wait up for me. I'll see you when I see you." I turn on my heel and head toward Pike.

"Gigi," Tamara yells out, barely audible above the music and chatter of the people around me.

I don't stop, though. I walk straight up to Pike, taking in his vintage T-shirt, torn jeans, road-worn black biker boots, sexy bed head, and just fucking spectacular beard and eyes and say, "Wanna get out of here?"

He pulls the beer bottle back from his lips, eyes sweeping up my body before his lips curve again. "Thought you'd never ask."

2

PIKE

"FANCY PLACE," THE GIRL SAYS AS SHE WALKS INTO MY hotel room, glancing around like she's waiting for something to jump out and bite her because it's a shit hole.

"I can take you back to your friends if you want." I can see she's not comfortable.

The chick—Gigi, I think she said her name was—drops her purse on the green carpet and turns to face me straight on. "I don't want to go. I'm right where I want to be." She sways as she speaks, clearly on the verge of drunk.

Why in the hell she asked me to take her to my hotel is beyond me. I'm not looking a gift horse in the mouth, though. When a hot chick asks me to get out of somewhere with her, I'm no fool; I take her wherever the hell she wants to go.

Drunk sex can be fun, but drunk sex with such a young chick may not be all it's cracked up to be. Besides being plain fucking stupid. I'm not an idiot. I've been with enough women, drunk and sober, to know when they want it and when they aren't quite sure.

Right now, the way she's looking at me, I'm not sure she wants what she's asked for. I grab the bottle of Jack Daniel's and pour two glasses, one for her and one for me, as she walks toward me. I push one in her direction, lifting the other one to my lips.

She takes the glass, staring at me as she moves slowly, lifting the rim to her mouth. "Pike, right?" she asks.

"Yeah, darlin'," I mumble into the amber liquid, gazing at her as she tips the glass back and takes a mouthful.

"I don't usually do this," she says, wincing as the burn slides down her throat and mine.

Those words, I believe. There's nothing in her body language that screams one-night stand. She didn't leap into my arms, attaching her lips to mine as soon as we walked through the door. I almost feel guilty having her here even if she asked me to bring her exactly where she's standing.

"Figured as much." I move to the bed, sitting on the edge, resting the glass of Jack on my knee as I look at this mint-ass chick with the wild brown hair, big blue eyes, and killer rack. But the thing that gets me most is those long-ass legs, smooth and shiny, dark from the sunshine kissing her skin.

"But I want to be here," she says quickly, moving to stand in front of me, but not close enough to where I could reach out and touch her.

"How old are you?" I ask, noticing the flawlessness of her skin as she stands near the bedside light.

"Twenty-two," she says, not meeting my eyes.

She's right at the edge of my limit. At twenty-six, anyone younger feels just plain wrong. I don't care how much they push their pussy in my face, I ain't looking for jailbait.

I take another sip, eyes locked on hers as she stares at me, shifting from foot to foot just a few feet away. "We can watch TV or just talk," I offer, trying to be a gentleman.

This wasn't exactly how I imagined the night going. When a chick like Gigi leaves a bar with me, I always assume there's pussy coming my way. And before tonight, I've never been wrong.

"You want to watch TV?" she asks softly, finally stilling and staring at me with her head cocked and one eyebrow higher than the other.

I shrug, staring at the beautiful creature before me. She's like a Greek goddess, wild yet subdued, with hair rolling down her shoulders, covering her breasts in long waves. "Wasn't how I planned the night to go, but I'm down with whatever. This doesn't seem like your thing."

Her foot starts tapping, fast and loud. "What's that mean?"

"Just what I said. We don't have to have sex. We can just hang out."

Why is this girl busting my balls so damn hard? Usually, a girl's already in my lap, lips on mine, riding my cock through my jeans and begging to be filled. But not this one. She's staring at me, putting more than a few feet between us, not moving a muscle or throwing herself into my arms. I'm trying to be a gentleman, but she's making it damn hard to keep my shit together.

She slams back the Jack, slides the glass onto the nightstand, and moves in front of me with her legs touching my knees. I glance up, and it's my turn not to move.

"I want you," she says softly, placing her hands on my shoulders. Her eyes warm as her fingers touch the tender skin on my neck near my collar, stroking slowly back and forth. "I want you to fuck me, Pike."

I don't know what I said that made her flip a switch. Thirty seconds ago, I could've sworn we were going to watch a movie, or at the very least, we'd be heading back to the bar.

But now… Now she's staring at me with hungry eyes and nothing but determination.

She moves forward, lifting her legs one by one, planting her knees near my thighs as she climbs onto the bed. I slide my hands to her waist, steadying her as she settles onto my lap, pressing her sweet pussy against my dick.

The kiss is sloppy, her lips tasting like Jack but her breath laced with tequila. Her movements aren't smooth, sending up red flags all over the place.

I glide my hands up her sides to her arms before hauling her backward. "Are you drunk?"

"No," she says quickly, gasping when I tighten my hands around her upper arms as she tries to get to my mouth again. "Are you?"

She's a sassy thing, ready to throw words back in my face without hesitation.

"Darlin', it doesn't matter if I am. I'm a sure thing. But it matters if you are."

She tries to wriggle free of my hold, but I keep her pinned, my hands on her arms with her body moving in my lap, making my hard-on worse. "It doesn't matter for me either. I just want to have sex."

The last thing I want is to be someone's regret. Tomorrow, when she wakes up, I don't want to be the biggest mistake of her life or even this week. I want to fuck a woman because she wants me, not because liquor gave her the courage to step outside her comfort zone for a walk on the wild side.

In one swift move, I have her in the air and then flat on her back in the bed. But I don't dare join her. I stand quickly, moving away from her as she blinks up at me in shock.

"What the fuck?" she hisses, trying to sit up but falling backward. "What's wrong with you?"

"I don't do drunk chicks." I run my fingers through my hair, pacing a path in front of the bed.

She grunts. "I'm not drunk."

By her behavior, I can tell this isn't her typical scene. Throw in alcohol, and this shit could blow up in my face big-time.

"Fuck."

"Well," she says, waving her hands over her body. "Hell yeah, baby. I'm waiting for that."

I grab the bottle of Jack, walking toward the table and two chairs near the window. "I need a minute to think." I'm trying to buy some time and a way out without pissing off this chick completely.

She's not timid or meek. She's quick with her words, and I know if I say the wrong thing, she's liable to go off half-cocked, completely losing her shit.

"Pour me one," she says, trying to sit up again, but she falls back down, letting out a loud sigh.

I fill my glass, collapsing into the chair after I set the bottle back on the table. "No. I think you had enough for one night."

"You're not my father," she snaps, fisting the comforter in her thin fingers and squeezing her eyes shut.

"It's a good thing I'm not. I'd tan your hide for doing what you're doing."

She throws up an arm. "Now he has a conscience."

"I always have a conscience." I bring the glass to my lips and look toward the doorway, wondering if I should just leave her here or take her back to the bar.

I'm leaning toward leaving her, letting her sleep off the liquor. The last thing I want is for her drunk ass to be on the back of my bike, sliding onto the pavement because she's too fucked up to stay on.

"Mr. Badass Biker Dude has a conscience," she says before she starts to laugh. "Mr. McHotterson doesn't want to fuck me because I had a few drinks." She pauses, and her laughter turns into loud giggles. "Maybe more like five or seven drinks."

I slide my gaze to her, but her eyes are still closed as she lies flat, unmoving except for her laughter inflating her chest. "However many you had, it was too many."

Her eyes open for a moment, still unfocused as she

looks to her side, watching me. "That's priceless coming from you."

I down half the glass of Jack, trying to get my shit under control because this girl is seriously getting on my nerves. "Coming from me?"

What the hell is wrong with me? An hour ago, I didn't give a shit if she was annoying or not. I wanted to fuck her until I passed out. But now she's lying in my bed, hurling insults and compliments in my direction because I'm trying to do the right thing.

"Well, yeah. You're a badass biker dude."

"What the fuck with that badass biker dude shit? I'm just a man looking to fuck."

"See." She waves a hand in my direction before dropping it to the bed like a ton of bricks. "Totally a badass biker dude thing to say." She closes her eyes again, and I stay silent, knowing the argument is useless. "I just wanted to get laid and get Erik off my mind. Is that so much to ask?"

She wanted to have breakup sex. She wanted to forget. I can understand that even if I've only had a handful of women who ever came close to breaking my heart.

I don't bother asking about Erik. I don't give two fucks about the guy, and at the moment, I don't give a fuck about the mouthy chick in my bed either. I sit here in complete silence, pouring myself another drink as she keeps on talking.

"There must be something wrong with me. Erik was awful in bed, or was I the one who sucked so bad I couldn't even get off?"

She's clearly way beyond tipsy based on the way she's spilling her guts. I'm not engaging in this conversation, but she has no problem continuing.

"If the badass biker dude won't even fuck me when I'm throwing myself at him, maybe I'm the problem. Two guys. Two cheaters. What else can it be but me?"

I'd love to tell her it's in no way her fault. She's beautiful even if she is a pain in the ass. I don't know a guy in his right mind who wouldn't explore her body for hours on end until he gave her a damn orgasm—or so many orgasms she passes out from lack of oxygen.

I lift the glass to my lips again, mumbling into the liquid as quietly as possible because I don't want to engage in her ramblings. I'm thankful when she doesn't say anything else and nothing but her soft snores fill the room.

"Thank fuck," I whisper, glancing toward the ceiling and wondering what I did to deserve this shit tonight. "Dodged that fucking bullet."

All I wanted was a good time. And instead, I'm saddled with a girl I don't even know passed out in my bed, snoring away like she's got no cares in the world.

I'm tempted to leave, go back to the bar, and finish the night the way I'd planned. But I can't bring myself to do it. We may not know each other, but I can't leave her in this room alone. When she wakes up, the last thing I want her to think is something happened when it didn't.

I'm not a gentleman, but I'm also not a complete asshole. I don't need any more trouble in my life. I had enough of that growing up and trying to break free of my parents.

I tip my head back, downing the rest of my drink before climbing to my feet and making my way toward the closet.

"Way to go, Pike." I pull out the spare blanket, ready to bed down on the shitty couch near the door.

This may be one of the longest nights of my life. And I have a feeling tomorrow morning isn't going to be any better.

3

GIGI

"Oh shit," I whisper, turning my head to the side, seeing the hottie from last night passed out on the couch.

Did we do it?

That's a big nope since I still have on my clothes from last night and they reek of tobacco and the day-after drunk stench.

My head throbs as I start to sit up, and I instantly collapse backward, wishing I hadn't had the tequila. "The bad news is, I have a headache. The good news is, I'm still alive," I whisper again, staring up at the ceiling.

Maybe I can slink out of bed and make it across the room without waking up the badass biker. I place my foot on the floor, my body still flat against the mattress and comforter that probably hasn't been washed since before I was born. I push that thought right out of my mind as my toes dig into the dirty shag carpet, and I slide out of the bed like I'm doing a fire drill. It reminds me of the old stop, drop, and roll they used to teach us during fire safety week in elementary school.

I keep my head up, trying not to focus on the damn stickiness of the carpeting on my palms as I inch closer to the door while crawling on my knees. I hold my breath, trying not to wake the guy and wincing the entire time because it feels like there's a little garden gnome playing the drums inside my skull.

I glance at the guy as I reach for the door, still on my hands and knees, holding my breath. My fingers are an inch from the metal knob when I lift up into a crouching position, feeling my escape almost at hand.

I don't want to be here when the guy wakes up. He's probably pissed because we didn't do it last night. I came back here fully expecting to bump uglies because Mallory had pissed me off so much, and I figured it was spring break and the perfect time to do something reckless.

"Where ya goin', darlin'?" asks the voice from last night, still sounding like sin, but deeper from sleep.

I freeze. "I thought I'd let you sleep."

He reaches behind his head, arm thrown over the back of the couch, and grabs my wrist before I can turn the handle. "You in a rush?" His touch is light. "I figured we could get some breakfast."

My eyes widen and my mouth falls open. "You want to have breakfast?"

His fingers tighten around my wrist, but not painfully. He's holding me with such a light touch, it catches me completely off guard, and I do nothing to pull away. "That's what people usually do in the morning."

"But…" I swallow, hating to bring up last night but thinking it needs to be out in the open. "But we didn't do it."

"Do it?" He repeats my words, rolling his body without letting go of my wrist until we're eye-to-eye. "Seriously?"

I nod and shrug, feeling like a bigger moron than I probably look. And that shit is pretty hard considering I'm on my hands and knees, trying to sneak out of his room without even brushing my hair.

The guy laughs. "No, darlin'. We didn't *do it*, but I'm hungry, and I'm sure the hangover you're nursing needs some hair of the dog, along with something greasy."

I blink a few times, wondering if I'm hearing him right or if I'm still drunk and not quite understanding what he's saying. "You want to take me to breakfast?"

He lets go of my wrist and rubs his forehead, leaning over the couch with his elbows resting on his knees. "Clearly she isn't as smart as she seemed last night," he mutters to himself. "This is what I get for wanting to bang the hot girl."

I rise up higher on my knees, my back straight, still blinking at him with my mouth hanging open. "I'm the hot girl?" I ask.

He lifts his head enough to see my eyes. "Are you shitting me with this?"

"Pike, right?" I ask because last night is a little fuzzy, which is odd because I didn't have *that* much to drink. But it had been a while since I'd drunk something stronger than beer. He nods, and I continue as I finally climb to my feet. "I am not shitting you. Are you shitting me?"

He throws his body back into the couch and runs his hand through his still hot-as-fuck bed head. "About breakfast?" he asks.

"About everything."

His gaze intensifies as he stares up at me with those dreamy green eyes. "I'm hungry. Are you?"

"Yes."

"Then let's eat."

"Okay…" I whisper as my stomach growls.

It won't be so bad sitting across from Pike and sharing a meal. We don't have jack to talk about, but at least I'll be full and can buy a little time before I go back to my room and have to face Mallory.

"And, babe," he says and pauses, sitting motionless.

"Yeah?"

He's on his feet, hand on my jaw, eyes locked on mine. "You were one of the hottest chicks there. You're a little fucking loony and can't hold your liquor worth shit, but you're off-the-charts hot."

My knees wobble a little like I'm drunk on his gaze and the words he just spoke. "Now you're really shitting me," I whisper, swallowing hard because I suddenly want to launch myself into his arms and finish what we started last night. "But I could eat."

The corner of his mouth twitches as his thumb grazes my bottom lip whisper-soft. "I could eat too."

Oh, fuck me dead. I know he's not talking about breakfast.

"So, breakfast..." My mouth's suddenly dry. My stomach isn't growling anymore; it's fluttering like a horde of tiny butterflies have taken flight inside it. I start toward the door, but he hauls me backward and in front of him again.

His eyes move down to the floor, but mine are firmly planted on his face. "You're probably going to need shoes."

I close my eyes, wishing I could start the last twelve hours over again. There's so much I would do differently, and maybe I wouldn't look like such a newb in front of this hot-as-fuck badass biker guy.

My face heats, and I want to crawl into a hole and die. "Yeah. Shoes would be good," I whisper, unable to take my eyes off him.

He releases me, but I don't move right away. It's like he's cast an invisible net around me, holding me to him. Maybe it's the fact that I haven't had any action in months, or the fact that every time he looks at me, I can see the hunger in his eyes...and he's not thinking about bacon and eggs.

"Sandals," he says as he sits on the couch and pulls on a boot.

"Yeah," I say, still not hauling ass because I'm too busy watching his every move. The way his muscles dance under his ink-covered skin is completely hypnotic.

"Do you need me to put them on your feet?"

"Yeah," I whisper again because my brain is fried, and I'm not thinking straight. "Wait, no." I wave my hands when he starts to stand. "I got it."

"Thank fuck for small miracles," he teases, putting his ass back on the couch as he grabs the other boot.

I silently chastise myself as I walk around to the side of the bed, finding my sandals placed neatly together, facing outward like he cared. I slide my toes between the plastic and close my eyes, trying to calm the fuck down. "Is it a far walk?"

"Nope. We're taking my bike. That a problem?"

Something about that makes me smile. Erik and Keith didn't have bikes. They both preferred their souped-up sports cars to the roar of a motorcycle. But they were boys, and Pike is all man.

"Nope," I repeat his words and tone. "Just let me make myself halfway presentable."

I don't wait for his approval before I take off toward the bathroom and shut myself inside. Leaning against the door, I allow myself a moment to freak out. Once I've whispered "Holy shit" for the tenth time, I move toward the sink and get a glimpse of my post-tequila face. I scrub away the smeared mascara with the little soap that is still in the wrapper next to the sink. As soon as my face is dry, I almost squeal when I find his toothpaste and place a drop on my finger, scrubbing my teeth and the rancid taste of last night away. "It'll do," I say to myself in the mirror, wiping away the toothpaste from my lips.

"Let's hit it," he says near the doorway, ticking his head toward outside as soon as the bathroom door opens. "I'm starving, and the day is wasting."

"What time is it?" I ask him as I brush past him and shield my eyes from the blazing sun.

"One."

"One?" I gasp, realizing I slept half the day away. "In the afternoon?"

He's right on my heels, laughing because I'm an idiot and making no moves to try to hide how stupid I can be, especially around him. "No, darlin'. The sun decided to come out at night just for you."

I slap his chest as soon as he's next to me. "Don't be a dick."

"Don't make it so easy."

"I don't make shit easy, Pike."

He reaches into his pocket and taps the cigarette packet into his palm. "No shit. I'm learning that quickly, and the hard way," he teases with a smirk, and it takes everything in me not to smack him again.

"Um, Pike."

"Yeah?"

I tuck a lock of hair that had fallen free behind my ear. "Can you not smoke?"

"Seriously?"

"Uh. Yeah. I don't like it, and it's not good for you."

He tilts his head but doesn't put up much of a fight before putting the cigarette back in the pack. "It can wait."

I try not to smile at my victory.

An hour later, we're jamming pancakes down our throats like it's an Olympic sport and we're both aiming for the gold medal.

"How old are you?" I ask Pike.

"Twenty-six. You?"

"I told you last night I'm twenty-two." Which was a

lie, of course, but I'm not going to tell him the truth now after everything that's happened. I am a month shy of my twenty-first birthday, even if the fake ID in my pocket says otherwise.

Pike nods, shoving another forkful of pancakes into his mouth, chewing slowly as he stares at me across the table. I squirm in my seat because I expect him to call bullshit, but he lets it go. "Where ya from?"

"Miami. You?"

"Up north."

"Northern Florida?"

"A little farther."

I roll my eyes. I lied about my answer, but at least I was more specific than "down south."

"Are you a badass biker for a living?" I set my fork down, knowing if I don't stop eating soon, I'll need a nap and probably assistance wobbling out of this dive.

Pike laughs, and it's the most beautiful thing in the world. Serious Pike is hot as fuck, but laughing Pike takes my breath away. "Nah, darlin'. I'm not a biker in that way. I ride because I love it. I'm not in an MC or anything."

"So, what do you do?" I ask again because he's cagey, and I'm not getting much out of the guy.

"I'm a tattoo artist."

My eyes widen because I know the community is both big and small. Sounds like an oxymoron, but I know the probability of most tattoo artists in the South knowing my family is pretty damn high. Inked is one of the most well-known shops in the South after being featured in dozens of magazines over the years.

"That sounds fun." I lean back in the booth, fidgeting with my napkin.

"What do you do?"

"I'm between jobs right now, but I'm looking for work as a graphic designer." Technically, I'm not lying. I am between jobs, but I leave out the bit about my college classes. I will be doing graphic design, but not on paper or in a digital format. I'll be tattooing skin just like him.

"What's your medium?" he asks, running his last forkful of pancakes through the lake of syrup on his plate.

"I'm a traditionalist. I like drawing by hand."

"Me too. Those girls from last night old coworkers?"

"Shit. I forgot about them." I pull out my phone from my purse, but I don't look down at the screen. "One is my cousin, but we all work together and figured Daytona was the place to be this week."

I glance down, finally seeing the five missed calls and ten text messages from Tamara. My eyes widen at the level of crazy in her text messages.

Are you okay?

Hey asshole, I'm getting worried.

Are you alive or dead?

Fucker… You better reply to me!

I know you're busy sucking cock and all, but use those fingers to text me back, bitch.

Goddamn it. Should I call the police?

Your ass better be dead since you're not replying.

I'm going to kill you when I see you again.

OMG. If you're dead, your father is going to kill me, and then my father will kill me.

I'm too young to die. I hate you.

"They lookin' for you?" he asks as I chew on my bottom lip, typing out a reply.

At breakfast. I'm fine. Great, even. Don't worry so much. I'll text you later, and we can meet up for drinks.

"Nah. They're good. They know I'm always safe."

"You know that shit last night was *not* safe."

I lift my gaze to Pike. "I'm alive, aren't I?"

He nods. "If you'd have gone with someone else, you might not be. You can't just walk up to a stranger in a bar, ask if they want to get out of there, be shit-faced drunk on top of it, and think you're definitely going to walk away unscathed."

"But I did." I shrug as my phone vibrates in my hand.

Thank fuck. I was about to call Uncle James or Uncle Thomas.

"You didn't look like a serial killer."

Pike's face grows serious as he kicks back into the booth, crossing his arms over his chest, showing off that ink and those muscles. "And what does a killer look like?"

"Fuck if I know, but not you." I smile because he's right, but I feel a lecture about to start, and I'm not going to listen. "I'm alive and breathing."

"Because it was me you left with. Anyone else and shit could've been way different."

I lean forward, pushing my empty plate to the side, and stare at the hottie who's now preaching to me on personal safety. "You're not my father, Pike, and while I appreciate the lecture, it's not needed. I was looking for a good time, and while it didn't end the way I'd planned, shit turned out just fine."

We're headed to Froggy's in an hour. Meet us there, and bring the hot guy and his friends if he has any.

"Fair enough."

"Now, my friends are going to Froggy's if you want to go too. But I imagine after last night, you probably want to ditch me for someone else. So, if you can just drop me there, you can do your thing and I'll do mine."

"You going to pull that shit you did last night with someone else tonight?"

I shrug and give him my best poker face. "I don't know. The day is young, and the night is long."

Pike's jaw tightens and his eyes flash. "I'm coming," he says quickly.

"Don't put yourself out or anything. I don't need a bodyguard, especially not someone I don't even know. I've survived this long without you watching over my shoulder. I think I'll last another night."

Pike leans forward, our knuckles touching on top of the table. He studies me. "I know you don't need me to watch over you, but if you're going home with anyone, it's going to be me, darlin'. We never finished what we started last night, and I'm a man who likes to follow through."

"That's so romantic," I tease, rolling my eyes.

"You want romance, I'll give you romance. You want to fuck, I'm the man to fuck you. Whatever you want, I'll be the one giving it to you."

"Why?" I blurt out, wondering why this hot-as-fuck biker guy wants to saddle himself with me all day.

"Because you seem hell-bent on a good time, and there's no one more equipped to give you that good time than me. You want to let your hair down and get wild, baby, I'll be right there with you. The one thing I won't do—" he touches his hand to his chest "—is let another man be the one to give it to you."

I suck in a breath, feeling like he's punched me straight in the gut. I should hate him. I should tell him to go to hell. I can have fun with any guy here. And trust me, there're thousands of them here this week to pick from.

"Okay." He's hot as fuck, and like Mallory said… The best way to get over Erik is to get under someone else.

That someone else might as well be the hottie across from me, who's staring at me like he's starving even though he ate a stack of pancakes it shouldn't be humanly possible to consume.

He leans back and reaches into his pocket. "Let's blow this joint and get the party started, yeah?"

"I don't want to go to the bar."

The thought of drinking right now makes my stomach turn.

"I'll take you anywhere you want."

"Take me back to your hotel room."

4

PIKE

I OPEN THE DOOR TO THE BATHROOM, TUCKING THE edge of the towel around my waist and stop dead. Gigi's standing in the middle of the room with her towel still wrapped around her body, hair damp and wild as she pushes her fingers through her locks.

"Do you have a brush?" she asks.

My gaze travels up her body, taking in her long, tanned legs as she turns to face me.

"I don't." I barely get the words out because she's still in the damn towel.

She said she was going to get dressed before I headed into the bathroom to wash off yesterday's grime. When she left the bathroom, she had her dirty clothes pulled tight against her chest like she was using them as a blocker between us.

"Figured you wouldn't with that hair." She ticks her chin upward, smiling at the mess that's on my head. It's always in a state, and I gave up a long time ago trying to tame the style in any way.

I rub the back of my neck, trying to do something with my hands besides ripping the towel off her body and having my way with her. "I can run and get you one."

"No," she says, taking a step closer to me. "Don't go."

I still haven't moved from the doorway to the bathroom. It's like my feet are glued to the floor. Besides my chest heaving and my heart pounding frantically, the only other thing moving on my body is my cock.

She reaches for my face, but I grab her wrist, needing to set her straight. "Darlin', don't start something I'm not sure you want to finish."

The warning is gentle and soft, but necessary. After last night and standing here in our towels now, I want her so badly, I'm aching to bury myself deep inside her.

Her eyes burn with just as much need as mine do. "What if I don't want to stop?" she challenges, stepping even closer so her towel brushes against my chest. "Maybe I want this just as much as you do."

"Maybe isn't a yes, Gigi. I don't want there to be any miscommunication about what's going to happen. I'm wound so tight right now, I might break."

Her free hand moves to my towel, groping my cock through the rough fabric. I suck in a breath and close my eyes, tightening my hold on her wrist. "Gigi."

She moves her fingers up and down my shaft, causing my legs to tremble. "I want you, Pike. I've wanted you since the moment I laid eyes on you."

I open my eyes, peering down at her beautiful face and soft smile. "You don't know what you're asking."

"I'm asking you to fuck me." She tightens her grip, moving her hand faster until I'm so hard, I'm almost panting. "I know exactly what I'm asking, Pike. But if you can't give it to me..."

"I can give you everything." I lift my hand to cup her face and angle my mouth close to hers. "I want to taste your mouth." I run my thumb along her bottom lip. "I want to taste you everywhere."

She moves her hand to the top of my towel, pulling the material apart as my lips crash down on hers, getting the taste I've been dying for since last night. I slide my hand into her hair, holding her face to mine as I swallow her moans and my own. Her towel falls away, pooling near our feet as her skin touches mine. It's like a million little electric shocks go off at once.

Her hands are on my hips as I slide my other hand to her back, memorizing the dip of her spine as I move my palm to her ass. "So fuckin' soft," I murmur against her lips.

"So fuckin' hard," she murmurs back as her fingertips move up to my abdomen, toying with my V.

My stomach clenches at the way her fingers trail over my flesh, sending goose bumps scattering across my body.

She's hesitant. I can tell by her movements this isn't her usual thing. Most women would be grabbing at my cock, but not her. She's busy touching my body, exploring what I have elsewhere and not what's the usual main attraction.

I pull my lips away, knowing I have to give her another out. She's a big talker, but maybe the reality of what we're about to do has finally sunk in. "We don't have to do this."

She shakes her head, staring up at me with hooded eyes. "I want this. I just need to take it slow, okay?"

"I'm not looking for fast, darlin'. You take all the time you want because I know I will." I smirk, our faces only inches from each other.

There's something so intense about staring at someone this close. Something so intimate about it. Rarely have I ever done this with anyone. I never care about the emotion in their eyes or the tenderness they need. But Gigi is different. I am different with her.

She lets out a shaky breath, lifting up on her tiptoes to give me her lips again, and this time, I don't hold anything back. I slide my tongue along her bottom lip, loving the way she tastes of mint and strawberries.

Then she pulls away. "I have to be honest with you," she says, holding my sides but keeping her eyes locked on mine. "I haven't been with a lot of guys, and I was always in a relationship if I slept with someone. This is all new to me. I need you to know…"

"I don't need to know anything."

"But what if I'm bad?" She blinks up at me like she's surprised by my words.

"You can never be bad at anything. There's no such thing. Do what feels right and good. Do what comes naturally, and I promise you it'll be good for the both of us."

She nods, seeming satisfied by my statement. I've never understood that way of thinking. I've never had a bad time in the sack, no matter the level of skill or number of partners the person has had before me. I don't care if she's been with one or a dozen guys as long as her mind, hands, and body are only on me.

"No more talking." We've already said too many words, and I can't go another minute without my body attached to hers in some form.

Her tits press against my chest as I take her mouth again, claiming her long and deep with the kiss, showing her how I feel and how badly I want her, experience be damned.

She slowly slides her hands over my stomach, moving to my abdomen before gliding them across my trail of hair, finding my hard cock. The moan that escapes her lips along with the soft warmth of her skin makes my dick twitch in anticipation.

"You're big," she mumbles against my mouth because I don't give her a chance to get away this time. I knead her ass cheeks, humming my appreciation at the way her hand strokes along my shaft. When her fingertips find my piercings, she freezes.

"Oh. My. God." She pushes me away with one hand, cock still firmly in her grasp with the other. Her eyes are glued to my dick and are wide, her mouth hanging open. "I didn't know you had…"

I move my hips toward her, and my cock bobs, showing off the shiny jewelry that has often gotten a mixed reaction from the ladies.

"Can I?"

I don't think anyone's ever asked for a better view, but if that's what she wants, she can do whatever the fuck she pleases. "Anything you want."

She folds her legs, kneeling before me on top of the towel that had fallen near our feet. I place my hands on my hips, stopping myself from pulling her in and jamming my dick, piercing and all, across her pretty pink tongue.

"You've never seen a pierced dick?" I ask.

She shakes her head. "Not this close, but I have seen them. Never touched one, though."

"Figured all the college boys were into shit like this."

"Shh," she says, peering up for a moment with her eyebrows drawn together before she goes back to staring at my cock. "It's an apadravya, right?"

"For a chick who hasn't seen many, you sure got the name nailed."

She shrugs, toying with the metal. "I know a little about this type of stuff. It's always fascinated me."

I can't take my eyes off her fingers as they move around the tip of my dick. The girl is a conundrum. She's innocent. There's no denying that. It's not an act either. But she knows shit too. Shit someone with her level of innocence probably shouldn't know. I don't ask because I don't care. There's a hot chick on the floor, eye-to-eye with my junk, touching me. That's all that fucking matters.

Her tongue pokes out of her mouth, sweeping across her bottom lip, and I grip my sides harder, trying to control myself. "I've heard it's pleasurable."

"There's one way to find out." I'm about done with show-and-tell, but then I remember I have to be patient. Something I've never been known to be.

"Can I lick it?"

Oh. My. Fucking. God. This girl is too much. "Of course." I'm not a fucking idiot. "Deep-throat it if you want."

She gazes up the length of my body, looking small kneeling before me. "Let's not get extreme."

"A guy can hope." I smirk and then hold my breath as she leans forward, that cute-ass soft tongue coming out from between her lips, reaching for a taste of my cock.

I can't take my eyes off her. The curve of her breasts as she moves toward me. The slenderness of her fingers as they wrap around my shaft, milking me as she tentatively touches the tip of her tongue to the head of my cock.

My body rocks forward, wanting her warmth and the wetness only her mouth can deliver. I close my eyes because watching this sweet, pure girl take me into her mouth is too much for me to handle.

"Fuck," I hiss as she slides her tongue over the tip, across the shaft, taking me slowly, inch by inch between her lips.

The warmth is instantly gone. "Did I do something wrong?"

I blink down at her in confusion. "Don't stop, darlin'. It was the closest to heaven I've ever been."

She smiles, liking the praise, but then something passes across her face. "I've been told I suck. Not in the good way either."

"Whoever told you that should be shot. There's no such thing as a bad blow job." Technically, I'm lying.

There is such a thing, but I doubt this girl could do anything wrong.

Her tongue's back on my dick a moment later, and I breathe a sigh of relief. If there's any more talking, I might lose my mind.

Her lips close around my shaft as she sucks me deep. No teeth with the perfect amount of suction and tongue. I'm in heaven, loving the way she uses her hand, not leaving an inch of my cock untouched.

"Just like that, baby." I tangle my fingers in her hair. I can't keep my hands to myself anymore. I want to touch her. I need to touch her.

"Darlin'," I say softly in a shaky breath as her tongue dances around the piercing, sending shock waves throughout my system. "Up, baby."

She blinks up at me with my cock still nestled between her lips, eyebrows drawn inward like she's confused.

"I want to taste you."

The corners of her mouth tip up, grazing the underside of my shaft with her teeth. I don't wince or grimace at the sensation because the last thing I want this girl to think is that I'm not enjoying myself.

I reach down, helping her stand before wrapping my arm around her back, hauling her toward the bed. My mouth is back on hers as our bodies fall backward, bouncing when we hit the bed. She lands on top of me, but she never stops kissing me as her hands slide across my shoulders, holding on to me.

I roll, pinning her underneath me, careful not to crush her with my weight. I kiss a line down her jaw to her neck, licking at the soft skin below her ear. Her fingernails dig into the skin of my upper back as she arches her back like she's offering her chest up to me and not satisfied with my mouth anywhere else.

Lifting up on one elbow, I stare down at her tanned skin, shining like a beacon underneath me. I slide my finger across the swell of her breasts as her breathing accelerates, and her eyes are fixed on me.

"You're so beautiful." I gaze down her body, letting my eyes linger on her wonderland of flesh.

"I could lose…"

I shake my head. "You're perfect the way you are." Suddenly, I'm a Chatty Cathy too, whispering sweet nothings to a girl I'll never see again.

She's fierce, yet unsure about everything sexually, almost like she's a virgin. I gulp at the possibility, hoping like fuck she's just had dipshit college boys in her life and that she's not entirely new to sex.

"Have you really done this before?"

She nods, giving me a small smile. "Yes, Pike. I'm not a virgin. I just…"

"Had shit boyfriends."

She nods again. "It was never like this."

"Like what, darlin'?"

"Slow and soft."

Fuck.

The last time I took it slow and soft was back in high school when I didn't know my ass from my dick. But here I am, going slow and soft for this girl because she needs it. Lying here naked with her, I'd do anything she asked without question.

"But I ache, Pike." She shifts her legs, rubbing her knees together and driving me crazy with desire. "I ache for you like I've never ached before."

"I'm going to make you feel good," I promise, leaning forward and swiping my tongue across her nipple.

She gasps, pushing her tits upward and against my mouth as I run my tongue around the outside edge of her nipple.

She burrows her fingers in my hair, pulling my head down against her skin. "Don't tease me, Pike."

I gaze down at her, noticing her rosy cheeks and the sheen of sweat across her skin. "I'm not teasing, I'm savoring, darlin'."

She growls a response, but I ignore her, going back to what I was doing and enjoying the fuck out of it. Her skin is warm and smooth against my lips, but her nipples are hot and hard on my tongue. Her body shakes as I close my lips around the tip, sucking with the right amount of pressure to drive her wild and have her on the brink.

Her nails claw my skin as her legs rub together, her body begging and needing more as she writhes underneath me.

I slide my hand down her side, making my way to her brown curls before slipping between her legs. Her knees fall to the sides, meeting the bed and giving me access to all of her.

The girl is wet. Almost dripping with need and I've barely touched her. I have to test her and figure out what she can take before I try to fuck her. The last thing I need is to hurt her, and she seems so sketchy and unsure about sex, I'm not sure I believe her depth of experience.

She rocks into my hand as I slide my fingers through her folds, parting her skin and stroking the pad of my thumb over her clit. She gasps, jumping like I shocked her at the contact.

I glance up, but she smirks with hazy, lust-filled eyes. "Don't stop," she begs me.

I mumble words against her skin, nipple still in my mouth, so I don't make a bit of sense and I don't care. I'm too busy exploring her flesh, tasting her body, and enjoying the fuck out of myself to speak or stop.

She tenses as I slide a finger down through her wetness and around the promised land, but as soon as I start to push inside, she relaxes and spreads her legs even wider.

She's tight, but not virginal tight. She may not have been with too many guys, but I'm not the first one to enter this territory. She doesn't even grimace as I push my finger all the way inside her body, relishing the warmth of her skin on mine. She moves with me, meeting every thrust of my fingers as her pussy contracts around me.

I pull out, adding a second finger, going slower this time and sucking harder on her nipple. She moans, pushing her ass upward and head backward like she's in heat.

"God, Pike. I want you so bad. Fuck me. Fuck me, please. I can't wait any longer. Don't make me beg."

I lift my head, fingers still buried inside her, rubbing

her G-spot. "I'll never make you beg." I smirk, loving the way this girl reacts to everything I say and do. "Unless we're playing that game."

"Not now. Please."

I reach across her, grabbing the condom I'd left there last night when I thought I had a sure thing coming back to my room. Gigi moves both hands to my cock, jerking me as I place the wrapper between my teeth and tear it open.

"You want the honors?" I ask her, loving the way she touches me.

She shakes her head and pulls away, leaving my cock feeling cold and alone. "Not with the metal. You do it."

I lean back, watching every movement. I make quick work of the condom after years of practice, barely noticing the piercing as I roll it down over the tip and shaft, readying myself for what I know is going to feel like heaven.

She places her feet on the bed, spreading her legs open as I slide between her thighs and line up our bodies. I can't take my eyes off her face as I lean forward on my elbows, ready to fuck this girl, but knowing I have to take my time.

I lower my mouth to hers, kissing her soft and gentle as my cock nudges her opening. She moans again as I press inside slowly. Inch by inch, I sheath my cock in the warmth of her pussy, causing my eyes to roll back from the tightness and pressure I haven't experienced with anyone else in a long time.

Her fingernails are on my skin, raking across my back as I push all the way inside until I'm fully seated.

She gasps into my mouth, and I swallow down her pleasure, taking it as my own.

I rock my hips, thrusting in and out as slowly as I can with as hard as I am. Sweat breaks out across my skin as the mix of pleasure and torture washes over me. She locks her ankles around my ass, holding me to her, not giving me much leeway to be aggressive.

I roll my hips, moving any way I can in this position. She pulls her lips away, staring up at me as I rock into her. I thought our moment was intense before, but it's nothing compared to this. Being buried balls deep, staring into each other's eyes, I'm momentarily winded from the intimacy.

My heart pounds as I realize I could like this girl. Not just like her, I could spend more than one night staring into her big blue eyes, listening to her babble about whatever she'll talk about. I could spend forever between these legs, fucking her, and never get bored.

I push my thoughts out of my mind, needing to stay in the moment and not think about tomorrow. We never promised each other more than this. More than a fuck at a shitty-ass motel in Daytona. She's a career girl with hopes and dreams that probably didn't include a guy covered in tats, working nights at a tattoo shop.

Get a grip, Pike. My mind keeps straying, and I have to remind myself to let shit go. Gigi grounds me, bringing me back to the moment when her tongue runs along the skin near my collarbone.

"Harder," she pleads, digging her heels firmly in my ass.

I pull back, breaking the bond her ankles have around my back and slam into her.

"Yes!" she screams, bucking against me, grinding her pussy against my body. "Fuck yes!"

It doesn't take but a few more minutes for me to teeter on the edge of orgasm. With one hand, I reach between us, rubbing her clit as I thrust inside her, deep and sharp, quickening the pace each time.

She gasps for air as her body locks up, following me over the cliff into bliss. "Jesus," I murmur as I nearly collapse on top of her.

"Again," she says almost immediately.

"Little tiger," I whisper, staring down at the most beautiful girl I've ever seen.

"I hope you're up for more, big boy, because I'm nowhere near done."

"I could go all night."

She pushes me backward, climbing on top of me. "Let's see if you mean what you say."

I slide out from underneath her as she paws at me like she's going to pull me back to the bed. "I'm going to need to get rid of this condom and get another."

"Take your time. I'll just stare at your ass and touch myself."

I turn, looking over my shoulder to see she's a girl of her word. "Fucking incredible," I whisper, running to the bathroom because I'm nowhere near done fucking her.

5

GIGI

FIFTEEN MONTHS LATER

THE DAY I STEPPED OFF THE STAGE WITH THE DIPLOMA IN my hand, I felt like I was finishing a chapter and starting a new one. The grown-up part of my life I'd been waiting for since I was a little kid.

The only thing I'd ever dreamed about was working at Inked. My artistic skills, I clearly got from my dad. He'd sit with me for hours when I barely reached his hip, watching me draw picture after picture as I tried to copy his work. He was a patient teacher and an even better father. There isn't a time in my life I remember art not being part of my world.

My poor mother didn't have a creative bone in her body. She was a numbers girl, and math bored the crap out of me…much to her disappointment. She dreamed of me growing up and becoming some dull corporate suit, slaving away for someone else instead of being tied to Inked.

After four years of college and four summers

interning at Inked, I am finally ready to take my rightful spot, or should I say chair, at the shop.

"I don't understand why you need to move out," my mom says as I sit down at the kitchen table with a cup of coffee, trying to get time to pass a little quicker.

I can't wait to get to the shop. My uncle Bear decided he would be my first official customer, and I couldn't be happier. But I could probably ink a piece of shit on him, and he'd still love it.

"I love living here, Ma, but I want to have my own place. You're great and Dad is the best, but I haven't lived under your roof and with your rules in four years. I just think it's the next step I have to take in my new life. Living here feels like taking a step backward, and I'm all about moving forward."

"Can't you stay a few weeks? I've missed you." She leans against the counter and sips her coffee, looking just as beautiful as ever.

"I'm picking up my keys before work today, but it'll take me a few days to get everything in order, so I'll be here until the place is ready to move in."

"Take your time, baby," she says softly before letting out a long and very dramatic sigh. "Make sure it's perfect before you officially move out."

I want to tell her that I moved out four years ago, but I don't. My mom is a big softy, and by the way she's looking at me, she's about to cry.

"Did you move back home after college?" I ask her.

She shakes her head. "I love my parents, but there was no way I could ever live under their roof again. I knew once I left for college, I'd never go back."

"Even if they were great parents, could you have gone backward after having a taste of freedom?"

She slides onto the chair next to me and places her cup on the table. "I don't think I could've gone back." Her lips pull downward because she realizes where I'm coming from, and no matter what she says, I won't change my mind. "Maybe we could build a guesthouse out back for you."

"Mom, come on now. I already signed my lease. And I'm sorry, I love you both, but living in the backyard won't work for me."

It's a sweet gesture and completely my mom, but in no way, shape, or form will that type of living arrangement ever work for me. I'm already going to be spending all day working with my dad. The last thing I want is to see him every night, checking up on me, and living under the Gallo microscope.

"I worry about you living alone."

"I'll be fine, Ma. Tamara is going to live with me for the summer, and when she's home on break too. If all goes well, when she graduates next year, she'll move in with me too. Where's Dad?" I change the subject because there's no way I'm living at home, and I know the mention of my cousin's name will get Mom off my back…at least for a little while.

She wraps her hand around her coffee mug and stares out the window overlooking the backyard. "He went in early. There's a new artist starting today, and he wants to train him before everyone gets there."

"Maybe I should be there too. Why didn't Dad ask me to go?"

Mom laughs. "Baby, you grew up in that place, and you've been working there for four summers. I'd hardly call you a new employee." She laughs and brings her gaze back to me. "I'm pretty sure you could train this boy yourself."

I push away from the table, about to stand, when she covers my hand with hers.

"Stay a little longer. You don't have to be there for thirty minutes, and I feel like we never have quiet time like this together."

"I don't want to be the last one there on my first day, Mom. How about we go shopping on my day off and buy some stuff for my new apartment?"

I'm grasping at straws here, but the last thing I want to do is sit here another twenty minutes, listening to my mother hem and haw about how I shouldn't move out. I figure if I ask her to help decorate my new place, she'll feel more invested, or at the very least, like she helped me.

That's the thing about Suzy Gallo. She's not one to sit idly by when her loved ones are in need. It doesn't matter that I only need help to pick out the perfect throw pillow or the best pots and pans, she wants to be included.

Right on cue, her face lights up. "I would love that. I know all the best places we can go too. We'll make a day of it."

"It's a date, Mom. I'm off Friday, if that works. But if not, I completely understand."

"Luna and Rosie have cheerleading camp starting

on Wednesday," Mom says, looking pained and moderately horrified that her two daughters are cheerleaders. "So, I have all day on Friday to be with you."

"Perfect." I push away from the table and walk toward the sink. "I better run. The landlord is probably waiting for me, and I want to make a good impression."

Mom follows me, leaving her coffee mug where it was sitting on the table. She leans against the counter, staring at me as I rinse and place my mug in the dishwasher. "I'm proud of you, sweetheart. I'm proud of the independent woman you've become."

My insides warm. "That's because I had two kick-ass parents."

Her smile falters.

I know she wants to chastise me for my crude language, because she's never been one for cussing.

"We want nothing but the best for you."

I lean over and kiss her cheek because, hell, I love my mother. "I couldn't have asked for a better mother. I mean it, Mom."

She wraps her arms around me, hauling me close. "I love you, baby. I can't believe you're old enough to move out. I never wanted this day to come, but now that it has, I couldn't be prouder."

That's my mom. She's full of all the goodness in the world. She never has a mean thing to say about anyone or anything. She wears rose-colored glasses when it comes to life. There are times where she's a little overprotective and worried about everything for no good reason, but I wouldn't change a thing about her.

"I have to run, Mom." I pull away from her embrace even though she tries to squeeze me tighter. "I don't want to be late on my first day."

Mom laughs. "Well, at least you know the owners. I'm pretty sure they won't fire you if you're a few minutes late."

"Mom, I don't want to be treated any different."

"Different from whom, baby girl? Besides Kat, everyone is family and works by their own rules."

I shrug. "The new guy. I don't want to set a bad example, ya know?"

She nods. "Go and have a great first day at work."

It's all silly. I'd worked at Inked for four summers, but interning is entirely different from earning my seat at the shop. Today feels like the first day of my adult life. No more school. No more classes. No more homework. Only freedom and time lie before me.

I had the same feeling the day my parents dropped me off at college. I watched their SUV pull away, and I waved at them frantically, filled with excitement and possibility. I had so much freedom, I didn't know what to do with myself the first few days. I didn't have a schedule. No curfew. No reporting my whereabouts to anyone. The only rigidity I had in my day were classes, but they were a breeze and mildly interesting.

But this, my first job and new place, will be the first time I get to make all the rules. I set my own hours at Inked, have my own place, and don't have to walk around my apartment in anything at all if I don't feel like getting dressed.

By the time I make it to the leasing office, Mr.

McNamara is waiting at his desk, paperwork ready and keys lying right next to the pen. "Are you ready to sign, Miss Gallo?" he asks as I slide into the seat across from him.

"I've never been more ready for anything in my life, sir."

Five minutes and a dozen signatures later, I have the keys in my hand. I thought graduation was the sweetest moment of my life, but I have to admit, being officially handed the keys to my new place tops even that.

"Shoot me over an email of any issues you find in the apartment. I'll get them fixed right away and add them to your paperwork, just in case. I did a walk-through this morning and found everything to be in working order, but it's still important you do the same in case you spot something I didn't."

"I'll be back after work later and will check everything out. I won't be staying here for a few days, though."

He smiles, but I know I'm rambling, and this man couldn't care less if I am going to use the apartment or not. The only thing he cares about is getting his rent check on time every month.

"Whatever you'd like, Miss Gallo."

I thank him with a firm handshake, something my dad taught me to always do, and excuse myself because I only have a few minutes to make it to the shop and not be late.

I blast the radio as I drive to Inked, weaving in and out of traffic, belting out the lyrics to "Truth Hurts."

The day just started, but it can't possibly get any

freaking better. I have the keys to my new place, and I am headed to my new job. I've dreamed about this moment for so many years, it feels surreal to finally be living it.

6

PIKE

"Any questions?" my new boss asks after giving me the rundown on how he likes shit to go.

I can't blame the man. He is the owner. He spent years with his family building up Inked to be the most sought-after tattoo parlor in the state of Florida. Their reputation is what drew me to this place. Well, that and starting over after shit went south in the last place I settled down.

"Nothing yet."

"My kid is starting today too. She's been interning during her summer breaks, but today, she officially has a chair. So, you won't be the only newbie in the place."

"Cool."

Fucking great. The first week at any new place is hard, but add in the owner's kid, and shit can become a whole lot more complicated in a hurry.

"She's bossy as fuck, but just remember she's not your boss, I am."

I nod because what he's saying is technically true,

but I'm pretty sure the kid will have his ear. If I fuck up and get off on the wrong foot with her, she can and probably will make my life miserable. I have to decide if I want to make friends with her, whoever the hell she is, or if I want to steer clear of her entirely to lessen the chances I'll get my ass canned in a heartbeat.

"I put you and her next to each other. I figure you two can help each other out. I know you're not new to this business and the craft, but sometimes people become intimidated working with so many family members."

I rub the back of my neck and try to pull on a smile. "It won't be a problem," I mutter, but nothing about the way I say the words is convincing.

"I'll be right next to you two, so I can be close if you have issues or questions."

Maybe I'm in over my head here. Working at a place like this, one with a crazy-good reputation, has always been a goal. No one wants to work at a run-down shop, scraping by and waiting for new clients to walk in the door. Inked has a two-month wait before someone can plop their ass in a chair and get the tat they've been craving.

The front door opens, and a beautiful woman steps inside, carrying a box of donuts and talking so fast on her phone, I can barely make out the words she's saying.

"That's Izzy, my sister. She's a ballbuster, so watch out for that one." Joe, my boss, laughs. "She may look small and weak, but the girl will no sooner have your balls in her hands, making you wish you could black out from the pain."

My eyes widen. "I'll steer clear of her, then."

I can't stop looking at her, though. There's something familiar in the way she talks, hand moving through the air like the person on the other end can actually see her. She's wearing a skintight white skirt, a pair of kick-ass boots with a heel long and pointy enough, she could do some damage with the fucking thing if she wanted. For an older woman, she's smoking hot.

Joe laughs louder. "There's no such thing. Once you're on her radar, you're on it. There's no hiding. So, prepare for that because, guarantee, she'll have her sights set on you at some point. I just hope, for your sake, she lets you get your feet wet before she decides to make a pet project out of you."

"Sounds great," I mumble, finally tearing my gaze away from the person who's going on my list of people to avoid while working here. "I'm sure we'll be great friends."

"Just don't get too chummy. She'll have you on the ground, begging for mercy, but it's her husband who will have you pleading for your very life."

Sounds fantastic. "Got it."

Izzy places the donuts on the front counter before telling the person on the phone she'll talk to him later. As soon as she ends the call and tosses her phone next to the donuts, her eyes are on me. "Well, well. I see the new kid finally showed."

"Ma'am," I greet and avoid correcting her on the fact that I'm nowhere near close to being a kid.

I'm twenty-seven and have been on my own for over a decade, with no one around to look out for me even longer than that. But I do the smart thing and keep my mouth shut.

"Ma'am?" Her mouth gapes open. "For real? What do I look like, your mama?"

I can't hold back the smirk as I run my fingers through my hair, trying to do something…anything… not to put my goddamn foot in my mouth. "No, ma'am. My mama looks nothing like you."

I can feel the judgment in them as she tries to make a decision if she likes me or wants to rip out my throat already with her blood-red fingernails.

"He just had to poke that bear," Joe mumbles behind me.

"I brought donuts for you assholes. That goes for you too, *kid*." She smiles.

I know she's going to call me that forever, just like she'll always be ma'am to me because that's how I was raised. As a Southern man, you don't have good manners unless you call a lady a proper name out of respect. I may have shit parents, but my grandmother taught me to be a gentleman. Because if I didn't, she'd smack me right upside the head.

I glance back at my boss, but he only shakes his head slowly like I need to let the conversation die and take what she's saying like a man. I make a quick note that Izzy, who's also Joe's sister, is the one who rules the roost.

"Where's my baby girl?" Izzy asks as she walks by us. "I thought she'd be early."

"She had to pick up the keys to her new place before work, but I'm sure she'll be here any minute."

I head to my station, unpacking a few personal items

and the tools I brought with me that I've carried from place to place for the last nine years.

"She's really moving out?"

"Yep. I can't convince her to stay."

I keep my head down and do my best not to listen, but I also want to know the family dynamics so I can figure out which land mines to avoid in the future. Plus, I never had a family that could stand one another in even small doses, let alone work together every day. The entire thing is fascinating and completely foreign.

"She's independent and grown, Joe. You had to know this was coming. Once she had a taste of freedom, how could she ever move back?" Izzy says, grabbing the only donut with sprinkles and then proceeding to pick one off and throw the pink sugar into her mouth.

Joe sighs. "I know, but she's my little girl. I thought I had a few more years of waking up to see that beautiful face." He leans back in his chair, crossing his arms. "You know what I miss the most?"

"Her attitude?" Izzy laughs.

"Hell no. I blame you for all her piss and vinegar, sister. I miss sitting with her at the kitchen table, drawing together and talking about life."

Izzy leans against the counter, still picking apart the donut and eating it in small bites. "You can still have those moments. They just won't be random."

Their gazes move toward the front of the shop as an engine roars, and a sleek black pickup pulls into a parking spot out front.

"She's here," Izzy says, tossing the massacred donut into the trash can and brushing her hands together.

"Finally, some new life in this place. The kid here—" she tips her head to me "—and the other kid are just what we need to liven things up around here."

I grumble under my breath, busying myself again. I have my first client booked in thirty minutes, and it's a piece that'll take me all day plus another session to finish. My back's already aching thinking about the hours upon hours I'll be hunched over the woman's back, giving her the angel wings she's requested.

"Sorry I'm late," the female voice says, coming through the front door.

"No problem, doll," Izzy, her aunt, says.

I doubt I'd get the same response if I'd shown up late today too. But that's what you get for being family. Special privileges are the way it goes. Who knows if this girl has any real talent or if she rode on the coat-tails of her father, not earning the chair based on her skills.

"Thanks, Auntie," the girl says as she makes her way toward her father and me. "Hey, Daddy."

Joe rises from his chair as I watch his boots move across the floor in front of me toward a pair of sexy boots much like Izzy's. "Are you ready for your first day?" he asks her.

"I've been ready for this day since I was a little girl."

I'm sure she has. Most kids dream of following in their father's footsteps. I, for one, did not. My dad was the only attorney in a small town. He was also a bastard and not someone I ever wanted to be like. As soon as I could, I got out and as far away from him and my mother as possible.

"I have someone I'd like you to meet," Joe says, and I know it's my cue.

I stand slowly, running my hands down the front of my jeans before I finally lift my gaze upward.

No fucking way.

My eyes widen, and so do hers.

"Gigi, this is Pike." Joe motions toward me with his hand. "Pike, this is my little girl, Gigi."

Fuck me.

She looks like a deer in headlights as her mouth opens and closes, but no words come out.

She can't be here.

I run my fingers through my hair, staring at the beautiful girl I'd tasted and fucked more than once, but then she vanished without even leaving me a phone number. All I had was a first name and memories after Daytona last year. Hell, they were some great fucking memories too.

I narrow my eyes as I sweep my gaze from her face and down her body, remembering exactly how perfect her skin is underneath the scraps of cloth she's wearing. I don't linger on her body too long before I bring my eyes back to hers. "It's a pleasure to meet you, Gigi."

"Mm-hmm. You too, Pike," she says like the words are acid, stinging her tongue. She's staring at me as the shock wears off and the reality of what we've done in the past is hitting her square in the face.

"Do you two know each other?" Izzy asks as she walks to our side, staring at us, but neither of us looks at her because we're too busy gawking at each other.

"Don't be silly," Joe says, wrapping an arm around

his *little girl.* "Pike isn't from around here. He's new in town."

I fucked the boss's daughter. Way to go, big man.

"Are you sure you don't know him?" Izzy asks Gigi.

Gigi shakes her head, eyes still locked on me. "Never met the gentleman," she says easily, lying without hesitation.

She doesn't know Pike the gentleman. She's well acquainted with Pike the man. She'd spent days in my bed, pleasuring me and taking what she wanted without apology.

"Iz, I had a question about the schedule. You got a minute before we get slammed?" Joe asks.

"Sure," Izzy says, drawing out the word but not moving as quickly as Joe does. I can feel her eyes on us for a moment before she finally steps away and follows Joe into the office.

Gigi and I stand here, staring at each other, listening to the slow march of her family members' feet across the tile until they're on the other side of the shop.

"It's far too quiet in here," Izzy yells before loud music fills the shop.

Fuck my life.

"Are you stalking me?" Gigi whispers, getting right up in my face.

"Don't be fucking crazy." I wave her off and walk back toward my chair.

Gigi's right on my ass, practically glued to my back. "Don't fucking lie to me. You came here on purpose."

I turn to face her, leaning my head down so our faces are close. "Babe," I whisper, staring straight into her eyes so she knows what I'm saying is one hundred percent the truth. "Let's get a few things straight. You're a great fuck and you have a hot little bod, but I'm not chasing a piece of ass all the way across the state because I need another taste. I'm also not planting roots and finding a new job just to get closer to that piece of ass either."

She blanches. "You're crude."

"I thought that's what you liked best about me. At least, that's what you said when you were riding my cock and moaning my name, baby."

7

GIGI

His words are like a punch to the gut. There's truth to what he's said, but that doesn't mean it isn't devastating. I'd thought about Pike for months after spring break last year. Months of lying awake in my bed, replaying all the naughty things we did together, touching myself to the memories.

I knew Pike wasn't a gentleman, but the words he just threw in my face prove that simple fact.

There was nothing about him that screamed manners in the time we spent together. But there was a sweet side to him when he wanted to show it, which wasn't very often in the short amount of time I spent in his bed. He was a conundrum to me. I knew very little about the man.

Even though we spent days together, we didn't talk too much about our personal lives. I knew a few basic details about the badass biker with a cock so damn good, he could charge admission for a single ride.

I raise my hand, about to strike him, when he grabs

my wrist and holds it in midair. "You're an asshole, Pike," I hiss, ripping my hand from his grip. I take a step back, knowing I need more space between us. "I don't know what game you're playing, but I'm not interested in spending more time with you."

He smirks. The bastard actually smirks when I say those words. His gaze moves toward the office where my father and Izzy are talking. "Babe," he pauses and steps closer. "I don't play games. I don't need to." He lifts his hand and runs the backs of his fingers across my cheek, but I don't move away. "And based on the color of your cheeks and the way you're looking at me, I'd say you'd like to be back in my bed and riding my cock."

I slam my palm into his chest, knocking him backward because kneeing him in the balls isn't an option. At least, not now, but I'm not above using that move to bring him to his knees. Pike's not fazed in the slightest. He just stands there, still smirking like an asshole, looking just as delicious as he did fifteen months ago.

"I will not be *riding your cock* ever again, asshat. You scratched an itch when I needed you, but I'm so over this—" I wave my hand between us. "Whatever we had, no matter how short, is all we'll ever have. Don't even look at me sideways, or I'm going to make you wish you hadn't packed up your life for a fresh start. You may have skill, but that doesn't mean my daddy wouldn't fire your ass in a heartbeat. Especially if he knew…"

"How good I fucked you?" He raises an eyebrow.

The growl creeps up my throat and slides out from between my lips before I can stop the sound from leaving my body.

"Everything okay?" Aunt Izzy asks, stepping back into the room.

I nod and turn my face toward her. "Just talking about the shop," I lie.

Her eyes move between Pike and me, and I can tell by the look on her face, she isn't buying what I'm selling. "It looks like a little more than that," she says, running her fingers across her chin.

"Auntie, it's just a little friendly competition between us. We're both starting on the same day, and neither of us wants to look like the bigger asshole...even if that's going to be Pike. You know how men are. They never like to be showed up by a woman."

Izzy walks between us and faces Pike. "Is that all this is?" She stares at him, watching his every facial feature for a tell. I know my aunt, and she misses *nothing.* One misstep and Pike's days could be numbered before he's even had a chance to finish unpacking his tools.

"That's all this is, ma'am."

Oh shit. There are things my aunt hates and then things she loathes. Being called ma'am is a surefire way to set the woman off like she's got a wick coming out of her ass, ready for ignition. She's going to blow like a Roman candle on the Fourth of July.

Her entire body stiffens. "Pike, sweetheart," she says, but her tone isn't friendly, "don't ever call me ma'am. I get where you're coming from, being a Southern gentleman and all."

I snort, but it dies as she glances over her shoulder at me for a moment.

"But around here, I'm Izzy, Iz, or boss. Do not ever,

and I mean never, call me ma'am. Got it, kid?"

I pull my lips into my mouth, biting down on them to stop the laughter that's bubbling up the back of my throat. First, because Pike's getting his ass chewed out in the nicest way possible by my aunt, and second, because Izzy just called him a kid.

"I'm sorry, Izzy," Pike says without sarcasm. "I didn't mean to offend you."

"Your looks may get you a free pass with some women, but I'm not so easily charmed by a pretty face or that Southern drawl. Her daddy—" she pitches her thumb toward me "—will be even less impressed if you do something to piss off his daughter. So, word to the wise, kid, either steer clear of Gigi, or learn to make friends with her. You do something to make her mad, and it'll be your made bed you'll have to lie in as the door kicks you in the ass on the way out."

Pike nods, those beautiful green-blue eyes that have haunted my dreams for months showing no emotion. "Got it. Loud and clear, boss."

Izzy smacks her hands together and moves away from Pike. "My work here is done. We have a full schedule today, so it's time to get your asses in gear and your shit set before they walk through the door. No more time for girl talk. You two can finish your bullshit later. Got me?"

I'm staring at Pike, smirking because my aunt shut his shit down, but when I look at her, any glee I felt dies. She's staring right at me, looking like she knows something isn't on the up-and-up.

"There's no bullshit to finish later, Izzy. We're solid,

and I don't have time for anything else. Bear's coming in this morning to get that piece he's always wanted."

"Who's Bear?" Pike asks.

"A real badass biker, Pike. You may want to take notes on how one acts instead of being a wannabe." I walk toward my chair and away from Izzy's penetrating stare.

"You two ready?" my dad asks, walking into the main room, completely oblivious to everything that's been happening. "I prepped your station last night, sweetheart. Figured it would make your first day less stressful."

I pop up on my tiptoes and kiss my dad on the cheek. "Thanks, Dad. You're the best." I wrap my arms around him and hug him tightly. I peer over his shoulder, catching Pike's eye and sticking my tongue out at him.

Not the most grown-up thing to do, but I don't care. I'm not into impressing Pike. I've already taken what I wanted, and now whatever we had, which was only a few days, is done. Over. Caput. Finished. There was no dipping my toes back in those waters again, no matter how fabulous the orgasms were.

And they were ridiculously great.

Every orgasm I'd had before Pike, I gave to myself. It had always been me and my hand until Pike rocked my world and showed me how it could be. Or should I say, how it should be.

"I'm here, baby girl," Bear yells as the bell above the door chimes so loud it's like my aunt purposely wants to scare the shit out of everyone every time it rings.

"Back here, Bear," I yell back, trying to be heard over the bell and the death metal my aunt feels is appropriate for this early hour.

By early, I mean noon. Nothing happens in the shop before noon. My family has a different idea of time. In college, I took the earliest classes possible so I'd have the rest of the day free. Now, I'm trying to reset my internal clock to be on Inked time.

"I'll grab Bear," Dad says as he pats me on the shoulder. "Get your shit together because Bear may love you, but don't put it past him to be on your ass on your first day."

I nod. "I'll be fine. I'm ready for whatever he's going to throw at me. You know I've spent my life handling men like him." I smile, because my father's friends aren't for the faint of heart, and I've perfected wrapping them around my little finger.

Bear's no exception. He and my dad go way back. They've been friends for almost thirty years, back to my dad's single life when he was an even bigger badass than he is now.

When I was little, Bear married my great-aunt Fran, my grandfather's sister. No one was happy about their relationship at first, and I remember more than a few screaming matches, but people calmed their shit after a while and gave them free rein to be happy. I love Bear and Aunt Fran together. She is absolutely perfect for him because I don't know if anyone else could *handle* Bear the way she does.

Bear may be a biker, but he is the very best kind of person. He is sweet beyond compare—but only if he likes you and you have a set of tits. He is a horndog. It doesn't matter how old he is or that his beard is almost completely gray, he's never lost his thirst for the females. But he is a one-woman guy, and that woman is my aunt Fran.

"Got a handout for your first client. Must be nice to ride on everyone's coattails," Pike says when we're alone again.

"Why don't you just fuck right off?" I glare at his reflection in the mirror. "I can't help it if my family owns this shop. I'm sorry that pisses you off so badly, but I earned this spot just as much as you did, Pike. So, get the fuck over yourself." I plop down in my chair, pulling the bottle of black ink out of the cabinet I stocked last week, ignoring whatever face I'm sure Pike's making at me.

"There she is," Bear says as he walks into the back, holding out his arms, waiting for me to jump into them like I did when I was a little girl. "Come and give me some love, baby girl."

"Hey, Uncle." I smile at Pike so he'll eat shit. I want him to know that I plan to have everyone eating out of my hands, whether they're related or not. The only person who's not going to like me is Pike, and for that… I don't give a shit. "I've missed you."

Bear hugs me tightly. "Not as much as I missed you."

Pike's gaze flicks upward as he slowly shakes his head, muttering something under his breath. I can't wipe the smile off my face, because knowing he's annoyed has me over-the-fucking-moon ecstatic.

I pull away, still holding on to Bear's arms. "You

finally ready to let me scar you for life?"

Bear's eyes light up. "Been waiting for you to leave your mark on me for years, kid."

"Still putting it on your shoulder?" I ask.

"Well, it's either there or my ass. I figured I'd save your young eyes and stick with the shoulder."

I love my uncle, but there's no way in hell I'd tattoo his ass. I know it comes with the job. Men and women will walk through the door and ask for ink in places no human should have to see, but I am not prepared to go there with Bear. I'd never be able to sit across from him at another family dinner or holiday and not think about his pasty white ass.

"I have your design all ready." I grab my sketch pad from my bag and flip through the pages until I find his design. "I'm so excited for you to finally see it. I can make any changes you want." I tear out the page and hand it to him.

Bear holds the paper with both hands, gaze sweeping up and down and back up. His mouth twists at the corners, and his pink lips disappear, replaced by his white teeth. "Damn. You did good."

I let out the breath I've been holding because I wasn't sure if Bear would like the design, and I knew he wouldn't hold back. I may be his niece, but one thing Bear isn't is a liar. He doesn't sugarcoat shit. He doesn't spare anyone's feelings, and it's one of the things I love most about him.

I don't like people who are full of shit. Family or not, I want to be told the truth, and if Bear says it, I believe him.

"Do you want black or some color, Uncle?"

"Whatever you want, kiddo. Just not fucking pink." He shakes his head. "I fuckin' hate pink. No purple either. Not into having pansy-ass colors on my skin."

"No chick colors. I got it, Bear. You want it bigger or smaller than it is?" I ask, taking the paper from between his fingers.

"It's perfect. Let's get this show on the road. I have to be home in time to take your aunt Fran to dinner, or she'll have my balls in a sling, sweetheart."

"Get comfortable and take off your shirt. I'll be back in a minute, and we'll get started."

Bear sits down and pulls his shirt over his head before leaning back and throwing his hands behind his head, staring right at Pike. "What's your name, boy?"

I snort as I walk toward the back room to put the design on transfer paper.

"Name's Pike."

"Pike, huh? Where ya from?"

"Tennessee."

I stand close to the door, listening to them shoot the shit and trying to get whatever details I can on Pike.

"That your hog outside?" Bear asks.

"Yep."

"It's nice."

"You look like a man who knows his way around a machine, and that is one of the best."

"Had to cost you a pretty penny. I'm impressed someone your age could save enough for a classic like that."

"I don't spend my money on bullshit. I like a few

things in life, and riding is one of them. I don't cheap out when it's something I want, and I wanted that bike since I was a kid."

Bear laughs. "A kid with an attitude. I don't know if this shop can take more, but you're going to fit right in here, Pike."

"So, Gigi's your niece?" Pike asks, and I move closer to the hall.

"By marriage. I've known her since she was born. She's like one of my own, and I can tell by the way you've been looking at her since I walked through the door, you better turn your eyes elsewhere."

"Ain't looking at her, man. She's not my type," Pike lies because from the way Pike fucked me, I'd say I was very much his type.

"She's every man's type," Bear tells him, calling him on his bullshit.

I laugh as I grab the paper, but I don't walk out of the back room yet. I'm enjoying this exchange way too much to interrupt.

"And I know her daddy, and he won't like you staring at his daughter like you want to devour her. So, word to the wise, kid. Look elsewhere. Don't shit where you eat, and do not—and I mean, absolutely do not—make goo-goo eyes at my niece, or you'll be packing up quicker than that young pecker of yours can come."

"Noted," Pike replies.

I cover my mouth to hide my laughter as I stroll back into my station, holding the design, ready to give Bear the best tattoo I can. I also plan to fuck with Pike as much as possible to make the day even more kick-ass.

8

PIKE

My client, Piper, has headphones on, and she's trying her best to last one more hour in my chair before she calls it a day. She's sweating profusely and on the verge of hyperventilation with her eyes squeezed tightly shut.

"It doesn't look like she's going to make it," Joe says, standing behind me and watching over my shoulder.

I don't look up. Every second is precious now, and I'm doing my best to finish the outline of the massive piece before Piper quits. "She said she can take it. I've asked her every ten minutes if she wants to tap out and finish another day."

"She pukes, you're cleaning that shit up," Joe tells me. "You have two hours before your next and last client arrives." He walks away, going to the front of the shop where everyone is standing around, shooting the shit.

Everyone except Gigi. She killed the design on Bear's shoulder and finished four other small pieces on various clients. Each design was better than the last. I'd assumed she'd gotten the chair because she was related and for no other reason. But I was wrong. The girl has talent and tons of it. I have nine more years under my belt than her, but she is so skilled, I would've guessed she'd been doing tattoos for years.

I glance up as Gigi feverishly types away on her phone, tongue poking out, sweeping across the corner of her mouth. She's barely said two words to me since our little chat before the shop opened. It's probably for the best anyway.

Of all the damn shops I could've planted new roots in, why in the hell did it have to be the one where I'd fucked the boss's daughter? I was psyched when I got the call that there was a free chair at Inked because they needed extra hands to keep up with the demand for their services. This is a dream job for me. Every artist wants to be at a place that's brimming with life.

That was my main reason for coming to Inked. That and starting over, getting away from the bullshit of the last five years, and finding a new place to call home.

"I'm done. Stop," Piper groans as she pulls off her headphones, almost making me fuck up a wing tip.

I lean back, looking over the massive piece, knowing the shading will take a fraction of the time the outline did. "We can finish it when we do the shading."

Piper's facial features relax immediately as she sits up, holding her T-shirt against her chest. "I need a month before I can come back and go through this shit again."

I scrub my hand across my face, catching Gigi's eye as she watches us across the room. "Take all the time you need. When you're ready, we'll finish what we started. I've got nothing but time. Let me just cover this piece, and you can go."

Gigi's eyes narrow. I don't know if the words I just spoke were for Piper or Gigi. I don't plan on going anywhere, no matter how badly Gigi says she wants me to. What happened last year between us feels nowhere near finished either.

That's the biggest problem.

I didn't do a damn thing to the chick. At least, nothing she didn't beg for me to do to her. Yet, she's treating me like a piece of shit. A distant memory. A huge fucking mistake.

Piper pulls her shirt over her head as soon as I finish covering the back piece, facing away from me but giving Gigi the full view of her tits. "Can you put me down for one month from today? I want to have something solid in the books before I leave."

"I'll grab you a water and put you down." I stand, stretching my back and legs because they're stiff and ache like a motherfucker.

Piper follows me back to the front, standing on the other side of the counter as I pull up the scheduling software I've had five minutes of training in how to use.

"That piece is going to be killer when it's finished," Izzy tells Piper, chatting with her as I fumble my way through the screens, trying to find next month.

"I'll be happy when it's over. I always forget how much this shit hurts until my ass is in the chair and the needle is pulling at my flesh."

"But it's totally worth it. And Pike does some of the

best damn line work I've seen in a long time. You'll be happy when the work is finished and you can show it off to the world."

Piper shakes her head. "This one is for me. I don't plan on showing it off."

"Oh?"

"My husband died last year, and this tattoo is for him."

Izzy gasps. "I'm so sorry. I didn't know."

I glance up as Piper gives Izzy a pained smile. "It's not something I share. I'm still not ready to talk about everything that happened. He always wanted me to get this tat, but I was too much of a pussy to do it until now."

"Well, it's beautiful," Izzy says, placing her hand over Piper's. "The tattoo and the sentiment."

Finally getting the computer program to work, I tell Piper, "There's a spot open on July 5th at noon if that works."

"It's fine." She nods quickly. "We'll be done after that?"

"Yes, ma'am."

I get the side-eye from Izzy, and Piper's face falters for a moment. What the fuck is it with the chicks around here? Why is ma'am such a shitty word? Where I come from, every woman is a ma'am. You'll get yourself smacked upside the head if you call a woman by any other name. But here, in the middle of fucking nowhere Florida, the women act like you're physically hurting them every time you speak the word.

"Just Piper, kid," she throws back my way, just like Izzy did.

"I keep telling him," Izzy says, giving me a satisfied smile.

I scribble the date and time on a business card before handing it to her. "I'll see you in a month, Piper."

"Thanks for helping me push through it today, Pike," she says as she heads toward the door.

I nod, smiling at the pretty lady whose face displays all the layers of pain and grief for the world to see.

"You have just enough time to grab something to eat," Joe says as he stands across the counter in the same spot Piper just was. "Why don't you take Gigi and go grab some dinner?"

"I'm fine." The last thing I need is to be alone with her tonight.

"You both need to eat. I have a client coming in, and no one else is free. Just take Gigi. She knows this area, and maybe you two can be friends. It's always nice to have someone at work to talk to who isn't related."

I don't want to tell him that she and I have nothing much to talk about. We could fuck like monkeys, but beyond that, I'm not sure we have much to say to each other. Based on our earlier conversation, I'd say there are no words left to be spoken.

"I can just grab something next door."

Joe shakes his head. "I want my kid to eat, and it's important to me that you two are friends."

"Joe, let the kids work their own shit out," Izzy tells him, grabbing on to his arm and handling him with her words and body. "You can't force them to like each other."

"Gigi!" Joe yells out like his sister didn't say anything to him.

Gigi's in the front, standing behind her father and glaring at me within a few seconds. "What's up, Dad?"

Joe dips his head in my direction, not turning around to see his kid. "Go with Pike and grab something to eat. Show him some of the local places that serve the good shit. No fast food."

"Go with Pike?" Gigi whispers. "Why?"

"I want you two to be friends."

"Are you fucking serious?" she whispers, eyes turning icy fucking cold, but she's staring at me and not her daddy. "For God's sake, why?"

Joe glances toward the ceiling, muttering under his breath. "Just do as I ask," he tells her.

She lifts her phone and shakes it in his direction as he turns toward her. "They have food delivery now, Dad. You don't actually have to go anywhere. I'll just order us something to eat."

If he knew what he was asking, if he knew what we'd done, he wouldn't be forcing her to leave this place with me. But I never plan on breathing a word of what we'd done to anyone. I'd have my ass booted from the shop, and my name blackballed from every tattoo place in the state.

"Just let her order in," Izzy says, looking at me and then at Gigi. "You know kids today, Joe. They don't like to actually do anything for themselves." Izzy laughs nervously.

By the way Izzy's acting, I reckon she's read something in our body language and has assumed we aren't the strangers we've made out to be. She seems like someone who can figure things out quickly and see through bullshit quicker than most.

"Grab me a burger from that place down on County Line. You know it's my favorite, and they don't deliver up here."

"That's fifteen minutes away," Gigi whines.

"It's a good fucking thing you both have over an hour, isn't it?" He shuts down any argument either of us can make on why we shouldn't head out alone.

Gigi curls her lip as she glances at me. "Fine. We'll go, but you've used up your asks for this week."

Joe takes a few steps toward his kid. I haven't moved an inch, just stood there, staring at them both. "I'm not asking as your father, baby girl. I'm telling you as your boss."

My eyes widen, and so do Gigi's.

"So, grab me my usual," he says, looking down at his kid, standing a foot away from her.

"Fine," she snaps.

"Oh lord," Izzy whispers and shakes her head. "Clusterfuck. Total and complete clusterfuck."

I rub the back of my neck as I walk around the counter. "I can go alone," I tell Joe, not needing Gigi's pissy attitude because her daddy forced her to go with me. "I can find the joint and grab your food."

But any other words I have on the tip of my tongue die quickly as Joe glares at me. "No, you won't. She's going too. I don't know what bad blood you two have, if it's from both being new and starting on the same day, but this isn't a competition. This is a business, and you two have to work together. Whatever bullshit, imaginary beef you have ends here and now. Do you understand me?"

I nod because I'm not arguing with the boss. No way. No how. If he wants me to take a ride with his kid to hell and back to get him a bottle of water, I'll fucking do it. It's not like Gigi is hard to be around. Keeping my dick out of her might be an issue, but it isn't a hardship spending time with a pretty chick who could do more with that mouth than sass.

"I understand, Dad," she says softly. "I'll play nice."

Joe's lips turn up and his shoulders relax. "Now, get moving. I'm starving. Ask everyone else if they want anything before you go."

"I'll grab my keys."

"Oh no." Gigi shakes her head, still glaring at me like she wants to rip off my head. "I'm driving."

"Why?"

She crosses her arms, tilting her head to the side, eyes traveling up and down my body. "Let me guess," she says, her tone all full of piss and vinegar. "You have the bike, yeah?"

"Yeah."

"We're getting food for everyone, and I'm not fucking holding it while we weave in and out of traffic just because you want to take your bike."

I shrug. "I have a compartment."

"It's a big nope for me. We're taking my truck."

"Whatever makes you happy." I'm not going to

stand here another ten minutes arguing about which form of transportation we're going to take. "I could give two shits how we get there as long as we get there."

"Smart kid," Joe says.

"Or the dumbest one ever," Izzy whispers before shaking her head at me.

Hopefully, whatever scenarios Izzy has swirling around in her head, she comes to me about before blowing up my life. She and Gigi are close. I can tell that from the short amount of time I've seen the two interact. If Gigi spills the beans, my ass will be on the back of my bike, searching for a new job and a new town…again.

"I'll meet you out front." Gigi tips her head toward the door. "Black truck."

I don't stick around. I need some air and to get my head on straight before I go anywhere with this chick. She has me all kinds of tangled up inside. My brain is going a million different directions, most of which are bad, but they all end up in the same place…with Gigi back in my bed, moaning my name, and begging for more.

Fuck.

The door doesn't close behind me as I step outside into the damp Florida air. I don't notice I'm not alone as I start to pace.

"I don't know what's going on, but whatever it is, you better find a way to fix it or move the fuck on," Izzy says.

I jump, clutching my chest. "Jesus fucking Christ. You scared the ever-loving hell out of me."

She marches up to me, craning her neck to look me in the eye. "Did you hear me?"

I nod. "Uh, yeah. I said you scared the shit out of me, Iz."

"Listen, kid." She points to the window of the shop. "Gigi's gunning for you. She doesn't like you, and she doesn't hate many people. So, whatever you did to fuck shit up, make it right. I don't want to lose you already, but she's family."

"Yeah. Yeah. I know how it goes." I run my hand through my hair and sigh.

"It's not my business. She's my niece and you're both adults, but mark my words, fix whatever you fucked up, or you won't be here more than a week."

I don't deny that there's history. I won't lie to Izzy again. She's smart. I won't be going into detail about all the ways I'm acquainted with her niece. I won't tell her how I know the way she tastes, how she kisses, and the perfect curve of her ass.

"I'll fix it." I jam my hands into my pockets, trying to figure out exactly how I'm going to do that.

Maybe I need to remind Gigi of how perfect we are together. I don't get why she's so fucking pissed. I did not stalk her across the state. Hell, I knew her first name but nothing else about the girl.

She lied to me, in fact.

First, based on the fact that she just graduated from college, her first lie was about her age. She told me she was twenty-two and was about to graduate last year. Second, she told me she was from Miami and stayed there to work. I know there were a million other lies she told me that week, but I wasn't exactly open and honest about my life or my past either.

We both knew what we were doing. The week in Daytona was all about pleasure. About being in the moment. Our pasts and futures didn't matter. The lies we told were of no consequence because there was nothing more than that moment, in that hotel, tangled in sheets and coated in sweat.

But now…our paths are intertwined. My fate and future lie in the hands of the boss's little girl, the same chick I'd banged until my legs barely worked anymore.

"Do whatever you need to do to make shit right," Izzy tells me before walking away and disappearing inside the shop, leaving me out front with my dick in my proverbial hands.

She said do *whatever*, but I wonder if the whatever includes being with her niece.

I know the spark is still there.

I caught Gigi staring at me more than once. Not with rage, but curiosity. Watching my hands as they touched Piper's back, maybe remembering the way they felt sliding across her skin.

Whatever there is between us…I'm going to leave her alone until I find out.

9

GIGI

Fuck. I love my dad, but come on. Why does he have to be so gung ho about the happy family vibe at the shop? What does it matter if I like Pike or not? I don't remember my dad going to this much trouble when they hired Kat. But what I do remember is my aunts going bananas about a young little hottie working so close to their men.

But now my dad wants us to be all kumbaya, holding hands, and one big, happy freaking family. If he only knew…

He'd fucking kill me, and then he'd murder Pike.

"We going to talk about this?" Pike asks from the passenger seat of my pickup truck.

"I think we said everything we needed to say already." I stare straight ahead, keeping my eyes on the road instead of on the hottie next to me.

Why the hell does he have to smell so good?

Pike shifts his body, but I don't dare sneak a glance. I know his eyes are on me and nowhere else. I can feel the weight of his gaze like a warm blanket, covering my skin. "Darlin'," he says with a hint of a Tennessee twang in his voice. "I have a lot more to say to you."

"Well, you talk, and maybe I'll listen while I drive." I shrug one shoulder, wrapping my fingers tighter around the steering wheel. "It's not like I have a choice, do I?"

"I like a captive audience," he says sarcastically. "First, I didn't follow you. I'm not a stalker."

"That's what you say, but how do I know?"

"Gigi, how the fuck would I even find you?"

I shrug again. "Anything's possible."

"You told me your first name. You also told me you were from Miami, and the last time I checked, we're hundreds of miles away from there."

"There are other ways."

"What other ways?" He turns and his knee is almost touching mine, but I have nowhere to go. No way to fight back because he's making all the sense in the world, and it's aggravating as hell.

"I don't know. My uncle's a private investigator, and I'm sure he could've found me with very little to go on."

Pike laughs, and I can see him shake his head out of the corner of my eye. "Listen, babe."

I growl, which only makes Pike laugh. *Ugh.*

"You like darlin' better?"

"I don't like either. My name is Gigi or Giovanna," I correct him.

"Giovanna is kind of an uppity name, which right about now, suits you."

"I changed my mind." I reach for the radio because

I'd rather listen to anything other than his sexy as all get-out voice.

He tightens his fingers around my wrist, peeling my hand away from the buttons on the console. "I didn't have anything to go on. I figured what we had was nice, but it wasn't anything that would go the distance. The last thing I'd do is stalk you to try to get another piece of that fine ass."

My gaze slides to his face for a moment before going back to the road. "Nice?" My voice is high, almost shrill. "What we had was *nice*?" I ask, grinding my teeth and ripping my hand from his grasp.

"Well, not really." He pauses, and he's lucky as hell I can't lunge across the seat and wrap my hands around that beautiful neck of his. "It was fucking spectacular. The shit you did..."

"Stop." I shake my head, grinding my teeth so hard, my jaw aches. "I was there. I don't need a play-by-play."

Pike laughs again, practically making my blood boil. "I'm just saying, I didn't track you down. I figured you had your fill and were through. So why would I bother to track you down?" He pauses, but I don't reply before he continues. "I don't chase pussy. Never have. Never will. It's not my style, darlin'."

"Thanks for that little nugget of truth, Pike."

"You're acting like I did you wrong. You were the one who just up and left without even so much as a goodbye."

I cringe when he says the last few words. I did do that to him. I told him I was running out for some coffee, and I didn't look back before I got in my car, picked up the girls, and headed back to FSU. But in all fairness, when I rolled over that morning and saw his phone with a text from some skank that read, "When you're done with the little girl, I'll be waiting for you," that shit set me right off. I knew I was just another piece of ass to him in a long line of pussy waiting to take my place.

For half a second, I thought we had something more than a casual fling, but that text reminded me I was nothing more than another notch on his bedpost.

"I waited in that hotel room for three hours before I figured you weren't coming back. I felt like a fuckin' fool too."

"I'm sorry."

I didn't take into account how he felt or if he'd even give a shit. I figured a clean break, no goodbye, no last kiss, and no more questions was the best way to end things with him. It was a coward move, but I'd never done anything like that in my life. I didn't know how to act or if there was a proper way to say *thanks for the cock, big man.*

"Who does that kind of shit?"

"Oh, please. I'm sure you've been with plenty of chicks who didn't kiss you goodbye."

"I've never had anyone run away without at least saying thanks."

My gaze moves from the red light to his face. He's staring at me with a hardness in his eyes, fingers moving across his beard. "Thanks?"

The corner of his mouth tips up, showing the white of his teeth nestled behind his facial hair. "Why not?"

I throw my head back and laugh. "I think you would've been the one saying thanks to me, buddy."

My words only make Pike laugh. God, he's so annoying. "I figured I gave you all the thanks you needed with so many orgasms you could barely walk when you went for that fake-me-out coffee."

I narrow my gaze on his handsome, smug face. "It's not like you're the only man on the planet who can give an orgasm. You're not God's gift to women, country boy. Hell, I can give myself an orgasm anytime."

"Do you think about me?" His smile grows wider.

I twist my lips, staying silent as I turn my eyes back to the road. I'm thankful we're two minutes from the burger shop because I need out of this truck and need distance between us. "Babe, when I'm touching myself, like really getting into it, fingers stroking away, and I'm craving to be filled…"

"Don't say things like that unless you want to be flat on your back, begging for my cock, sweetheart."

"You're so full of yourself." Fuck, he's so right.

We're trapped in the small cab of my truck, and he's so close to me, I can smell the musky soap on his skin. All the memories from that week come flooding back to me like the naughtiest and most vivid dream, but I push them aside, staying in the present with the more annoying version of Pike.

"Tell me you haven't thought about me once since you left Daytona, and I'll leave you be, chalking it all up to a good time and nothing more."

"I haven't thought about you once," I lie. "Have you thought about me?"

"Every. Damn. Day," he answers quickly, and I immediately regret asking him that question.

If I were being truthful, which I'm not because I'm not giving him any ammo, I've thought about him every damn day too. How could I not? After a week like we had, the way we had it, I couldn't think about anyone else but him.

He ruined me. I never thought I'd say those words, and I can barely admit them to myself sometimes. But he did. He ruined me completely.

Mallory had asked me before I met Pike if Erik was any good in bed. I said he was okay or maybe I said he was good, but now I know better. Pike did things to me that made my toes curl and my legs shake like I was having a seizure.

"We're here." I open the door and hop down from the truck's cab, leaving Pike behind as soon as I shut off the engine.

I move quickly, pulling open the door to the burger shop, trying to put as much space as possible between Pike and me. But no matter how quickly I move, he isn't far behind.

"We're not done," Pike says, almost plastered against my back in the impossibly busy restaurant.

I turn, glancing up and over my shoulder at him. "We are."

He leans forward, putting his face so close to mine, I can feel his warm breath tickle my skin. "I'm calling a truce for now, but that doesn't mean I don't want you in my bed again, lips on mine."

I suck in a long, deep breath, feeling a little dizzy,

remembering how his lips felt like velvet even with that beard. "It's never going to happen." Quickly, I twist my head, staring up at the menu and silently cursing myself because I very much wouldn't mind being in his bed with his lips on mine again. "Asshole," I mutter softly.

"Welcome to Burger, Burger, Burger," the guy with the dopiest outfit ever says on the other side of the counter. The name is cheesy, the uniforms are even cheesier, but the burgers they make are the best in the county. "What can I get you?" he asks with a grin so large, I know it's fake as fuck because ain't no one that happy to be working in this joint.

"I'll take a Double Swiss and Mushroom, a large onion ring, and a medium diet lemonade."

"Diet?" Pike says in my ear. I elbow him because he's close, and I don't feel like getting into it with him in front of everyone.

"What do you want to eat, Pike?" I ask, not turning around, but instead giving the same fake-ass smile back to *Jim*—or at least, that's what his name tag says.

"Besides you?" Pike whispers in my ear, which earns him a second elbow to the gut. "I'll get what she's having." His voice is strained, the two good shots I got in clearly having an impact.

"For here or to go?" Jim, the cashier, asks with his smile still firmly planted on his pimply face.

"To go."

"Here," Pike says over me, and Jim nods. "We also do need a few other things to go." Pike's fingers graze my ass, and I jump but stop myself from smacking him when I see the yellow sheet of paper in his hands. He rattles off the order for everyone at the shop before handing Jim a wad of cash.

"You could've just asked me for the list," I snap.

Jesus. When did I become so bitchy?

Pike brings out the worst in me. That week in Daytona, I felt more like myself. I didn't have to be anyone else but who I was. Although I told a few lies because I didn't know Pike at all, I was truly me. I didn't have to put on a good face or act like some happy party girl, ready to do anything Mallory wanted so I didn't have to listen to her shit.

"My way was more fun." He smirks, eyes blazing as he stares at my snarled lips.

"We'll bring it out to you when it's ready," Jim says because, clearly, we're done and stopping the flow of traffic.

I stalk toward an empty table, plop down in the chair, and stare out the window.

"We can be civil," Pike says, sliding into the chair across from me. "I want this job, and I'm not looking to get canned before I've barely had a chance to start. Your dad won't fire you, but he'll toss my ass out in a fucking heartbeat. I'm not trying to piss you off."

"That's news to me, Pike, and by the way, I didn't get the job because I'm related. I've been working my ass off at the shop for years, earning that damn chair."

"Your line work is amazing," he says, complimenting me on something that isn't sexual for the first time. "Especially with the short time you've been tattooing. It's impressive, actually."

"Thanks. My dad taught me well."

"You're lucky," he says, leaning back in his chair and kicking one leg out so it's practically touching mine. "My father didn't teach me shit except how to be an asshole."

"Ah, it's genetic, then," I tease, reaching over and pulling a handful of napkins out of the container just so I have something else to do besides stare at him.

"Ha. Ha. Very funny. I'm not an asshole." He pauses. I risk a glance at him and quickly realize I shouldn't have. The teasing, happy-go-lucky guy from a few moments ago is gone, and in his place is a man filled with sorrow and maybe…regret. "Well, not one like my father, at least. We're nothing alike. Thank fuck for small miracles."

"I'm sorry." I can't imagine growing up with a horrible father.

Joseph Gallo may be overbearing, but he is so damn loving that the amazing outweighs the bad. Sure, there were times I wanted to scream at him about his ridiculous rules, but I knew why he was being so over the top. He loves me. He also thought he knew better than me, which he probably did, although I'll never admit it.

I won the lottery the day I was born. I knew that much. I have a father who adores me and a mother who is the sweetest human being on the planet. I have an entire tribe of people who are mine, looking out for me, loving me no matter what shit I pull…and there's been a lot.

Pike shrugs one shoulder and then runs his fingers through his impossibly messy, yet somehow perfect, dirty-blond hair. "It is what it is. I put as much distance between him and me as possible."

"But what about your mom?" I ask, unable to imagine not being able to go home again.

"She's no better than him. Just a different type of asshole, but still an asshole."

"That's harsh."

"If you knew them, you'd understand why I'm not being harsh enough."

I stare at Pike, losing myself in his soulful eyes, wondering what made me the lucky one to be born into a great family, when there are others who got a shit deal the day they were born.

"Two burgers, two onion rings, and two drinks," a girl says at the side of our table, wearing the same hideous outfit as Jim and looking no less ridiculous.

"That's us." I reach for the tray because she's staring at Pike with wide eyes like a deer caught in headlights. She's not a deer and Pike's not a car, but she's no less mesmerized by him.

Yeah, girl, I know.

I take the tray from her hands, placing it on the table in front of us, but she doesn't move. She barely blinks, ignoring the fact that I'm sitting right here, like she's stuck to the floor, frozen in place.

"Can I get you anything else?" she asks him in an almost robotic voice.

"I think we're good," Pike says and looks at me, pleading with me with his eyes like I'm going to be able to chase this girl away. "You need anything else, darlin'?"

"I got everything I need," I reply, grabbing the burger from the paper basket, trying to ignore the weird girl who can't seem to do anything other than stare at Pike.

"Well," she says softly, blinking her eyelashes so quickly I'd think she has something stuck under her eyelid. "If you need anything, just ask for me." She smiles and points at her name tag. "Angie."

"Thanks, Angie," Pike says with a big smile, tipping his head to her. "I'll let you know if we need anything else. My girl and I are hungry."

Her top lip curls as Pike looks over at me, breaking the happy trance she was in and reminding her that he isn't alone. "Enjoy," she says flatly before stalking away from our table, thankfully leaving us in peace.

"Is it hard being you?" I tease him.

"Hard because people are nice?" he asks, grabbing his burger and holding it in front of his lush, soft lips.

"Hard because women seem to throw themselves at you."

"Sometimes it's great, while other times, it's a pain in the ass." He takes a big bite, chewing slowly, staring at me across the table as I do the same.

We sit like that, chewing and not speaking, but his eyes say everything that needs to be said. I could lose myself in his eyes. The deep blue-green like the Gulf of Mexico before a storm.

"Like the night I met you, that was one of the great times."

I'm mid-swallow, and the burger almost gets lodged in my throat, but I fight to get it down. "And when it's not so great?" I ask, wanting to talk about anything except us.

"Fuck," Pike mutters, burger in hand, cocky smile playing on his lips. "Who am I kidding? A face like this has its perks with very little downside."

I grab an onion ring and playfully throw it at his face, but Pike catches it before it can connect. "You're being an asshole again."

"Darlin', I'm always an asshole, but that's why you like me," he says with a straight face.

"Keep dreaming, buddy," I snarl and take another bite of my burger, chewing on my food and his words.

Do I like Pike?

I liked him enough to sleep with him…repeatedly.

I was attracted to him. That much was true.

I liked Daytona Pike way more than I like Inked Pike. But Daytona Pike also had an expiration date, whereas Inked Pike seems to be ready to settle in and stick around, putting down roots in my small town.

I can't chase him away. That would require me being open and honest with my father about what happened in Daytona and what went down between Pike and me.

Shit, my father didn't even know I went to Daytona, and the one thing he hates most is lying. I did my fair share of that in college, though. If they knew half the shit I'd pulled… Well, it's not like he could ground me. I don't live under his roof anymore and can make my own rules. But that doesn't mean my ass wouldn't get chewed out for the danger I'd put myself in.

I can't even imagine what he'd say about me

sleeping with a stranger, let alone going to his hotel room where I could've been raped or murdered. I'm sure my father would immediately go to the worst-case scenario and all the ways I could've fucked up my life by sleeping with a stranger.

I didn't get an STD or end up with a lifelong reminder, waking me in the middle of the night to be fed. What I did get was the best damn sex of my life—and now a constant reminder sitting in the chair across from me.

"Finish up. We have to get back. I have a client in thirty minutes," Pike says as he glances at his phone.

I take two more bites, trying to keep my eyes on the table instead of on his muscular, ink-covered arms, flexing with each movement. When I lift my gaze to his face, he's watching me and knows exactly what I'm staring at. I'm totally busted.

"I'm done." I toss the burger back into the paper basket before shoving an onion ring in my mouth. "I'm ready when you are," I say while chewing, hoping to pull off being as unsexy as possible.

I know I need to put space between us. The spark, the chemistry, the pull I felt toward him in Daytona is still there. That scares the shit out of me too. I'd never felt that invisible force pushing me toward someone when I was with Erik or Keith, but it's so strong with Pike, I'm not sure I can escape it.

"You're still hot," he says like he sees through my plan. "Still give me wood, darlin', even with that mouthful of onion rings."

I'm out of my seat, tray in one hand and the to-go

bag in the other before Pike can say another word. But I'm not alone for long. I don't even make it to the door before I can hear his heavy footsteps and feel the warmth of his body nearby.

"Fuck my life," I whisper into the glass door before pushing it open and stepping outside into the inferno that's a Florida summer day.

"Next time, we take my bike," he says, rounding the truck and opening my door before I can do it myself.

I stare up at him. "There won't be a next time." I stop myself from reaching out and running my fingertips along the coarse hair on his face.

Pike smiles, tipping his head and putting his face close to mine. "News flash, Gigi. Daytona was only the beginning."

10

PIKE

"Why couldn't you move to Nashville?" my grandmother asks as I stalk around my apartment searching for my boots. "There are plenty of places to work around here, sweetheart."

"Gram, it's still too close. I needed to put distance between myself and that shit-ass town."

"That mouth of yours, Pike. I know I didn't teach you to speak like that."

"Sorry, Gram." I pull on my boots as soon as I find them next to the couch.

"Nashville is two hundred miles from your daddy. It's not like you'd run into him."

My grandmother was the only saving grace I had as a child. She still is. How she's the same woman who raised my father, I'll never understand. Where she's sweet, he's cruel. Where she's soft, he's hard. It's like he decided to spite the world and do the opposite of anything Gram wanted for him.

"I know, Gram, I know."

"Just promise you'll come visit this old woman before I die," she says, laying on the guilt like she always does.

The woman has been talking about her death since I was in middle school. At first, she used it as a means to control me. It worked like a fucking charm until I got smart enough to realize she wasn't dying anytime soon. Then, she used it as a way to guilt me into doing shit like being around my parents when I wanted to be anywhere else in the world than breathing the same air as them.

"I promise I'll come see you before fall."

"That's three months away, sweetheart. A woman of my age could meet her maker at any moment."

"Why don't you come here? I have a spare bedroom, and I can show you around where I live. Have you ever been to Florida, Gram?"

"No, and I have more humidity and heat than I can handle here. I don't need to come to Florida so I can get more."

I laugh as I step onto my patio with a cup of coffee, closing the screen door behind me because the bugs out here are ridiculous and bigger than most rats I've seen crawling around near the gutters of Nashville. "Don't be dramatic."

"I'm always dramatic."

"From your lips to God's ears."

"Lydia is here to take me to the store. Call me tomorrow, and let me know how you're settling in."

"Okay, Gram. Tell Lydia hello." I lean over the railing and rest the coffee mug on the top. "Talk soon. Don't die on me today."

"No one is promised time, Pike. Remember that,"

she says, hanging up without saying goodbye like she always does.

She'd just turn me off. When I was younger, it bothered me that she never said goodbye. She was the only person I knew who never uttered those words. She said they were too final and not meant for casual conversation. That was the hard part of Gram, but everything else about the woman was soft and loving.

"Beautiful morning, isn't it?"

I turn my head, coffee cup close to my lips, finding a buxom blonde in a silk robe. She's leaning against the railing of her patio which touches mine, only separated by some iron spindles. Her hand is wrapped around a mug, but the robe is open, nearly exposing her breasts.

"It's something." I don't let my gaze linger too long because I don't know this chick or if she has a man inside her apartment who'd be willing to go five rounds because I looked at his girl wrong.

"New here?" she asks, sliding closer but still leaning.

"Moved in last week."

She extends her free hand, but I don't move a muscle. "I'm Cadence, but my friends call me Cady like Katie."

She wiggles her fingers, not getting the clue that I'm not interested in niceties, especially at this hour. "Well, Cady like Katie, it's nice to meet you."

"I won't bite," she says with a small laugh.

I've known plenty of women like Cadence, and they always bite. They take their pound of flesh in the end, and I am not particularly looking to have any more scars.

"Pike." I take her hand, giving her a quick handshake and nothing more.

"Well, Pike, I'm always around if you're looking for company."

"Sorry, Cady, I'm a taken man," I lie because it's easier than telling her I'm not interested.

She doesn't look like a woman who takes no for an answer. The way she's staring at me, I can tell she wants a piece of me for breakfast.

"Such a shame," she whispers and withdraws her hand from mine. "But if you change your mind…"

"I know where to find you."

"Nice ink, by the way."

"Thanks." I leave out the part about being a tattoo artist. The last thing I need is Cady's ass planted in my chair at Inked, tits hanging out, coming on to me in front of the entire Gallo family.

She gives me a once-over, eyes hungry and still burning as her gaze slides down my arms to my crotch. "You have a good day now, ya hear?"

"You too." I hold my breath, not daring to move until her screen door closes behind her.

I'm halfway back into my apartment, one leg still outside, when the patio door on the other side opens, and a familiar voice catches my attention.

"I know, Tamara. Can you believe this shit? Pike just shows up out of nowhere."

Well, fuck me.

If Gigi thought I was stalking her before, wait until she realizes I'm living next door to her. Out of all the places in this small-ass town, why in the fuck did she move in to my complex and right next door?

I pull my leg into the apartment but stay near the door and out of view. I don't dare shut the door because the last thing I want is for Gigi to see me or catch me listening to her.

"Yeah, he still looks delicious," she tells Tamara over the phone.

I fucking knew it.

"Tam, be serious for a minute here. Don't worry about Pike's big dick. Think of all the ways this shit can go south and bite me right in the ass."

There's nothing she can say now to wipe the big-ass grin off my face. Nothing. She can call me an asshole all she wants and pretend she doesn't want me, but I know the truth. She clearly told Tamara everything and is laying it all out for her again.

"You're so fucking funny." Gigi snorts but quickly sobers. "What if my dad finds out about Daytona? He'll fucking have my head."

Ah. The girl has a secret. Besides sleeping with me, her dad has no idea she was in Daytona last year for Bike Week. He'd probably shit a brick. I know if I had a daughter, I wouldn't let her anywhere near the place. Not when there're guys like me around. No fucking way would that ever happen.

I peek around the corner, getting a full view of Gigi's ass in the most spectacular pair of cutoff jean shorts ever. She's holding a coffee in one hand and her phone in the other, leaning against the railing near the corner.

"I can't sleep with him again."

I stand a little straighter.

"Because we work together, and Pike isn't the type of guy who settles down. I don't want to be someone's booty call forever, Tam. I want love. I want a relationship. I want what my parents have. What your parents have."

That's where she's wrong, but damn it, I can't set her straight right now. It would ruin everything that we built on yesterday. By the end of the day, she wasn't ready to rip out my throat. We'd made progress, and I wasn't going to do anything to fuck that up. And I most certainly wasn't going to scare the piss out of her by walking out on the patio and interrupting her most telling conversation.

"I'm not going for another ride on that cock just because I haven't been laid since the last time."

My eyes widen, and everything around me seems to disappear. Her words slam into me like a ton of bricks.

She hasn't slept with anyone else?

"My fling with Pike was a one-time thing because Mallory wouldn't shut the hell up about how I was a prude. I've embraced my prudishness now. I have exactly two notches on my bedpost, girl. Erik was a cheating asshole, and Pike is Pike. Best fucking sex of my life or not, I'm not rolling around with a man who can't commit."

To say I'm dumbfounded is an understatement. Very little surprises me in the world anymore, especially the shittiness. But goddamn, I was only the second guy Gigi had ever slept with, and she hasn't been with anyone else since.

How is that even possible?

I know three things for sure in this moment.

First, Gigi isn't exactly what she seems. She's not a party girl and has never been one to sleep around. I was the exception and outside her norm.

Second, I still have a shot with Gigi. She wants love. She wants romance. I could do those. I could be whatever she wants me to be. She is that badass. She is soft and hard, sweet and salty, and everything I want in a chick. She has balls and a mouth on her that could break a man's heart or have him panting with need.

And third, I need to find a way to make Gigi mine without getting my ass shot by her badass father. I know I could break down Gigi's walls, but Joe… He is another story entirely.

"Trust me. The women basically throw themselves at Pike. They go all stupid around him. It's ridiculous." Gigi pauses for a moment. "I did not go stupid around him. Shut up, Tamara. He scratched an itch, and that's it."

I don't know what Tamara is saying, but I sure as fuck wish I could hear her. Having one side of the conversation is fine, but damn…I want it all. I wonder what she told her cousin. How open she'd been about the things we'd done and how fucking fantastic it had all been.

"I'm not full of shit," Gigi barks.

Oh, but she is. She hasn't been honest about a damn thing with me since the moment I met her, and she continued the lies yesterday. Her mouth was saying she hated me, but now, talking to Tamara, she's saying the opposite. I knew by the way Gigi stared at me that she still wanted me.

"Anyway, when are you getting here? My mom's flipping out because I'm living alone and I told her you're staying with me for the summer until school starts again."

Fuck. Tamara could be a wrench in my plans to win Gigi over. But maybe not. From the sound of it, I think Tamara believes Gigi and I should be together, even if only sexually. I'll take what I can get, trying to win Gigi over piece by piece, orgasm by orgasm. Whatever it takes. I've never been a quitter, and when I see something I want, I go after it…full throttle.

"I'll have the place ready, but I'm only giving you two weeks to get your ass here. I don't know what the hell you're still doing up there."

I now have a timetable. I have two weeks to see what I can do to win the girl over before her cousin crashes the party. Maybe I can use the time to my advantage. If her parents, specifically her mother, don't like her living alone, maybe if they knew I lived next door, they'd feel better about her living arrangements. Knowing there was a friendly face and coworker right next door in case shit went bad wouldn't be a bad thing, would it?

"Dump Hank. He's a loser, Tam. You could do so much better, and you know it. You said you were breaking up with him a month ago, but there you are, staying at FSU for him." She pauses again, and I'm still plastered to the wall just inside the doorway. "You have two weeks to break his heart and get your ass here, or

I'm telling your daddy you're there getting your brains banged out of that pretty little head."

I reach out, slowly sliding the patio door closed and engaging the lock. I keep my body out of sight, not knowing if she's looking but taking no chances either. I need to get to the shop, and I want to be out the door, on the back of my bike, before she has a chance to leave. The last thing I need is for her to find me here, thinking I'm following her ass around.

I have to find a way to let her know I'm living here without her also knowing I was listening in on her conversation.

It's a giant clusterfuck, but a damn good one too.

I'm halfway to my bike when a door opens behind me, and I freeze.

"Pike?" Gigi calls out. "Is that you?"

Fuck. I rub the back of my neck and turn to face her. "Hey." I wave with my other hand, keys dangling from my fingertips like a dope.

She looks stunning in the early morning sunlight, the rays shining around her hair and illuminating her like an angel. But the look on her face isn't sweet.

"What the hell are you doing here?" she asks as she stalks toward me, arms swinging at her sides with each hurried step.

"Headed to the shop." I wait in the empty parking spot next to my ride.

"No." She crosses her arms, the anger coming off her in waves. "I mean, what are you doing here at Sunshine Vista?"

"I live here," I answer flatly, laying out the truth.

"Here?" She points to the cement.

"There." I point toward the building. Our building.

She narrows her eyes. "Which one?"

"On the end."

Her eyes widen. "Right fucking next to me?"

My eyes widen too. "No shit. Really? What a crazy-ass coincidence."

Please for the love of God, I hope she didn't hear my sliding door close, figuring out I was listening to her conversation. I'd like to get to work with my balls intact and my voice in a normal octave.

"You say you're not stalking me. But for real, Pike, it sure as fuck seems like you are."

"I signed the lease two months ago, and I moved in last week. You?"

"I'm just moving in this week," she tells me, balling her fists at her sides, and I slide backward because she looks like she's about to throw down.

"Why here?"

"There're only two apartment complexes in this small-ass town. The other place was…"

"Gross," she finishes my sentence, and I nod.

"Wasn't going to plant my roots in a shithole like that. So, I wasn't stalking you. This was the only place within a twenty-mile radius that was worth renting. Nothing more. Now, you want a ride to work today or not?"

"Not," she hisses.

"Suit yourself."

"Pike, how would I explain why I'm on the back of

your bike when we get to the shop? Think about it for a minute."

I slowly nod and swing a leg over my bike, sitting my ass down on the seat. "I wasn't thinking about much other than having you on the back of my bike, those sweet thighs rubbing against mine and your tits pressed against my back."

She tips her head toward the sky and groans, followed by a slew of curse words I haven't heard strung together in quite as creative a way before. "It's so not happening ever again," she tells me as she brings her gaze back to mine instead of the fluffy clouds floating above our heads.

Yeah, it will, darlin'. I don't utter those words out loud because she'll just deny how she's feeling and tell me I'm fucking crazy. But I heard her talk to Tamara, and I know the truth.

"Just go. I'm not ready for work yet. I have to do my makeup. I just ran out here to grab my makeup bag from my car."

My lip curls. "You don't need any of that shit on your face, babe. You're looking beautiful right now with the sunshine streaming through that brown hair of yours, kissing those cheeks."

Her cheeks turn a bright shade of pink, and the attitude that had been running all through her body seems to evaporate. "You're full of shit." She waves me off. "Go, and I'll be a few minutes behind you. Don't say anything about being here."

"Lips are sealed, darlin'."

"Gigi," she says as I throttle the engine, ready to take off.

"Sure thing, darlin' Gigi." I smirk, unable to hear her scream even though her mouth is open over the bike. I slide on my sunglasses, lift my chin to her, and walk the bike back slowly out of the parking spot.

She doesn't move from the spot she's standing in. Her eyes are on me, hands on her hips, body looking smoking hot in those jean shorts, showing off the perfect amount of leg. She looks like a goddess with her brown hair blowing in the soft breeze, watching me like a hawk as I pull away.

11

GIGI

"We're all going out after work to celebrate," Izzy says as I walk into the office to grab a cold drink after my last client of the evening finally leaves.

"I don't know," I mutter, reaching into the small fridge near the doorway. "I have a lot to do at the apartment, Auntie."

"We're celebrating you and Pike joining our team. So, there's no getting out of this one, kiddo."

I twist the lid off the soda as I turn around, gawking at my aunt as she sits at the desk. "I'm not new, and I don't think Pike will be here for very long."

She draws her eyebrows inward. "Why do you say that?"

I lift a shoulder. "Just a feeling I have."

She taps her fingernails against the wooden top. "Are you ready to tell me how you really know Pike?"

"I don't know what you're talking about."

I will deny the shit that happened between us for as long as humanly possible.

She pushes back from the desk and stalks toward me, crossing her arms, which is never a good sign. "I've been watching both of you for two days. Want to know what I see?"

"Not particularly."

She gets right in my face. "I see two people who know each other and know each other well."

I laugh, but it's a shrill, nervous one. My aunt's eyes flash, and I know I have to divert. "I don't know him. He's just hot, okay? It's been a while since I've been with anyone, and he's the only guy in the shop I'm not related to. It's that simple."

She stares at me, lips twisting like she's chewing on what I'm saying but not buying a word. "He is hot. I'll agree with you there, but there's more to the story. There's something you're not telling me. And about Pike..." She grabs my shoulders, moving closer. "He's sticking around, kid. He signed a one-year lease on that chair, and he's planting roots."

"Planting roots," I mumble because Pike has said those same words so many damn times over the last two days, I could scream.

"That man has been trying to get a chair here for three years, but we weren't ready for new blood. Now, we've got a spot for him, and he's staying as long as he wants unless he does something to fuck up majorly. But if he does, he still has to pay for that chair for the duration of his contract. So, settle in, sweetheart, the hottie's here to stay."

Three years? That kind of kills my theory that he

tracked me down, following me halfway across the state to get me into bed again.

"Fuck," I hiss under my breath, and Izzy doesn't miss it.

"So, you might as well tell me how you know him and why you want him gone before those roots are firmly planted here."

I know if there's one person I can trust to understand everything that happened and how I feel about it, it's Aunt Izzy. She wouldn't judge me for sleeping with a stranger, but she'd probably give me a lecture about safe sex and other uncomfortable topics I didn't feel like talking to her about. Then, she'd probably lay into me about being in Daytona for Bike Week, which I don't feel like hearing. Not yet, at least.

"It's no big deal. We just ran into each other somewhere. He has an unforgettable face," I lie because it's easier than the truth.

I don't want to make waves for Pike. He didn't do anything wrong. I took what he gave, and then I ran away without so much as a goodbye. If anyone should be pissed, it's him. But he's not. He doesn't seem angry with me about the entire ordeal. Maybe I should tell him about the fact that I hadn't done anything like that before and I wasn't sure how to handle saying goodbye to a man I never planned to see again. But here he is, and he's not leaving anytime soon.

Izzy hasn't moved, and she's still staring at me like she's a human lie detector, ready to call bullshit. "That's it?"

"Yep." I stare her straight in the eye when I speak because doing anything else will be a dead giveaway.

"What bullshit are you two cooking up?" Uncle Mike asks as he walks in the room, scaring the shit out of me.

"Just talking to Gigi about today. Making sure she's comfortable and happy."

Mike collapses on the couch behind me, kicking his feet up on the small coffee table and putting his hands behind his head. "She's not new, Iz."

"Thank you." I wave my hand toward him, proving my point to my aunt.

"Well, she is, but she isn't," Izzy replies.

I roll my eyes. "I don't know why we have to go out to celebrate tonight."

Uncle Mike laughs. "After you have kids, you'll understand that you'll make any excuse necessary for a night out."

I cross my arms, feeling like my entire family is ganging up on me in some way. "I'm sure Auntie Mia would rather you be at home."

His laughter gets louder. "Mia will be asleep, and so will the kids. I'm sure she'll be lying in the middle of the bed, enjoying the extra space for a few more hours. Pike's finishing his last piece, so we're out of here in thirty. Want me to close out the register?"

"I got it," Izzy says before bringing that hard stare back to me. "We're not done, baby girl. I know you better than anyone, and there's something you aren't telling me."

"Oh, I love a good secret," Mike says from the couch.

"There's no secret, Uncle."

"Want me to hold her down, and you can tickle it out of her, sis?"

I put my hands on my hips and spin around to face my uncle. "I'm not five anymore. That won't work."

"Kid, you know your aunt. She's like a rabid dog when she gets something stuck in her craw. You might as well spill your guts now and make it easy on yourself. And in my mind, you're always going to be a little girl."

"There's nothing to tell. I'll go clean up my station so we can get this celebration happening earlier rather than later. I have a lot to do, and time's wasting away." I march out of the room, not giving them another chance to say anything more.

Pike, Anthony, and my dad are cleaning their stations, talking about bikes because what else would they be talking about.

"Gigi, Pike just told me something interesting," my dad says as soon as he spots me.

I stop dead like my feet have been nailed to the floor. My heart starts to pound out of control, pumping so fast, I'm pretty sure it's about to burst. "What?" I ask, wincing because I'm not sure I want to hear whatever my dad is about to say.

Pike's gaze locks on mine, and I'm ready to blurt out something, anything, to lessen the blow. Why in the fuck would Pike tell my dad about seeing me in Daytona? I thought he wanted to be here, and although starting on a lie isn't great, telling your boss you fucked his daughter is just plain stupid.

"He got a place over at Sunshine Vista. So, you two are neighbors now. That'll make your mom feel better, knowing someone is close by that can look out for you."

A slow grin spreads across Pike's face, and I immediately want to smack it off.

My eyes widen as my gaze moves to my father. "Look out for me?"

"Well, yeah." My dad nods, smiling because he doesn't know the truth. "Your mom doesn't like that you're going to be living on your own, and this will make her feel better."

"He could be a serial killer, Dad. We don't really know Pike that well, and anyway—" I smash my hands together, pulling at my fingers to keep my anger in check "—I'm twenty-one and can look out for myself."

My dad shakes his head. "You're also a girl who's living alone. I don't care if you're thirty, your mom is always going to be your mom. You know how she is, and with knowing Pike lives close, even if you don't ever need his help, she'll sleep better at night."

I love my father, but he still has some backward ways of thinking. He has three daughters and has taught us all how to defend ourselves and be independent, but here he is, talking about how my mom will sleep better knowing I have a guy nearby. A dick has nothing to do with safety. Knowing I've got a bullet for whatever dumb fuckers try to fuck with me is all the security I need.

"She should sleep better knowing I'll have my Glock

in my nightstand, ready to shoot anyone who tries any shit."

Dad shakes his head, scrubbing his hands down his face and muttering a string of curse words under his breath. "First, you know she can't find out about the Glock."

"Dude, you never told Suzy about getting Gigi a gun?" Anthony says, staring at my father with his mouth hanging open.

"Nope, and we're going to keep it that way," Dad tells him.

"You know how to shoot with that?" Pike asks, leaning back in his chair, eyes only on me.

"You want to find out?" I smirk.

Pike throws up his hands. "Maybe we can hit the range."

"That's a hard no." I turn back toward my dad. "I don't need a man to keep me safe. Not when I have Lola."

Anthony almost chokes on the water he's sipping. "You named your gun Lola?"

"Of course. What did you name yours?"

"I never named a gun, and I don't have any in the house anymore. Max would skin me alive if she found one with the kids in the house."

All the badass men in my life pretend to be in control, having shit on lockdown in their lives. But it's all a lie. The women in their beds have all the power. Anthony won't even keep a weapon in the house because he can't win an argument with my aunt because she holds the reins, as well as his balls.

"Well, Dad taught me how to shoot a long time ago. When I went away to FSU, he bought me Lola as a graduation present."

"Classy," Anthony says, earning him a glower from my father. "Couldn't get her a normal gift like money or a car?"

"He doesn't do anything normal," I add.

"That ain't no lie. Tamara hates guns," my uncle says, but he couldn't be further from the truth.

I chuckle because Tamara, Anthony's daughter and my cousin, so doesn't hate guns. She loved going to the range with me, especially when we needed to let off some steam around exam week. The girl actually has killer aim, a born natural for someone who never spent much time shooting.

"Lily has a gun," Mike says. "It's good for a girl to know how to defend herself."

Izzy walks into the main room, arms folded, head cocked, ready to go off. "You assholes act like we're weak. I never needed a gun to bring a man to his knees. Don't start acting like we're delicate flowers in need of rescue. You taught your girls how to fight just like you taught me. Lord help any man who fucks with a Gallo girl."

"You got a gun, Pike?" Anthony asks, diverting the conversation from the weakness of the Gallo women and back to guns.

"Nope." Pike shrugs. "I have my fists, and they're the only weapon I need. Used to have one when I was a kid, but haven't felt the need in years."

I roll my eyes again. That was such a bunch of macho crap spewing from his mouth.

"I got you covered, Pike, ya know…in case you need rescuing." I smirk.

Pike's body shakes with laughter. "You're a funny chick, Gigi."

"We're leaving in ten. Whatever isn't cleaned tonight will have to be done in the morning," Izzy announces to the entire room. "There's a cold drink with my name on it, and you Chatty Cathys are wasting time."

"We're moving as fast as we can, Mom," Anthony tells her, earning a glare back for his attempt at trying to make a funny.

Ten minutes later, Izzy's shooing us out of the shop, locking the door behind us.

"Want a lift?" Pike asks as he walks next to me into the parking lot.

I gawk at him. "Are you serious?"

"Well, yeah."

"Do you want a lift? Because I'm not going on the back of your bike tonight."

"Does that mean you'll get on the back another time?" he asks with his face covered in shadows, but his white smile is clearly visible.

"No."

"Why don't you ride with Gigi, Pike?" Izzy asks, and I know she's testing me. Seeing if I'll lose my shit, which I'm pretty close to doing. "Since we're going to be having a few drinks, one of you needs to stay sober enough to drive. Might as well use one car since you're going to the same place."

I open my mouth to argue, but Pike jumps right on in. "Good idea, boss."

"Just put your bike behind the shop. No one will mess with it," she adds, staring at me as I glare at her, but she's sporting the biggest smile. "Gigi will follow you back there."

I look to my dad for a rescue, but he's climbing on his bike, either completely oblivious to the conversation or he agrees with my aunt and just isn't saying anything.

"Works for me," Pike says, throwing a leg over the seat, looking all too happy about the turn of events.

"I'm sure it does," I mutter to myself before climbing in my truck and letting out a stream of curses as soon as I close the door.

My aunt, God love her, is testing my patience and doing what she does best…sticking her nose where it doesn't belong and meddling in other people's lives.

What else could possibly go wrong?

12

PIKE

THERE ARE THINGS I KNOW FOR CERTAIN, AND OTHERS I'd only assume. I know Joe Gallo loves Gigi more than just about anything, except for maybe his other daughters and his wife. The way he looks at his eldest daughter, it's like the sun and the moon rise and set on her very existence. I don't remember my parents, either one of them, ever looking at me the way he looks at her. I was more of a nuisance to them than a source of pride. I could do no right in their eyes, and they made sure to let me know how they felt on a daily basis.

Even from the short amount of time I've spent at Inked, I also know the Gallos are a tight-knit crew. They love being around one another, busting the others' balls about whatever they could find. I can't imagine having so many people willing to have my back about anything and everything.

The closest I got to having something like that wasn't from blood relations. When I turned eighteen and left Tennessee, I landed straight in the middle of a group of bikers who were hell-bent on making me one of their own. Spent three years riding with them as I worked at various tattoo shops all over Florida, trying to better my artistic craft and my line work. They treated me better than the two people who gave me life. They didn't judge me, didn't expect anything but loyalty, and had my back no matter what shit went down. And there was shit. Plenty of it too. I was an angry kid with a massive chip on my shoulder, pissed off and ready to take on the world, no matter the consequences.

The guys adopted me in a way. As much as any group can when the person's not a child anymore. I was always open and honest, telling them the biker life wasn't for me. I had dreams, and nothing, not even my first real family, would derail me. When I finally found a shop that would hire me full-time, I started spending less and less time with the MC. They weren't happy, but they understood where my heart was, and it wasn't riding up and down the coast of Florida, wreaking havoc and raining down mayhem.

They weren't in my life on the daily, but I never said goodbye. I still met the guys every year at Bike Week, catching up like old friends who had a long history together. It was our own little fucked-up family reunion, because we had one another if no one else.

Over the last two days, I also realized Gigi's Aunt Izzy, the one with the giant attitude, liked to be in the know about *everything*. There wasn't a person's business she wasn't all up in. That included Gigi and now me since we were clearly throwing off some sort of vibe neither of us could hide, but we weren't about to fess up to anything either.

"This is my last beer," Mike says after he orders his second and another round, slipping a fifty to the waitress. "I finally feel as old as I am, and staying out late, partying my ass off, won't make for a happy Mike tomorrow."

From the little I know about Mike, he had dreams of being a fighter. He even lived out that dream, climbing to the top, getting the title, before marrying and calling it quits.

I'd thrown down with some pretty scary fuckers in my time, but no one quite as big as Mike Gallo. The man made every doorway seem small. But even with his imposing size, he has a kind smile and says shit that makes the smile slide easily across my lips.

"We're all leaving after this," Izzy announces, mothering us like she did all day at the shop. "This makes the second round, and anything more than this and none of us can drive."

"I'm good with the one," I add because although I'm not above mixing business with pleasure, I don't know these people well enough yet to match them drink for drink.

"Good, then you can drive Gigi home," Joe says from across the table with his daughter sitting right next to him, giving me the side-eye.

"I'm fine, Dad. It's only beer," she tells him and motions toward her half-empty glass sitting in front of her. "It's not like I'm about to chug the next one."

The first time I met Gigi, she had more than a beer

in her system. The girl could drink and had an appetite for alcohol, like almost every college kid in the country.

"I'll make sure she gets home safely." I know it's going to aggravate her to no end that I'm willing to be her escort home.

"It's amazing I survived college without a ride home after a beer." She rolls her eyes, pushing her beer farther away with her top lip curling. "It takes more than that to get me tipsy."

Joe covers her hand as it lays on the table in front of them. "Just do your old man a favor. Give me peace of mind tonight and let Pike drive you."

"Why? Because he's a man?" she grumbles. "That's such bullshit, Dad, and you know it."

"Just be happy you have two sisters and not two brothers, Gigi. Your life could be worse. So much worse," Izzy adds, sliding her fingers through the water drops running down the side of her glass.

"Whatever," Gigi mutters, glaring at me across the table like I'm trying to give her a hard time when I've done nothing but keep my mouth shut, letting our secret stay hidden.

"So, Pike," Anthony says, placing his phone on the table next to his beer. "What's your story?"

I blink a few times, staring at him in confusion because the question is loaded and totally open-ended. "My story?"

"Yeah." Anthony lifts his hand as his eyebrows pull downward. "You got any siblings? Parents still alive? What brought you so far away from home?"

"One brother. Ten years younger than me. My

parents are very much alive and still in Tennessee, hopefully where they'll stay until they take their last breath." I push my beer glass to the side and lean over the table, clasping my hands together.

"Your folks planning a visit?" Izzy cocked an eyebrow, staring at me, waiting for more details than I gave. She was fishing. Always fishing.

"Nope. I haven't spoken to them in years." I catch Gigi's eye. "My grandmother raised me since I was thirteen."

"Years?" Gigi mutters. "I couldn't imagine going that long without talking to my parents."

"That's because you have good parents. No, great parents, Gigi. You grow up with shit parents, living the way I did, you ride away and don't look back. The last thing I need is to waste any more of my life on people who couldn't give a shit if I'm alive or dead."

Gigi's eyes widen in horror at the harshness of my words. "That's awful."

It isn't the first time I've seen the pity on someone's face when they realize I'd had a bad hand dealt to me before turning everything around and making it what I wanted.

"If I'd grown up with an ounce of what you've got —" I dip my head toward her father and waving a hand toward her aunt and uncles "—I probably wouldn't be sitting here, having a beer in another state, determined to plant new roots far enough away I could never run into my past either."

The pretty little waitress sets the beers down on the table, her eyes moving from one person to another but not saying a word because she can probably feel the vibe at the table has shifted.

"Keep it, doll," Mike says when the woman tries to hand him his change.

"You're too kind, Michael," she says as a giant smile spreads across her pouty lips. "If I didn't love Mia so much…"

"It still wouldn't happen, babe. While you're pretty and sweet, you're way too young for an old fart like me."

She snorts. "Always a charmer."

I'm thankful for her interruption. Most of the table is busy shuffling around the beer glasses, hopefully forgetting everything I said moments ago. Everyone except Gigi. Her eyes are pinned on me, sweeping over my face with the small little creases across her forehead more pronounced.

"What about your brother?" Gigi asks as soon as the waitress wanders off because the woman can't leave shit alone.

I shrug. "He was seven when I left home. It's not like we had a close relationship."

"But if your parents were that bad, don't you worry about him being with them when you're not there to protect him?"

I laugh and shake my head. "My parents were shit to me, but not that kid. They love him. Treated him like the king of the castle. He could literally do no wrong in their eyes. He's fine right where he is, and it's not like I could've just taken him when I left. The road is no place for a kid."

Before I took off, I thought about taking Austin with

me, but I wasn't sure how I was going to feed myself, let alone a kid. I knew he'd be fine with my parents. They loved him way more than they ever loved me. They made sure I knew how much more on a daily basis too. My grandmother promised me she'd check in on Austin, and the moment their attitude went south and they started treating him like anything other than a little prince, she'd let me know. Then and only then would I go back for him, taking him wherever my ass ended up.

"Where have you been for the last nine years?" Gigi asks, leaning forward, resting her fist underneath her chin and studying me like I was a rarity instead of the norm.

"Here and there."

"Pike's been working at some of the best tattoo shops in Florida since he was twenty," Joe tells her, figuring my answer wouldn't satisfy his daughter.

"If they were so good, why is he here?" she asks like I'm not even at the table or able to answer.

"Because I only wanted to be at the best place, and that's Inked."

I hope it's enough for the conversation finally to shift away from me.

"And for the two years in between?" she asks like a bloodhound, suddenly interested in my life for the first time since I met her.

"He was hanging with the guys in the Disciples," Izzy throws out there like it is common knowledge and something I put on my resume, which I didn't, and I thought I'd covered my tracks enough that no one would find out. My gaze slides to Izzy, and she shrugs with a shitty smirk. "You didn't think I'd hire you without having my husband run a full background check, did you?"

"So, you all knew, but hired me anyway?" I lean back in my chair, stunned as I look around the table, all eyes on me.

"When we let someone into the shop, we're not only letting them into our business, we're giving them access to our family. No one gets hired without a full work-up, no matter how fucking great their work is," Joe tells me, his face hard and unreadable.

"I was never a prospect," I reply, feeling like I need to explain my checkered past.

"We know," Izzy says, crossing her arms in front of her chest, leaning back like me. "You wouldn't be in that chair if you had been."

"How do you know?" I'm pretty sure the things she's saying and thinks she knows aren't public knowledge or part of any record. At least not something someone could find out without digging into my background, finding the filth I wanted to stay hidden.

"Babe," she says, a shit-eating grin spreading across her face. "My husband may be an investigator now, but he was a DEA agent working the MC scene all across the South. If there's something he needs to know about a person or any club in the country, he's going to find it and not stop until he does."

"He asked around about me?"

Izzy nods. "He went right to the source, had a sit-down with Tiny."

My shoulders slump, and I let out a long, exasperated sigh. "He went to Tiny?"

Izzy nods. "Yep. Got all the dirt."

I raise an eyebrow because I'm sure he got some dirt, but he didn't get the steaming pile of shit that was my time hanging with the Disciples. "Tiny isn't much of a talker."

"Tiny and James go way back, and my brother Thomas and he go even further. They picked Tiny's brain, got the dirt they could get, and were satisfied enough with what he had to say that I got the okay to offer you that seat." Izzy pauses for a moment, shifting in her chair, leaning forward with her elbows resting just off the table. "And just so you know, the Feds watch those clubs every second of every day. You're in the files. Your name is there, pictures of you at their compound, riding with them, causing the havoc only the Disciples cause. If Tiny hadn't vouched for you, telling my husband you were just a kid who needed a home and help, you wouldn't be sitting where you're sitting."

"Still don't like that shit one bit," Joe says, glancing down at his daughter as she gawks at me like she didn't know a damn thing about my past.

She may not have known about the Disciples, but she knew why I was at Bike Week. It's not like we met at the ice cream shop, sharing wanton glances as we licked our cones. We met at a biker rally. One of the biggest ones in the country for fuck's sake.

"I was never in the life, and I don't plan on ever being there either. Those guys took me in when I had nowhere to go. They gave me a bed and a place to belong at a time when I had nothing and no one. They were a solid in my life when all I had was chaos."

"They don't do that shit out of the goodness of their heart," Izzy says, clearly knowing a lot about the life from her husband. "I spent enough time around those guys to know that life comes with strings."

"You know a lot of bikers?" I ask, trying not to laugh because the woman may be scary, but she didn't seem the type to be hanging out at compounds, sucking the cocks of random bikers for kicks.

"Someday, if you stick around, maybe I'll tell you about the time I spent with the Sun Devils. But that day isn't today, kid."

My eyebrows shoot up. "I know enough about the Sun Devils that I'm not sure I want to know about what shit went down between you and them."

"The fucking Sun Devils," Joe groans. "I hate those fuckers. They caused enough shit with this family that if I ever see one of them again, I'll…"

"They're all put away, Joe. Calm your shit. They can't touch us now," Izzy tells him like he doesn't have a reason to worry, which isn't entirely true.

"They have a far reach, Iz. Even behind bars, those fuckers have eyes and ears on the ground. I'm waiting for the next time they come after this family. And besides, it's not like they have life sentences."

I swallow down the lump that's lodged in my throat, thinking about the Sun Devils and the carnage they'd spread across the South back in the day. "They came after the family?"

Joe nods, eyes steely and cold. "Kidnapped Izzy and,

hell, Angel too, but in the end, they landed in the place they deserved. Should've known better than to mess with two DEA agents' family members, but they weren't always the brightest fucking bunch. They let their thirst for vengeance cloud their judgment and sealed their fate in pulling the shit they did."

"Happens a lot with men like that," Anthony adds as he lifts his beer glass to his lips.

The table goes on chatting about the Sun Devils as I sit there, staring at them in shock and amazement. I can't wrap my head around the fact that the MC went after the Gallos. They seem like the nicest people in the world, maybe wound a little tight and possibly a little too loving, but why the fuck would they come after them and kidnap two women who weren't even part of the world? It makes no sense. But then again, shit inside the MC world rarely made a bit of sense unless you were part of the life with axes to grind and anger to burn.

"I'm ready to go." Gigi stares at me across the table. "You ready?"

I nod, swallowing down the last sip of beer and pushing my seat back, standing. "Let's hit it."

"You two be careful on the way home," Joe says like he's said it a million times before.

A weird feeling crashes over me as Gigi waves goodbye. One of belonging. One of family. All about something I never had before but wished like hell I did. No one has ever given a shit if I got home okay or made it in one piece. The only person who cared was my grandmother, but she wasn't even that concerned, figuring I was a man who would somehow get myself through anything.

But Gigi grew up Gallo. She grew up surrounded by love, not knowing what it's like to have no one at her back. She is luckier than she could ever know, and I am kind of jealous of the life she's lived. The love she has. The acceptance that is freely given.

I'd give anything to have just a small sliver of that goodness in my life. I may not have been given it by birth, but I'll do whatever I have to do to get a little piece of it in my life now.

13

GIGI

"I LOVE THE LAST PIECE YOU DID TONIGHT," PIKE SAYS with his wrist on the steering wheel, looking like he's driven my truck a thousand times. The flash of oncoming traffic lights up his features, sending shadows across his face.

I stare at him in the relative darkness, taking in the slight bump on the bridge of his nose and the lushness of his lips. "I love when clients want me to design a piece. When they give me free rein to run with their thoughts and turn it into something original and meaningful."

"You nailed it. The coloring was spot-on too," he praises, and warmth blooms inside my chest.

"Thanks." I turn my head just as he turns his to look at me because I don't want him to know I'm staring at him. "I could use a little more practice at shading."

"Nah. It took me a couple years to get as good as you are now. In five years, you'll be featured in all the big magazines. Mark my words, Gigi."

"That's really nice of you to say, but you don't have to suck up to me. I don't plan on blowing up your world anytime soon, Pike."

He rolls the truck into the empty parking space in front of our apartment building and stops, turning to me as he cuts the engine. "I figured if you were going to, you would've done it already."

"Oh," I whisper, glancing at him when he shifts, sliding a little closer to me. "What are you doing?"

"Just wanted to talk alone for a few minutes." Pike stares at me in the soft glow of the parking lot lights, and I practically have to will myself not to leap into his lap.

Even after fifteen months, the pull to him is so heavy, the attraction so deep, I have to remind myself he's not for me. We have very little in common except for where we live and what we do. He comes from a different life. One without a loving family but with the Disciples in his past.

"You can talk from over there." I tick my chin toward his side of the cab, because if he gets any closer…

He scoots closer, and I hold my breath. "What's going to happen?"

My fingers work the fringe on the bottom of my denim shorts, and I remind myself to breathe. "I just don't think it's a good idea."

The one thing I know about Pike is he won't do anything I don't want. If I tell him to back off and it's not going to happen, he'll leave me alone. But then I remember the way his mouth tastes, the sensation of his lips against mine, and how much I want to feel his body pressing mine into the mattress.

"Sometimes, the best things never are."

"What if we get caught?"

He cocks an eyebrow. "Your parents have surveillance set up?"

I shrug, laughing nervously because the way he's looking at me is nothing short of hot and needy. "I wouldn't put it past my mother. My father is overprotective, but my mother is downright smothering."

His gaze drops to my lips as I speak, and heat sparks across my body. The needy ache I've felt for him since the moment I laid eyes on him again at Inked amplifies, and I'm pretty sure nothing but his touch will help chase the feeling away.

"Darlin'," he says, and my belly tumbles. I keep telling him how much I hate that word, but damn it, it's a lie. It's so much better than babe, and when Pike's saying it, there's nothing sweeter and it's a total turn-on. "Get your ass over here and kiss me already."

I gawk at him. It's like he's reading my mind because my body language doesn't exactly scream sex right now. I haven't moved an inch, too scared of what will happen if I do. The last time Pike and I kissed, we barely came up for air for almost a week. With my current dry spell, I'm confident it'll be much the same, but I don't have the luxury of time.

When I don't move, Pike slides closer until our knees are touching. "I'm going to kiss you, Gigi."

Oh God. Oh God. Oh God. Yes! Yes! Yes! I want to crawl

into his lap, wrap my arms around his neck, and kiss the hell out of the man until I'm gasping for air.

"Pike," I whisper, my eyes locked on his mouth as his tongue pokes out, sweeping across his bottom lip. "I…"

The words don't make it out of my mouth before his hand is on my jaw, caressing my cheek with his thumb. "Tell me no, and I'll stop."

"Pike," I repeat like my brain is fried and his touch alone has rendered me completely and absolutely stupid.

He leans forward, eyes locked on mine, hand on my face as the shadows pass over his face when he moves his mouth closer.

"Yes," I whisper so quietly, I can barely hear myself over the loud thumping of my heart against the insides of my chest.

When his lips connect with mine, so velvety soft and warm, I can do nothing but open to him. The man is hard everywhere. Hard arms. Hard features. Hard eyes. Hard cock. But the one place he's soft is his lips. His mouth is demanding, just like the rest of him, as his lips press against mine. He tightens his fingers behind my neck, pulling me toward him, and my body moves on its own. Without thinking, I crawl into his lap, straddling him in the front seat of my truck in the very public parking lot of our building.

My arms go around his neck like they were always meant to be there as I settle into his lap, pressing my chest against his, loving the demanding way he's kissing me.

I could get lost in him.

I did actually.

Fifteen months ago, I'd been in this same position, tasting his lips, figuring I'd never see him again.

Wrong.

He slides a hand around my back, gripping my ass roughly as his tongue moves across my lips, and my skin starts to tingle everywhere like his mouth is the lighter fluid and his touch is the match. My body's on fire, burning for the man below me.

I grind my hips as I open my lips, giving him anything he wants. It's been so long since I've been touched like this. So long since I've felt this kind of need for anyone. In all honesty, I haven't wanted another man since the day I drove away from Daytona, telling myself Pike was nothing more than a fling.

Pike's fingers slide up the back of my neck before tangling in my hair, securing me to him even though I'm not going anywhere. I'm right where I want to be.

"I missed this," he murmurs against my lips, sending a jolt of white-hot electricity down my spine like a lightning bolt of need coursing through my system. "Missed how sweet you taste."

I moan and tighten the hold I have around his shoulders, latching my lips back on to his to stop him from talking. We talked all day. What we didn't do was kiss. Now isn't the time for chatter. Now's the time to get what I've been thinking about since the moment I laid eyes on him again.

A man clears his throat, and I freeze, my eyes flying open and going wide. We stare at each other, our mouths still touching, but not breathing.

"Excuse me," the man says, not giving two fucks that

we're currently getting hot and heavy in the parking lot. "I'm looking for a Mr. Pike Moore."

Pike's lips move to the side, sliding off mine slowly, and I want to crawl through the open window and knee this guy in the balls for interrupting us. "I'm him."

The man reaches down, fishing something out of his pocket, and Pike's body stiffens under me. His hand is wrapped around my arms, hauling me off his body and to the other side of the truck, shielding me from whatever the man is about to do.

"I'm Special Agent Russo from the FBI. I was wondering if I could have a minute of your time." The man flashes his identification before snapping the leather wallet shut.

Pike growls. Flat-out growls like he's about to attack. "It's almost one in the morning, I'm sitting in the truck, having a nice time with my girl, and you pick now to bust my balls?"

The agent's eyes cut to me and then back to Pike. "Sorry for the bad timing, but I've been waiting around here all day for you, Mr. Moore."

"Bad timing," Pike mumbles, his hands balling into tight fists against his legs. "Understatement of the fucking year."

"I only need a moment of your time," the agent says, making no move like he's going to leave and let us finish what we began.

Pike's gaze moves to me. "Go inside, darlin'. I'll only need a minute."

"I'm not leaving." No man is going to tell me what to do, and like fuck am I leaving Pike out here alone with an agent without finding out what the hell he wants.

"It's about your dad."

If I thought Pike was stiff before, he's hard as granite now. His movements are slow, letting the man's words wash over him, soaking into his soul. "Is he dead?"

"He wasn't the last time we had eyes on him."

Pike moves his hand to the steering wheel, making no attempt to get out of the truck as I sit next to him, not moving and barely breathing.

What the hell could the agent want with Pike if it has to do with his father? Whether Pike likes the man or not, I can't imagine a cop showing up, asking me questions about my own blood.

"I don't talk to my father, so I don't know how I can help." Pike's eyes burn as they come to me. "I'm busy with my girl, so if you could come back tomorrow, maybe, and I mean maybe, I'll talk to you."

"Sir," the agent says and shakes his head. "I'm not leaving until we talk. If I have to haul your ass downtown to FBI headquarters to do it, so be it."

My hand clamps over my mouth as I gasp, and I try to cover my horror at the entire situation. "Is that really necessary?" I mumble against my palm with wide eyes.

The agent nods. "Actually, let's take a drive. I'd like to speak to you in private. It'll be safer downtown."

"Like fuck," Pike hisses, hand tightening around my steering wheel like he's trying to choke the life out of it.

"Don't go."

I stick my nose where it doesn't belong, but that's always been my way.

"Ma'am, do you want to take a ride in the back of my car too? You can wait in the holding cell where we keep the *good* criminals." He winks.

Pike's out of the truck before the guy can straighten his face again. "Leave her the fuck alone. If your beef is with me, keep it with me. Ya hear me?"

I lunge to the side, trying to grab on to his arm but miss, falling face first into the seat. "Let me call my uncle," I mutter into the fabric as I push myself upward to a sitting position.

Pike turns, his eyes flashing a warning that needs no words. I'm to call no one. "I'll be fine. Get your ass inside and lock the door." Pike ticks his head toward the apartment building like I'm just supposed to obey.

Is he for real? If the situation weren't so dire and the agent didn't look like such a giant douche, I'd laugh right in Pike's face. "Pike, I don't think…"

"He'll be fine, ma'am." The man dips his head, giving me a bullshit smile like I'm just going to take his word on that. He already said shitty things to me and hasn't been the nicest to Pike even though he's supposedly only wanted for questioning.

"Are you arresting him?" I blurt out as I slide across the truck, crawling to my feet just behind Pike.

The agent's gaze sweeps over Pike as he pulls at the cuffs of his dress shirt that are barely peeking out from his suit jacket. "Not yet, but stranger things have happened."

Well, isn't that reassuring?

"Just go inside, Gigi," Pike orders as I start to reach for my phone. "Call no one."

I let out a loud huff before jamming my phone back into my shorts pocket. "Fine."

"Let's go, son."

"Don't call me that. You're not my daddy," Pike says coldly.

"The longer you wait, the later it'll be when you get back."

Pike turns to me and grabs my hands, tangling his fingers with mine. "I'll text you when I'm back, darlin'. Don't worry. I'll be fine."

"I'll go with you." I take a step toward Pike before he tightens his grip, stopping me.

"Stay here in case I need you. Please," he begs with knitted brows.

What the fuck am I supposed to do from here? How can I help him if I'm thirty minutes away? He's crazy if he thinks I'm just going to stand by, twiddling my damn thumbs until he sends me a text message.

"Okay," I lie. "I promise," I lie again.

He exhales as his shoulders finally relax. "Thank you." He leans forward, placing his lips on my cheek and whispers, "I promise everything will be fine."

I don't know if I want to scream or cry as he releases me, backing up toward the agent, our eyes locked on each other. I want to beg him not to go. Beg him to stay here, but I know it's useless.

Pike folds himself into the back of the guy's unmarked car, staring at me through the window as the dickhead slams the door. I lift my hand and wave, wishing I could tell him everything will be okay. He may have whispered the words, but I know he didn't believe a word he spoke.

The agent smirks as he climbs into the front, revving the engine like that piece of shit Capri is a hot rod.

I walk toward the car, following as it slowly rolls toward the exit of the apartment complex. Pike turns in his seat, peering at me through the window, barely visible in the darkness.

I waste no time, grabbing my phone and dialing the only person I know who can help in this situation. The only one I know who can keep his mouth shut.

"It's fucking late. This shit better be good."

I wince. "Um, Uncle James. I need you." I look into the darkness as the taillights of the agent's car disappear.

14

PIKE

THE SOUND OF METAL ON CONCRETE SNAPS ME OUT OF the haze from sitting too long in a quiet room at four in the morning. Fuck, I need to be at work in eight hours, and I'm nowhere near my place and need to get some damn sleep so I'm not useless tomorrow.

So far, the asshat agent hasn't said much but has come in to bust my balls every few minutes just as I'm nodding off. I assume it's all part of his genius master plan, trying to deprive me of sleep so I'll tell him whatever he's fishing for just so I can leave.

"Sorry," a new guy says, plopping down in the chair, almost spilling the coffee he's holding in one hand. "Didn't mean to wake you."

Fucker. "Can we just get this shit over with so I can get out of here?"

They took my phone as soon as I got here. I'm pretty sure there's probably dozens of texts from Gigi, possibly a few missed calls, all growing in levels of panic. I wasn't looking forward to having her chew my ear off for ordering her ass inside and telling her to mind her own business, even if I said it in a nice way. Or at least, the nicest way I knew how.

The man flips open a folder, fingers a few pages, staring down at the words. "Your father is Colton Moore?"

"Yes." I grit my teeth together, slouching over in the chair and rapping my fingertips on the metal table. "I thought we established this."

"I'm the new shift." He peers up for a moment as he turns a page. "Have you ever worked for the firm of Moore, Justice, and Sanders?"

I glare at this dumbass. "Do I look like a lawyer?"

"I guess that's a no," he says, pulling a pen from a pocket on the front of his shirt. "Have you ever spent time in his office?"

"Recently? I mean, my ass is in Florida, so that would be a no."

Is this guy fucking serious with these dumb-ass questions?

"Ever, kid. Have you ever spent time in his office?"

"When I was a kid, sure. He is my father."

He scribbles something on the paper, flipping to the next sheet. "Have you ever heard the name Dominic DiSantis?"

My face doesn't move because I've heard that name a million times in my life. Dirty Dom. That's how my father always referred to him, especially when talking with other friends and clients he'd bring back to the house. The man was a criminal and my father was his attorney, but half the shit my dad did for him wasn't covered under the umbrella of a normal attorney-client relationship.

They thought I was too young to understand when they'd talk in my presence. Just figured I was some dumb kid who was too busy pushing around the same shitty toy truck I'd had for three years to know what they were saying, but I heard every word and took it all in.

"I've heard the name," I tell the guy who is staring at me across the table, waiting for me to lie.

I'm pretty sure he already knows the answers to the questions. A quick background check would've told him I haven't lived in Tennessee in almost a decade, and being Colt's kid, of course I heard names I probably never should've heard.

He raises an eyebrow. "Care to elaborate?"

I raise mine right back. "Care to tell me why?"

The man sighs, leaning back in the chair, pushing the folder of papers toward the middle of the table. "Dominic DiSantis is a mobster."

I nod because anyone who's anyone and pays attention to the national news knows this shit. He was popped a year ago and is awaiting trial for money laundering and a whole long-ass list of shit I'm pretty sure he did.

"He's currently locked up and awaiting trial."

"Tell me something I don't know." I kick back, putting my hands behind my head, acting as chill as I can so I don't lose my shit. "Why did you haul me down here to tell me something I already know? This is bullshit, verging on harassment."

"Your father was on retainer with Dominic."

"I know," I bark, losing my patience.

"We believe your father may be involved in Mr. DiSantis's criminal enterprises."

I lean forward, resting my arms on the table and glare at this buffoon. "Whether my father is or isn't, I don't know how you think I can help. Do you know how close I am to my father?" I pause for a second, and just as he's about to say something stupid again, I continue. "I haven't spoken to my father in over ten years. I lived with my grandmother as soon as I started middle school because I couldn't be around the asshole another minute. He may be my blood, but that doesn't make him my family. I know you want to nail him and DiSantis, but there's nothing I can say to help you."

The agent crosses his arms, studying me. "Whether you've talked to him in ten years or not, you know things, were privy to things no one else was. If you're not willing to help us, maybe we should visit your little brother at summer camp and see if he's willing to help us."

I force myself to stay in my seat because all I want to do is lunge at the asshole and wrap my fingers around his neck until he begs for me to let go. "Leave Austin out of this."

"We're running out of options, Mr. Moore. Either you help us, or we'll have no other choice but to speak with Austin."

"Talk to my mother. I'm sure she'll flip on him if you offer her something she wants, like a new life and an unlimited bank account."

"She's dead, son."

I blink a few times, thinking I must have heard him wrong. "Excuse me?"

"Died this morning. Gunshot to the back of the head after she dropped Austin off at camp. We figured it was an execution, sending a message to your father from Mr. DiSantis."

My head spins with the news as it slams into my chest like a ton of bricks. *My mother is dead.* She and I had a tenuous relationship at best, but I wasn't her favorite and always seemed more like a burden than a blessing. She never once stopped my father from putting his hands on me. Never once stopped the man from treating me like an outcast in my own home. If she had a maternal instinct, it didn't appear until Austin was born.

I never went to summer camp. I never got shit as a kid. There wasn't a new toy in my room until the ones I had were so worn out they basically fell apart. I don't remember being hugged or snuggled, even if I was sick or bleeding. The two of them were worthless. The day my grandmother caught my father, hand raised, ready to strike me, she took me in and I never looked back.

"You think DiSantis killed my mother, and you track me down, harassing me for hours, and don't even bother to mention that shit until now?" I ball my hands into fists, wanting to punch this fucker straight in the face. "And you make me leave my girl alone and vulnerable so you can haul me down here, not even thinking it's a good idea to clue me the fuck in on the day's events?"

"We have no reason to believe your girlfriend is in danger."

"Pardon me if that isn't reassuring. Did you think

my mother was in danger, or did you let her take one for the team?"

"Son…"

"Don't fucking call me that!" I yell, pushing back from the table and rising to my feet. "Don't ever fucking call me that. I want to talk to your superior."

The man's up, studying me as I pace around the room, running my hands through my hair to do something with them besides knock his lights out. "I don't think…"

"That seems to be the norm around here," I taunt, wishing he'd get pissed and swing on me just so I could land a good one on him.

He turns his back to me as the handle to the door turns and opens, and a man appears. "Agent Carson, the interview is over."

"Damn right, it is," I bark out, leering at the two men across the room from me.

"We weren't finished," Carson replies, turning and tossing his pen on the table that sits between us. "Just a few more minutes."

The other man shakes his head. "Can't let that happen. We have an issue."

"What kind of issue?"

"The Director called and isn't so happy about us bringing Mr. Moore in for questioning."

Carson stiffens. "How the hell does he know?"

The man gives a small shrug. "I guess the kid has a few connections. Calls were made. Favors exchanged, and we're to let him go or else…"

Connections? Favors? No one knows I'm here except for

Gigi. *Fuck.* She didn't listen to a damn word I said. By now, the entire Gallo family probably knows my ass is downtown, sitting in FBI headquarters for some unknown reason. I'll have a lot of explaining to do and a lot of begging if I am going to be allowed to stay at Inked and at least finish out the contract on the chair I so badly want.

Fucking perfect. If shit wasn't fucked up enough already, my mom dead, my brother motherless, and my father who the fuck knows where, my job is in jeopardy because Gigi couldn't let me handle my own shit.

"What the fuck? The Director knows how important this case is." Carson throws out an arm in my direction. "And we're just supposed to let him go?"

The other man raises an eyebrow. "You want to call him at this hour and tell him you think he's wrong?"

Carson glances toward the ceiling and lets out a loud grunt. "Fuck. This is bullshit."

"It's *all* bullshit," I mutter, still pacing so I don't go ballistic about the entire situation, including the two assholes in the room with me.

"We're sorry about your mother, Mr. Moore," the new guy says like somehow his condolences are going to make anything better.

My mother cut ties with me years ago. The last time I talked to her, I was already living at the Disciples' compound, which she snubbed her nose at, reminding me that she thought I was a piece of trash before and always. That was the last time I said goodbye to her, and that time, I meant that word completely.

I should be crying, shedding a tear that the woman

who gave birth to me is lying somewhere on a cold metal table, stiff and not breathing. But I can't bring myself to cry. I care, of course I do—she is family—but there's no love between us. There never will be now.

The thing I care most about is the fact that Gigi's out there and I don't know who's had eyes on me. If DiSantis was watching my parents close enough to off my mom, is he watching me too? Has he seen Gigi and me together? Would he use her to keep me quiet?

"You can go, Mr. Moore. If we need you further…"

I wave him off, pushing past Carson. "You know where to find me the next time you want to drop a bomb in my lap and harass me."

"The department truly is sorry," he says as I brush against him, wishing I could knock them both over as I make my way toward the sterile gray hallway.

"Save it. Just give me my phone and let me go."

"The receptionist at the front desk will give you your things before you leave."

I pause for a minute, waiting for someone to offer me a ride home, but they say nothing. I stalk down the hallway, happy to be heading toward freedom and to make my way back home to check on Gigi. I have to figure out what to do about her. Do I distance myself from her entirely? Distance myself from her family too? I don't want my father to put her and her entire family at risk because he's a money-grubbing asshole.

I'm staring at the floor, watching the black-and-white checkered pattern pass in a blur and thrilled as fuck to get out of here, even if I have to hitch a ride home with a stranger.

"Pike!" Gigi screeches.

I lift my head, catching sight of the beautiful brunette running toward me like we haven't seen each other in years. "Are you okay? Oh my God. I was so scared. I thought they were never going to let you go." Her gaze darts over my body, checking for some sign of wear and tear. "Did they hurt you? I was so worried, I didn't know what to do. I'm so sorry." She looks over her shoulder toward a man who doesn't look happy and is scarier than any dude in this place. "I had to call someone. Don't be mad at me," she finally pleads, sucking in a breath because she hasn't given herself a chance to come up for air and stop talking long enough to breathe.

"I'm not mad, darlin'," I whisper, mindful of the man looking a little like a caged lion and totally pissed off to be here at this hour. I want to wrap her in my arms, steal her away from this place, and put her where I know no one will find her, but the way the man she came with is staring at me, at us, I know I'd better keep my hands to myself.

Gigi turns toward the tall, dark-haired man behind her. "This is James," she says and pulls me toward him, locking her fingers with mine. "My aunt Izzy's husband."

My eyes widen. "You called Izzy's husband?"

She nods, smiling at me like her decision made all the sense in the world. "Izzy's not stupid. She knows something is going on. Plus, James worked for the DEA, and I figured if anyone had connections with the FBI, it would be him. What else was I supposed to do? Just leave you here?" She squeezes my fingers and gives me the sweetest smile, like it's going to make all this shit okay.

Fucking great.

"Well, yeah." I pull my hand from her grip because Uncle James hasn't taken his eyes off our connection, and there's no happiness on his face. "I would've figured something out sooner or later."

James stands taller, crossing his arms as he spreads his legs farther apart. "You two about done?"

"We're done." I look the man in the eye because he deserves my respect. No matter what, he pulled my ass out of a jam, getting up in the middle of the night to help a person he didn't even know. "Can you just take us home?"

James shakes his head. "You two are going to my place. Izzy's waiting, and she's probably climbing the walls right about now. If I don't bring you there, she'll have my ass. And besides losing sleep, I don't need her chewing my ear off all morning about dropping you off at home."

"I'm sorry," Gigi says again.

"It's fine," I lie because what else am I supposed to say? Nothing about this night has been fine. From the moment the asshole interrupted our kiss until the moment I walked out of the interrogation room, nothing has been fine.

"We're coming, Uncle James." Gigi turns to me, grabbing my hand, giving my fingers a light squeeze. "Okay?" She stares up at me, looking for my confirmation.

I nod. I'm not sure if it's something I want Gigi to

know because she'd flip her shit and rightfully so. Maybe I need to explain the situation to James, get his thoughts on what my next move should be and how we can shield Gigi from any potential blowback.

James practically punches the door open, walking into the thick night air with Gigi and me following behind him. She glances at me, giving me a small smile every few steps before staring at her uncle and frowning.

I know she has a lot to say. I know she wants to ask me everything, but she's holding back…for once. I have a lot to say too, but I'm not sure I can put everything into words just yet. There's so much swirling around my brain, I can barely make sense of it all.

"Pike, sit up front. You and I are going to talk," James says as we approach his kick-ass Challenger parked just outside the doorway since the place is deserted.

"Um," Gigi mumbles, wanting to say more but shutting her mouth when James turns his gaze toward her. "Got it. I'm in the back."

I fold the seat forward, letting her crawl into the impossibly small back seat, thankful I don't have to contort myself in crazy ways to sit next to her. I slide in under the watchful eye of James and stare straight ahead, feeling something strange wash over me.

"Seat belts, kids."

I don't argue with the man. I'm not stupid. I'm not even in the mood to tell him I'm not his kid because I'm almost certain he'd knock me upside the head, and I'd still have to put on my seat belt before he'd drive away.

Right now, all I want is a place to lay my head, sort out my thoughts, and say goodbye to this day.

"How do you know DiSantis?" he asks before we're even out of the parking lot.

"I don't." I shrug, staring out the front window as the oncoming cars pass in a blur. "My father worked for him."

"That's it? You never did any side jobs for him?"

"That's it. I was a kid last time I was around him, fifteen years ago, maybe. I forgot about the guy until I saw he'd been arrested splattered on the front page of the newspaper."

James adjusts in his seat, leaning forward, holding the steering wheel with one hand. "The Director and I go way back. We have a history together. He told me what he could about the case, why they hauled you in for questioning, and what they're hoping to gain."

"I don't have anything to offer." I shrug, placing my elbow on the door, resting my head in my palm because I'm so exhausted, I'm fighting to stay awake in the darkness.

"They told me about your mom," James says softer, his voice laced with sorrow. "I'm sorry for your loss."

Gigi gasps behind me, and I straighten. "Oh my God. Pike, I'm so sorry." Her voice wavers like she's on the verge of tears, but there's no time for crying.

I ignore her, because there's more pressing shit than fretting over a woman who gave no shits about me. "I'm worried about Gigi and anyone who's around me right now. I could use your help in figuring out what my next move should be, sir."

"Why are you worried about me?"

This time, James ignores her. "We have a lot to figure out and not a lot of time to do it. For the time being, the safest place for the two of you is at my house. You'll stay there until we know what we're dealing with. Got it?" James raises up, looking in the rearview mirror as we wait at a traffic light. "You hear me, Giovanna? I don't want any lip either."

Fan-fucking-tastic.

The night just went from bad to clusterfucked beyond belief.

15

GIGI

I YAWN FOR WHAT MIGHT BE THE HUNDREDTH TIME IN the thirty-minute drive home from the FBI headquarters. To say I'm tired is an understatement. I don't remember being this exhausted in my entire life. I never even pulled an all-nighter studying for college exams.

I've sat in relative silence as James and Pike talked around me, ignoring my every comment like I wasn't talking or even in the same car with them. They are both infuriating, cut from the same manly cloth, and it's annoying as hell.

"Be ready for the real grilling to start," James says as he pulls into the drive and his headlights land on Aunt Izzy.

She's pacing back and forth in the driveway, her head coming up as she's bathed in light from the car. The look on her face isn't friendly or even playful, but serious as a fucking heart attack and like she's ready to pounce at any second.

"Well, this should be fun," I mumble and wonder if I should've called Uncle Thomas instead. But I know Angel is shit at keeping secrets, and right now, I needed silence.

"Just let her say what she needs to say, answer what she wants to know, and you'll live to see the sunrise," James says, trying to make light of what totally isn't a funny situation.

I drag my hands down my face, trying to clear my mind and wake myself up for what's probably going to be hours of explaining and getting my ass chewed out.

"You handle your aunt while Pike and I talk in my office," James tells me as he cuts the engine and unlocks the car doors.

"Handle her?" I cackle, feeling loopy from exhaustion. "You know that's an impossibility, right?"

James's eyes slice to mine. "You're exactly like your aunt, kid. You two think alike. If I didn't know better, I'd think you were her daughter. You know how she thinks, so handle her. Tell her what you want, leave out what you can, and then get your ass to sleep." James turns toward the door as Izzy raps her fingers against the window before throwing her arms up in a *what the fuck* kind of way.

"I think I'm getting the better end of this deal," Pike says as he pushes open his door, climbs out, and pulls the lever to let me out of the crazy-small back seat.

"You so did," I whisper, brushing up against him as I crawl out, almost smacking my head before I find my footing. "I'll find you when you're done."

"You two better get your asses inside. You have a lot of explaining to do," Izzy announces before I've even stood straight and stretched my legs.

"I have a feeling I'm going to be done before you, darlin'," Pike says as the corner of his mouth quirks up.

I scowl because there's nothing even remotely amusing about the entire situation. From Pike being hauled downtown, the fact that his mother is dead and I have no fucking clue how or why, and that my aunt and uncle are now all up in my shit and Pike's too.

"Sweetheart," James says, grabbing Izzy by the waist and hauling her body against his. "Go easy on the kid. She's had a long, stressful night. She's tired."

Izzy glances at me over James's shoulder. "Good. She'll break easier that way."

"For fuck's sake," I mutter, rolling my eyes. "I'll tell you everything, Auntie, if you just let me sleep for a little while."

"Fat chance, missy. March your pretty little ass in the kitchen, and we'll have some coffee while we talk about all the shit you've left out."

Pike squeezes my hand, peering down at me. "Tell her what you want, Gigi. I have nothing else to hide. I'm pretty sure my ass is going to be fired anyway."

"Why?" I furrow my eyebrows as I glance up at him, my mouth hanging open.

"No one wants trouble coming to their door, especially from someone they don't know and just hired. Go with her. It'll all be better in the morning."

"Find me, okay? Promise me," I plead.

Pike nods, releasing my hand and pushing me toward my aunt. "Go."

Izzy's out of James's arms and around the Challenger within seconds, stalking toward me like a woman possessed. "Stop wasting time," she says, reaching for my arm and hauling me away from Pike like I'm a little girl again.

I glance over my shoulder, mouthing "I'm sorry" to Pike as I follow my aunt up the stairs to the front door of their house. He only waves, giving me a small smile like this is just another day and not one where his mother dies and his life may be at risk.

"Sit," Izzy says before I'm two steps into the kitchen, pointing at a chair near the island. "Coffee or water?"

"Coffee." I slump over, wishing she'd just give me a pillow and one hour to get a little sleep. But I know my aunt, and she ain't giving me nothing until I give her something in return.

She pours the coffee, her back to me, and I can almost hear her thoughts and the line of questioning she's about to hurl at me.

"Before we start." I clear my throat, staring at her back, wishing like fuck I was anywhere but here. "Can you not tell my dad?"

Izzy sighs, placing the coffee carafe back on the warmer. "They already know."

I gasp, eyes widening, and suddenly feel more awake than I ever have in my entire life. "What?"

"There was an agent waiting at your parents' house when he got home from the bar tonight. He knows Pike was hauled in for questioning. But we left some things out like the fact that you called James in a complete panic, begging for someone to help a guy you claim to hate."

"I don't hate him," I mumble, crossing my arms over my chest, trying to figure out how to crawl out of this miserable mess.

"I know, baby girl," she says, sliding the coffee cup in front of me. "I used to look at your uncle James the same way. Girl," she laughs, shaking her head as she leans across the counter, facing me. "That man had me all kinds of crazy and my head all twisted."

I laugh because she says that like she's normal now and Uncle James's effect has worn off. He's the only man who can shut my aunt up when she's on a tirade, which is more often than not, especially lately.

"So, start at the beginning and tell me how you know Pike." She pins me with her gaze, and I swallow the lump that suddenly forms in my throat.

I glance down at the mug, wrapping my hands around the warm ceramic, wondering just how far back I should go and how detailed I should be. I'm not about to get graphic with my aunt because she's my aunt and I sure as fuck don't ask about her sex life, even if I have heard about it.

"Well…" I pause, stalling but knowing she would wait an eternity to hear the answer. "I met him last year."

Her eyes flash. "Where?"

"In Daytona."

"When?"

"Last year."

"No, smartass. When were you in Daytona? I don't remember you ever mentioning it to anyone."

I shift, squirming in the chair because Tamara and I swore each other to secrecy and hadn't broken our promise for fear of our parents flipping the fuck out. "We went there for spring break," I squeak, cringing at my voice and the look that shifts across my aunt's face.

"You went to Daytona for spring break last year?"

"Yeah." I nod slowly, holding her steely gaze.

"In March?"

I nod again because I figure there's nothing else I need to say, and I know more questions are coming.

She moves her coffee mug to the side, flattening her palms against the cold granite countertop. "Wasn't that Bike Week?"

I nod again, biting on my lip to stop myself from saying anything more.

"Are you fucking stupid, little girl?"

I shake my head, figuring words aren't necessary and knowing she is going to say enough for the both of us.

"You went to Daytona for spring break, which just happened to be Bike Week, alone, and didn't bother to tell anyone?" She sucks in a breath, looking like her head is about to pop off. "Do you know how goddamn dangerous that was?"

"I wasn't alone," I whisper, staring back down at my mug as I play with the handle.

"You were with Tamara, weren't you?" she says

flatly because usually, wherever I go, Tamara isn't too far behind. We're a package deal especially since Lily decided to go to Miami instead of FSU like Tam and me.

I nod again.

Izzy pushes away from the countertop, cursing into the air as she starts to pace again. "Of all the stupid shit you two could do..."

"We were safe. We made it back in one piece. Nothing bad happened, Auntie."

"Thank fuck," she blurts out, stopping on her heel and spinning her body to face me. "I've been to Bike Week. That shit ain't no joke, Gigi."

"You went there?" I ask, fascinated that my aunt ventured into the biker world, but I shouldn't be surprised. She did end up married to one of the most badass men I've ever known besides my father. "To Bike Week?"

"I was almost raped at Bike Week. If it weren't for your uncle Thomas and uncle James, I don't know what would've happened to me." She hangs her head for a moment and takes a deep breath. "But I was older and should've been wiser. You weren't even twenty-one yet, and Tamara isn't even twenty-one now, so explain to me what the fuck you two were doing at Bike Week?"

"Lying on the beach." I don't even believe my own shit because my voice rises like I'm asking a question instead of stating a fact. Dead giveaway and my aunt doesn't miss a fucking beat.

"Gigi," she says flatly. "Stop the bullshit. Lay it out, and I want the truth."

"We went for spring break, but we honestly didn't know it was Bike Week when we planned the trip. We found out as we pulled into town and noticed all hell had broken loose and everyone was covered in leather and tattoos."

"Even if you didn't know it was Bike Week, why did you lie about going to Daytona in the first place?"

I shrug. "We figured Dad would get pissed and Uncle Anthony would throw a fit, so we just thought it would be easier."

Izzy chuckles softly, and I almost think she's going to let it drop, maybe let me go to sleep, but I'm dead wrong. "You should always let someone know where you are. You could've at least told me. A place like that at a time like that was risky, and you're lucky you two made it out unscathed."

"Yeah. I know that now." I'm trying to pacify her. "I'll never do it again."

"And how does Pike fit into—" she clears her throat "—lying on the beach in Daytona?"

"We ran into each other there," I lie and lift the mug to my lips, hoping to cover some of my face so she doesn't know I'm still not telling her the entire truth.

She straightens, crossing her arms in front of her as she stands there in a black tank top and yoga pants, her hair pulled into a tight, high ponytail. "So, you two ran into each other and then you looked like you saw a ghost when you ran into him again?" She narrows her eyes. "You think I'm going to believe that line of horseshit?"

"It's not horseshit," I mumble into my mug, staring at the black liquid because meeting her eyes is a little too much, especially when she's ready to start frothing at the mouth.

"You know the man better than just a quick passing hello. I wasn't born yesterday, Gigi. You better start telling me the truth, or I'll tell Joe about Daytona."

My eyes widen. "You wouldn't."

She drops a shoulder, a grin playing on her lips. "Sweetheart, I'll do whatever I need to do. It won't be my ass getting chewed out by him when he finds out."

I groan, knowing I'm not handling Izzy, but she sure as shit is handling me. Like a pro too. "Fine, we did more than run into each other."

"Did you drink together?"

"A little." I wince.

"Did he know you were underage?"

I shake my head. "We had fake IDs."

Izzy closes her eyes, pressing her fingers against her temples and rubbing. "Motherfucker," she whispers, drawing in a loud breath. "How many drinks did you have with Pike?"

"Which time?" I try to be funny even though I was also being honest.

She twists her mouth. "Stop being a smartass."

I shrug again. "The first night I met him, I think I had one drink."

"So, you weren't drunk?"

"Well…" I give her a nervous smile. "I may have been drinking before I met him. I said I only had one drink with him."

"On a scale of one to ten, ten being black-out drunk, where were you?"

"Before the drink with him or after?"

"For fuck's sake," she says, shaking her head, cursing again under her breath. "After you had the drink with him."

"A nine. I remember everything except for passing out, which I did because tequila." I laugh, trying to break the tension in the room, thinking Izzy will laugh because she's usually the fun one in my family.

She pulls her lips into her mouth, closing her eyes again, and groans. Clearly, I was wrong about the funny, and my aunt's sense of humor died somewhere between earlier tonight—or was that yesterday?—and right now. "You passed out with him, or were you with Tamara?" She's leaning over the counter, tapping her long black fingernails on the granite. "You can tell me, or I'll ask Tam when she comes home."

"I passed out with him." I don't want her questioning Tamara, and she'll find out anyway because Tam will crack like an egg under Izzy's pressure.

"Of all the stupid shit," she says, pushing off the counter and pacing again. "Did he hurt you?" Her eyes slice to mine.

I shake my head. "No, Auntie. He was a gentleman."

"A gentleman who took you back to his hotel room." She laughs. "You're priceless, kid."

"So, you've never had a one-night stand with a stranger?" I throw that right in her face because I've heard all about the night she met James at my parents' wedding. They weren't sipping coffee all night before she snuck right the fuck out of his room.

"We're not talking about me," she deflects. "Now, you had a drink with him, passed out, and then what? Don't leave anything out, or Pike will be out of this house and have his shit packed before your tired ass wakes up."

I take a deep breath and start at the beginning, telling my aunt every detail, minus all the crazy-amazing fucking we did. She doesn't need to know the details because she isn't my girlfriend, and it is already horrifying enough that I am telling her I slept with him. After what feels like I've been talking forever, I stop, finally looking at her in the eyes again. "That's it."

"Did you give him your phone number? Promise him anything?"

I shake my head. "He didn't even know my full name. Just knew me as Gigi, and I told him I was going for coffee one morning and never went back."

My aunt's face changes, and her eyes light up. "You said you were going for coffee?"

I nod, laughing a little and feeling guilty too. "I did. He said he waited for me for hours before realizing I wasn't coming back."

"You so should've been my kid," she says, holding her stomach, still laughing. "That's totally something I would've pulled back in my heyday."

"We're not talking about your heyday." I use air quotes on the last two words. If there's anything more horrifying than telling your aunt about a guy you banged, it's hearing about the guys she banged when she was your age.

"I was young once."

"You still are." I suck up. Something I've always done with my aunt and has typically worked.

"You're a shit liar, baby girl."

"Don't fire Pike," I beg because her mood has changed, and this may be the only time I can beg her for mercy. "I promise he didn't do anything wrong."

"I need to talk to your uncle before I can make you a promise about Pike and his future at Inked."

"That's bullshit. I'm either an adult, or I'm not. You can't treat me like a girlfriend one minute, laughing about the way I left a guy with his dick literally in his hand, and then in the next breath, tell me you can't make me a promise until you discuss something with my uncle. Why not just throw Dad in there too?"

"Pike's future is going to be a family decision, Giovanna. We all own Inked. I don't get the final say in anything that happens to that man without the others getting to say their piece."

"Fucking great," I groan.

"I won't tell them about your spring break activities, but they will know what happened tonight and the world of shit surrounding Pike."

"You won't tell them that we were making out tonight, will you?"

When her eyes widen, I slap my hand over my mouth, realizing I hadn't told her about that and she had no way of knowing. *Fuck. Good going, dumbass.*

"I won't tell them about that either if you want Pike to still be breathing, but they're going to have questions, and you're going to have to woman up and answer them."

"Fine."

"But there will be lots of questions—especially now that Pike's worried about your safety."

Sounds like a fan-fucking-tastic time. I've always wanted to tell my dad about the lies I've told him and the guys—even though they've been limited—that I've banged. I'm totally looking forward to the most uncomfortable situation of my life. *Not.*

I would rather have my hair pulled out strand by strand while being tied to a chair of nails sticking in my ass than talk about any of this shit with the men in my family, especially my father.

"Speak of the devil," Izzy says as the door creaks behind me.

My eyes widen and I freeze, unable to move as if somehow I'll disappear and won't have to have this talk now instead of later.

"Giovanna," my father says, his voice washing over me like I'm a little kid again, waiting to be punished for my stupid shit.

I don't turn around because Joe Gallo is a sweet man, but every guy, even my dad, has his breaking point. I'm pretty sure I've punched right through that ceiling without even trying. "Hey, Daddy."

"You and me, outside."

"Just talk here and grab a cup of coffee. I'll go see what's taking Pike and James so long." Izzy catches my eye, giving me a small wink before she sashays right the fuck out of there, not even worried that my dad's going to blow a fucking gasket.

"Daddy…"

"Save it, baby girl."

I bow my head, staring at my coffee, and ready myself for the biggest ass-chewing of my life.

16

PIKE

"We have a problem," James says into the phone, staring at me from across the desk with his lips set in a firm line. "You're the only man I could think to come to about the situation."

I bite the inside of my cheek, rubbing my hands against the wood of the chair my ass has been planted in for hours, taking James's questions in rapid-fire succession.

"I know what fucking time it is, but I couldn't wait until your old ass decided to get out of bed."

My mouth falls open. No one has ever talked to Tiny, the President of the Disciples MC, that way. At least, I'd never heard them do it, because Tiny would've pounded their face in until they were black and blue, sucking their food through a straw for the next two months.

James laughs. "You never were an early bird, ya old fuck."

I blink a few times, wondering who the fuck James is

to Tiny, and how they know each other well enough that they can laugh while insulting the hell out of each other.

"I have your kid Pike here." James pauses, eyes sweeping over my face. "Yeah, he's in one piece, alive and breathing, sitting right in front of me."

I begged James not to call Tiny. Pleaded with him not to get the Disciples MC involved, but he told me not to be a fucking moron and picked up the phone like it meant nothing to call in a favor.

"Just sit there and keep your mouth shut," James told me before he dialed Tiny's number from memory, surprising the fuck out of me.

So, here I sit, watching James as he takes my business into his own hands, giving help where I didn't ask. But this isn't just about me; this is about his niece and the pile of shit she landed in just by being near me.

"He has an issue with DiSantis and needs somewhere to lie low." James taps the pen he's holding against the pad of paper he'd been taking notes on like he was working my case too. "Couldn't think of anyone with enough manpower and weapons, outside of law enforcement, who would look after the kids except you and the boys."

I shake my head, surprised James is asking Tiny for help. Not just Tiny, but a motorcycle club that has many wearing the badge shaking in their fancy, polished boots.

"It's serious. Pike's mom ain't breathing no more because of the shit his father's in with DiSantis."

I close my eyes, rubbing my fingers into the corners, wondering where the fuck my normal life has gone. Now, my mother's dead, lying somewhere cold with a bullet lodged in the back of her head. My brother's God knows where, hopefully with my grandmother, and my dad's gone missing because he's a fucking coward and a criminal.

"My niece is involved too, Tiny. She'll need safe haven and a guarantee you'll protect her with your life. I'm trusting you more than I've ever trusted anyone who isn't blood by asking you for this favor."

That shit ain't no lie.

Gigi said her uncle worked for the DEA but had since retired, now owning a private investigation firm. But from the sounds of it, he's not entirely out of the game.

"I'll owe you, and you know I always pay my debts," James tells him, still staring at me with a look I can't quite place, and I'm not sure I'd want to even if I could.

"I'll drive them over after nightfall. You're going to have to keep them out of sight until this shit blows over. I don't want them traceable. No eyes can fall on them. The FBI has already questioned Pike, and I don't want them getting their hands on him again. No man, no matter how much he hates his father, should be put in this position. Just keep them safe, and I'll come for them when shit blows over."

"James." I want to argue with him because I'm not sure hiding out with a badass biker crew at their compound is the best idea.

He covers the phone with his hand, mouthing, "Not now. Just keep quiet."

I raise my eyebrows and twist my lips, biting back the words I want to say so badly.

"We'll be there around one. Be ready for us. I'm dropping them off at our meeting place and heading out. I'll have two cars following, making sure no one is on our tail. I want them untraceable."

James leans back, laughing with Tiny before he presses his finger to the phone screen, ending the call. "Go get some sleep. You have a long day and night ahead of you," he tells me, not even wanting to discuss the plans he made on my behalf.

I don't move because I'm not ready and I'm sure as fuck not used to being ordered around. "How exactly do you know Tiny? Because from what I can tell, neither of you run in the same circles."

"You know I worked for the DEA, yeah?"

I nod.

"We most certainly weren't friends back in the day, but there was a mutual respect because I wasn't out to pop him or his club for the dumb bullshit they were pulling back then. The Sun Devils were our target, and they were the mortal enemy of the Disciples. Let's just say Tiny was happy to see that MC put behind bars."

"Wait, he helped you?"

James shakes his head. "Fuck no. He's not a narc, but when I started my own company and needed information, I went to Tiny, made peace, and paid him for intel I couldn't get through any legal channels."

"That's it? You paid him for information, and now you're sending us there, thinking Tiny's going to protect us?"

James studies me as he leans forward, putting his palms together, elbows on the desk, and his mouth resting on the tips of his fingers. "When I went to Tiny about you because Izzy asked me to look into your past before she took you on, I'd never heard the man speak so highly about someone who wasn't a brother." He drops his hands to his desk, squaring his shoulders, eyes still on me. "He talked about you like you were his own kid. A man like Tiny doesn't do that unless you crawled under his skin and made him feel shit he hasn't felt in years. You're up to your neck in shit, and by default, so is my niece. You need to hide out, lie low until shit with your father and DiSantis blows over. I can't think of a better place to put you than a spot that has enough brute force and an arsenal to handle an attack if the man is stupid enough to go after you inside their compound."

"I'd think a man like you would have us under FBI protection instead of the Disciples."

James gives a slow shake of his head. "Even though I worked for the government back in the day, I know how corrupt the system is and how easily people can be bought. I'm not putting my niece somewhere unless I know they can handle the blowback."

I've got nothing left to say. What he's saying is true. If DiSantis wants me dead, I'm a sitting duck unless I hide out, and there's no better place to disappear from radar than at the Disciples' compound.

"Now the sun's up, the day's already fucked because I've been up for hours, and I'll have to listen to Izzy for an eternity as she tears me a new asshole. We'll roll out just after sunset. You tell no one where you're headed, and I mean no one. Not even your grandmother, Pike."

I nod. "I won't tell a soul. Gigi's safety is all that matters."

"If DiSantis's men come…"

"I'd throw myself in front of a bullet if it meant she'd be okay."

She wouldn't be in this shit if it weren't for me.

"I'll hold you to that. If you don't, I'll make you wish you had taken that bullet instead of what I'd do to you."

I stand, rubbing my hands down the front of my jeans, feeling the day's events finally starting to wash over me. "Understood, James."

"Now, go. I have shit to do," he says, not moving from his chair and lifting his chin toward the door.

I turn the knob, swinging open the door, and come face-to-face with Gigi's father. Our eyes lock, and I wait for his fist to make a beeline for my jaw, but he just stands there, staring at me. "We'll have words when this is done," he says, all joy gone from his voice.

"Yes, sir."

"Now, get gone so I can talk to my brother-in-law." He ticks his head toward the empty hallway. "It's best if I'm not around you right now."

By the hardness in his jaw and the coldness in his stare, I'm guessing he knows what went down with Gigi and me in Daytona. This isn't a conversation I want to have with him after being up all night. It's actually not a conversation I want to have with him anytime, but it's one that's going to come whether I like it or not. It's also not a conversation I've ever had to have with a woman's father because relationships weren't really my thing and the women I've slept with were usually older and not so attached to their fathers.

"Got it."

"Izzy's waiting for you in the kitchen," he says, brushing past me and stalking into James's office before slamming the door right in my face.

I expected nothing less. If Gigi were my kid and I were face-to-face with a guy who'd done the shit I did to her, I'd want to rip his fucking throat out with my bare hands. I couldn't fault the man.

I make my way down the long hallway and head toward Izzy's voice. If she weren't talking, I'm not sure I ever would've found the kitchen because the house is probably the biggest one I've ever stepped foot inside.

"There you are," Izzy says as soon as she sees me rounding the corner. "I was beginning to think James was never going to let you out of that room."

Gigi's sitting at the kitchen table, quickly running her fingertips over her cheeks. "I'll show him to his room," Gigi says to Izzy with her back to me.

Izzy raises an eyebrow, eyes moving from me to Gigi. "Your dad is still here. Watch your step, little girl. If you want Pike to still be breathing when the sun sets, don't get cute and try to crawl into his bed, curling yourself around the man for comfort."

So, Gigi did spill our entire sordid, although brief, history together. I'm surprised she kept her shit together this long, even though it's only been two days. I'm sure it was impossible for her to maintain the lie about not knowing me, especially after she lost her shit tonight once I was taken in for questioning. Even more, she was probably shaken up after hearing the shit James and I said in the car. All that together was just enough to have Gigi blabbing every last detail.

"Got it, Auntie." Gigi finds her footing before turning around, showing me her tear-stained cheeks and red, puffy eyes.

"You okay?" I ask as my eyes sweep across her face, knowing I'd caused her tears.

She nods. "Let me show you to your room," she says, ignoring the look I'm giving her and the fact that she's been crying. She dips her head toward another hallway, adding to the maze that is James and Izzy's house. "We'll talk after we get some sleep. I want to know that you're okay."

I walk inches behind her, following her wherever she's taking me because I don't care if it's a closet, as long as there's enough space for me to stretch my legs and close my eyes. "I don't know how I feel just yet. Shit's pretty fucked up, and now you've been pulled into the same mess."

She stops near an open doorway, leaning against the wall, staring up at me with glassy, bloodshot eyes. "I'm sure Uncle James has a plan."

Reaching out, I wipe away a tear that's resting near the edge of her lashes, ready to fall. "Do you know what his plan is, darlin'?"

She shakes her head, not moving away from my touch when I let my hand linger.

"He's sending us to the Disciples' compound to lie low."

Her eyes grow big as saucers. "He's what?"

I nod, just as fucking shocked by that reality as she is. "He said it's the safest place. Can't say I disagree with him either, but the compound isn't a place for a girl like you."

She wrinkles her nose. "A girl like me?"

I sweep my thumb just under her cheekbone, loving the softness against my skin. "You're good, Gigi. Pure, even. The Disciples' compound is no place for a lady."

Gigi's eyes sparkle, and she snorts in the most unladylike way. "I've been around bikers my entire life, Pike. I think I can handle whatever happens at their compound without losing my shit and rockin' myself in a corner."

"These aren't recreational bikers, Gigi. They're hard-core. They live the life. All full of violence, mayhem, booze, drugs, and so much pussy, it'll make your head spin."

She wraps her hand around my wrist and pulls my arm away from her. "You used to live there, yeah?"

I nod.

"We'll be safe there. And right about now, I could use a big fucking drink, so the compound sounds like a good place to get lost and forget all this shit."

"I don't think James is sending us there to party, babe."

She draws her lower lip between her teeth, biting the tender flesh gently. "Then he should send us to a convent. I'm not going into that compound to sit in a dark room day and night, playing the role of a scared little girl. I'm letting my hair down, immersing myself in whatever they have to offer for however long they're offering it. You don't like it? Then you can sit in that dark room alone."

Oh fuckin' boy. This girl is clueless about so much. She's probably binged every motorcycle show available online, thinking she knows how bikers are. But even Hollywood glorifies the life. If she thinks she can handle watching a guy do blow off some chick's ass while she's stretched out on the pool table for everyone to watch, so be it. She's going to get a hard lesson in the real MC life, and it may be eye-opening if not entertaining.

"Just know I'm not leaving your side. You're out of your room, I'm on you like glue."

She grins. "I'm counting on that, Pike."

"But first, we gotta live long enough to get to that compound." I grab her by the shoulder, moving her away from my doorway. "Now, you need to get gone so I can get some sleep before your father finds you outside my room and I end up next to my mother."

Gigi stares up at me, eyes glistening in the bright light. "You want to talk about her?"

I shake my head. "Another time. Maybe once we're settled, but not tonight."

"Okay, but I'm always here to talk," she says sweetly, and I want to wrap my body around hers, surrounding myself with the goodness and warmth only she can offer.

"Night, darlin'." I fight the urge to plant my lips on hers, letting all the day's shit leak out into that kiss.

"Night, Pike," she whispers and takes a step back, staring at me like she's pleading with me to give her what I want to, but I can't because I want to live to breathe another day. "I'll be right next door."

"Got it." I dip my chin, waiting for her to disappear through her doorway before I take a step inside the bedroom, ready for this day to be fucking over with.

Tomorrow starts a whole new shitshow. One filled with Gigi's family, Tiny and the Disciples, and us running for our lives, ducking for cover in a den of sin.

17

GIGI

"Don't you think this is excessive?" I ask Uncle Thomas, which earns me a hard stare in the rearview mirror. "I mean, seven cars behind us is a bit extreme. Even you have to agree with me." I turn to Pike, but he doesn't say a word because he's not rocking any boat, especially not after the way my uncles and father gave him shit before we left Izzy's house.

"Seven cars and twenty men is not excessive when you're dealing with a man like DiSantis," Uncle James says as he sits beside Uncle Thomas in the front seat of the car.

Pike's hand finds mine in the darkness, and he squeezes my fingers. "They're just being safe."

"Don't give me no shit, little girl," James barks.

That's my new name…little girl. I thought I'd grown out of it about the time I started to grow tits, but now it's back, and I have a feeling it's not going anywhere either.

"If I get word that you try to leave that compound…"

"You'll spank me?" I sass, smirking as soon as his eyes cut to mine in the mirror again.

Uncle James and Izzy get their freak on. I know all about their sex life now, after finding his profile on a BDSM website I'd used for research when I had to write a paper for my sexual psychology class at FSU. The textbook only went so deep, and the library was absolutely no help because many of the books they carried were by men who preferred the missionary position and knew nothing of real kink. So, I went right to the source, clicking my way through the biggest kinkster site I could find.

A few clicks later and I was on Master James's page, looking at shit I could never unsee and learning things I never wanted to know. That's not something you can just wipe out of your head. Can't erase the images and words with any amount of alcohol, and I should know because I tried and failed.

"Fucking hell," Thomas mutters, shaking his head. "You have a mouth on you sometimes."

"I'm just practicing for my stint at the Disciples' compound. I figure I can't walk in there all meek and mild. I have to be balls to the wall, ready to sling some shit with the best of them. Yeah?"

Pike's eyes flash as I glance at him with a big smile. "Fuck," he groans, which only makes my smile even bigger.

"It's best if you just stay in your room," James says, like that's going to fucking happen.

So, I keep poking because I have to do something to pass the time, and this drive has officially turned into the longest one of my life. "Why didn't you just lock us up instead, Uncle James? I mean, if you want us to be prisoners, why not just keep us home, locked in our rooms like the little kids you think we are?"

"I get you're pissed, kid, but I don't need your lip right now when I'm trying to do everything to keep you and Pike alive. You don't like the situation?" He pauses, but I don't fill the silence. "Too fucking bad. Sometimes, as adults, we have to do shit we don't want to do so we can live another day. You think a jail cell is going to be better than the compound?" He barks out a bitter laugh. "You have a lot to fucking learn."

"Three minutes out," Thomas says into the phone, sending a voice text to everyone who's following behind.

"Still all clear," my father's voice says back.

And I mean everyone. Not only are my other uncles and Dad in the cars behind us, but so are the guys from ALFA. Even Uncle Bear tagged along for the ride because he's down with anything that could end up with his ass shot. The man is crazy, searching for danger and driving my great-aunt Fran absolutely batshit crazy.

"I promise I won't cause trouble," I say softly, knowing my fate is sealed and our imprisonment within the walls of the compound probably won't be as bad as I'm making out.

"Just stick by Pike. He lived at the compound for a few years and knows what situations to steer you clear of."

"So, you want me at Pike's side at all times?" I clarify

because it's sounding like I have the stamp of approval to be in Pike's bed.

"Gigi," James warns, knowing where I'm going, because of course he does.

"She's trying to get me killed," Pike whispers.

I squeeze his fingers, trying to hide my laughter because this shit is heavy. I'm using the only coping mechanism I have…my humor and my sarcasm.

Who wants to be running for their life?

Not me.

Who wants to hide out because there might be a bullet with their name on it?

Again, not me.

The only upside to this entire situation is that I'll have Pike at my side. But if he thinks he's bossing me around like I'm his woman, he has another thing coming.

"Let's go over a few things before you step out of this car."

"Of course." I roll my eyes, getting a hand squeeze from Pike because he's not happy either, but somehow, he's remained silent.

"Absolutely no drugs."

"Uncle James."

"I'm serious, Gigi. They're into some heavy shit there. Stuff is just lying around, easy to get, and even easier to take. If I get word that you're sniffing coke or taking some shit you shouldn't be taking, I'll have your ass back in this car so fast…"

"I promise, Uncle. I've never taken anything before, and I don't plan to start now."

Pike raises his eyebrows because my admission has to be shocking to everyone in the car, especially him. I mean, what person my age hasn't at least dabbled in drugs besides me? Probably no one except Tamara. It has to do with the way our parents raised us and the fear of them finding out and the ass-chewing we'd both get over it after a very lengthy and boring-as-fuck punishment.

"No drinking either," Uncle Thomas adds.

My mouth drops open, and I gawk at the back of their heads, blinking like somehow it'll make those words any easier to swallow. "You've got to give me something. I'm old enough to drink and it's legal, so I don't understand the issue."

"Cut the girl some slack," Uncle James says, which shocks the hell out of me and Thomas too.

"Are you serious right now? She's going to be in the middle of a crazy scene, and you're giving her the okay to drink?"

"She's grown, Thomas. We can't stop her from drinking."

"Or doing drugs," I add because fucking with them is too easy, and maybe if I fuck with them enough, Thomas will relent on the drinking. "But I promise I won't get drunk."

"Just don't do anything stupid. Stay inside and out of sight."

"I'll sit at the bar day and night." I smile, earning me a few curse words from all three in the car.

"They're here," James says, ticking his chin out the windshield at a long-ass line of bikes and an unmarked, windowless van parked in an abandoned lot.

"Guess we're doing this," I whisper, glancing at Pike as he stares back at me.

"We're going to be okay," Pike says sweetly, squeezing my fingers gently. "I promise."

I believe what he's saying, and from the huge army waiting for us, I believe they'll do what's necessary to keep us safe. Unless DiSantis brings an actual army, they'll have a hard time outnumbering the men waiting in the parking lot and probably even more still back at the compound.

"Out," Uncle Thomas barks as soon as he throws the engine into park, letting it idle. "We're making this quick. Drop and dash."

Uncle James helps me from the back seat, looking no less badass than the other men standing in this parking lot. "Behave, Gigi," he warns before releasing my hand. "I love you and don't want anything bad to happen to you. Something goes sideways, and we're all going to be in the shit."

I swallow the lump his words cause to lodge in my throat. The last thing I want is for my entire family to be in the proverbial shit because I slept with a guy who has a questionable father and a possible order for his assassination.

"I'll be good. I promise," I rasp.

He gives me a quick nod before stalking toward a giant man with a potbelly, no doubt caused by all types of excessive drinking. I assume it's Tiny because that would make total sense as there's nothing small about him.

My father is at my side before I can follow Uncle James. "This is it," he says, balling his hands into fists as his eyes dart to Pike and then back at me. "I've said what I needed to say."

I don't correct him and tell him it was more of a lecture than a good old-fashioned chat. My dad chewed my ear off for hours about my trip to Daytona and throwing myself in the path of countless bikers and into the arms of one in particular.

"I'm sorry this is happening, Daddy. I never meant to cause any trouble."

His face softens. "Baby, sometimes trouble finds us, no matter how hard we try to stay away. This isn't your fault. It's not Pike's fault either."

I blink up at him in surprise. "You're not pissed anymore?"

His jaw ticks, which answers my question before he even opens his mouth. "I'm not happy about any of this. Pike and I will be having a long talk when you two are back home."

So, he is still pissed, but at least he isn't talking about murdering the guy anymore. In my book, that's progress. For my dad, that's a huge step. The man has the patience of a saint sometimes, but when it comes to men and his daughters, he has zero. I've probably had it easier than my sisters will because I'm like the trial kid where they can fuck up and see what works, tweaking their plans for the next in line. Luna and Rosie aren't going to stand a chance, but they're crafty little shits even at their age and will adapt easily before my father knows what hit him.

"Go easy on him, Daddy."

My father's eyebrows draw together, causing the wrinkles on his forehead to deepen. "You want me to go easy on Pike?"

"Yo, we gonna do this, or what? Eyes are everywhere, and I don't feel like being a sitting duck," Tiny yells across the parking lot.

"Gigi," Pike calls, motioning for me to move my ass before things start to get heated.

"I'm coming." I wave and stare back up into my father's piercing eyes. "Pike's no different from you, and I'm no different from Mom." I pop up on my tiptoes, planting a kiss on my father's cheek and throwing my arms around his shoulders, squeezing him tightly. "Well, maybe I'm a little different from Mom because I have two kick-ass parents."

"Baby," he whispers, wrapping his arms around my back and holding me so tight, I can barely breathe. "Go. Stay safe. Don't do anything stupid."

I nod, pulling out of his embrace ever so slowly. "I love you, Daddy."

"I love you too, baby girl. One call a day to me on the burner phone. You understand?"

"I'll call around noon every day. I promise." I start to walk backward. "But don't worry so much. I won't do anything stupid, and these guys—" I pitch my thumb over my shoulder toward the horde of badass bikers "—will keep us safe."

"Tiny, Gigi. Gigi, Tiny," James says, looking between

the two of us as I walk toward them, almost faltering when I get close enough to realize the true size of Tiny.

"Holy fuck," I whisper. "Well, aren't you a big fella." I wink, throwing that out there because I know bikers, and they love a compliment.

Tiny's lip twitches ever so slightly, but the man keeps up his tough-guy exterior with his arms crossed, making him look even bigger and downright scary. "She'll do fine," he tells James like I'm not even standing here.

James extends his hand to Tiny, and the men shake as I turn my gaze toward Pike, who's also shaking hands with a man about his age and his size, but with a bald head and a tattoo across his forehead that does nothing except make him look so frightening, I can't imagine getting pussy is real easy.

"You." Tiny juts his chin at me as soon as we make eye contact. "Ass in the van. We gotta roll."

"And Pike?" I ask, because where he's going, so am I, whether Tiny or any of these other bikers agrees.

"He's in the van too. Can't have you bein' seen before we get you within our walls."

"Sure thing, boss man." I smile at the big guy, because if it's the last thing I do, I'll get the old bastard to smile back.

"She's a handful," Uncle James tells him, shrugging his shoulders and throwing out his arms like he doesn't know how to handle me and is sorry to put me off on someone else.

"I got a kid her age, but mine isn't so...pleasant. Anyway, Pike will keep her ass in line, and if he doesn't, I'll make sure she's under control."

I roll my eyes at their conversation, and Pike mutters, "Good fuckin' luck," at my side.

"Let's get this shitshow on the road, boys." I wave my hand in the air and look at Pike with a smirk. "This is going to be one hell of a time."

Pike keeps step with me as I stalk toward the van. "This isn't a vacation, darlin'."

"Don't give a fuck. We're spending time in a biker compound, and I plan to enjoy the fuck out of it because I'm not spending all day in my room worrying about some asshole trying to kill us. Now turn around, put a smile on your face, and wave to my family." I spin on my heels just outside the back door of the van, my eyes sweeping across the line of cars brimming with my family and the ALFA guys. I wave a little too happily, which earns me more than one glower. "Bye, I love you," I call out, knowing they'd all cuss me out if they could and probably will the next time they see me.

My father's near the car, talking to Uncle Thomas, shaking his head at my antics, knowing shit isn't going to be as PG as he hopes. "Just behave, kid," he yells out, knowing damn well there's a snowball's chance in hell that's going to happen. "Now, get your ass in the van, and get the fuck out of here."

I salute him before crawling inside, nestling against the side wall of the filthy van. They could've at least cleaned up a little bit seeing as they were going to be transporting two people in here instead of whatever the fuck was here before us.

"We're only twenty minutes away," Pike says as he

settles next to me, legs outstretched and his shoulder touching mine.

"Good, I could use a drink." I plaster a smile on my face because I don't want my father or uncles to know I'm terrified.

"Already?" he asks, staring at me as the doors slam shut.

"Already?" I gawk at Pike, happy I don't have to put on a good show anymore. "We're in some deep shit, Pike. What the fuck do you mean, already? Don't you want to drink that shit away?"

Pike shakes his head. "I have to stay focused. Shit can happen at any time, and I don't want to be three sheets to the goddamn wind when all hell breaks loose. They come for you, I need to be ready. I'll throw myself in front of whatever they hurl in our direction, shielding you so you can walk away without a scratch."

My mouth's hanging open as I blink at Pike like I'm trying to focus, but everything's crystal clear. "You'd give your life for me?" I whisper as Tiny slams the front door, shrouding us in darkness.

"I'd give everything for you, darlin'."

18

PIKE

"THIS PLACE IS LIKE DISNEY WORLD FOR CRACK whores, career criminals, and lost souls," Gigi says casually at my side, almost making me spit my mouthful of beer across the bar.

"Keep your voice down." I wipe my lips with the back of my hand, glancing around to figure out if anyone overheard.

"They can't hear above this classic rock, Pike. Half of them are probably hard of hearing, and the other half are so trashed, they're probably unable to form coherent thoughts."

"You're on a roll tonight, sweetheart." I lift my mug, glancing over my shoulder at a few guys who are sitting close, most likely assigned the task of keeping an eye on us while we're under their protection.

I'll have to talk to Tiny about that. While I appreciate his concern and security, when we're within these walls, hidden from view, we don't need extra eyes on us, watching our every move. Gigi most certainly doesn't need any men loitering near her, making her feel any more uncomfortable than she already does.

"They your friends?"

I shake my head. "Nope. Never seen them before. I haven't been around here in years. Based on the lack of patches, I'd say they're prospects."

"Oh. I saw that on television," she says, confirming everything I assumed she thought this place would be. "How long do they have to do that?"

"As long as Tiny and the guys want them to."

"There's no time limit?"

"Babe, this isn't a job. Bikers don't put time on anything unless there's money involved."

"Where's the little fucker?" a familiar voice says, and we both turn, watching him finish tucking his cock into his pants before he zips his fly.

"I guess you're the little fucker, yeah?" Gigi giggles, peering at me over her shoulder.

I set my beer down, climbing off the stool to greet Morris before he sets eyes on Gigi and tries to get his hands on her too. "Morris. Lookin' good, man."

"Morris?" Gigi asks, not hiding her shock that the guy with the crazy-ass salt-and-pepper hair and goatee to match doesn't have a biker name like the rest of the guys.

Morris shakes my hand and pulls me in for a bear hug before slapping my back so hard, I'm almost winded. "Who's this fine piece of ass you brought with you, kid?"

"This is Gigi, my girl, Morris. Don't start no shit, and there won't be no shit."

A slow, wide smile spreads across Morris's face, showing his white teeth with a big enough gap between the two front ones it's hard to mistake him for someone else.

Morris throws his hands up as he steps away from me, and his eyes sweep over Gigi again. "Wait a second, isn't she the chick from…"

"Yeah, man. Don't say it. It's a long-ass story."

"Hello," Gigi calls out, waving her hand at Morris and me because we're talking about her like she isn't sitting right there, and she hates nothing more than being ignored.

Morris slides next to her, moving onto the barstool so smoothly, it's like he practiced the maneuver a thousand times. "You're even more beautiful than the last time I laid eyes on you."

She blinks at him in confusion, moving back slightly when he reaches for her hand and brings it to his lips. "I'm sorry, I don't remember…"

"You probably don't remember a lot, mama. You were pretty trashed the night I met you—and damn fucking mouthy too." Morris laughs, placing a soft kiss on the top of her hand and getting a growl from me.

Gigi laughs, looking like a little kid next to the old man who will stick his dick in just about anything as long as he can get off. "It was spring break. I was letting loose."

"And so you did, sweetheart." Morris grins, eyes only on her and not on me at all.

Gigi grabs her drink as soon as Morris releases her hand and rests her chin in the palm of her free hand, elbow propped against the bar. "Why Morris? Why don't you have a tough name like the rest of the guys?"

Morris grins at Gigi, motioning to the prospect behind the bar for a drink, but he never breaks eye contact with her. "Because every MC has a Tiny, Rooster, Reaper, and so on, but only the Disciples have a Morris."

Gigi's nose wrinkles. "That's the reason?"

"Doll, I'm one of a kind. Who wants to be lumped in with those sorry fuckers when you can be the only one?"

Gigi shrugs, lifting the drink to her lips, and his eyes follow the movement. It's time to shut down the flirtfest Morris is having with my girl, so I slide in behind her, wrapping my arm around her middle and hauling her ass backward so she's pressed flush against me.

"You happy to see me, baby?" she asks playfully, tossing a glance over her shoulder.

"I figured I needed to remind Morris who you belong to, darlin'," I whisper in her ear, causing her to shiver, but my gaze is on Morris. "I don't want this dirty old man to get the wrong idea."

"My head only has room for wrong ideas," Morris says with a laugh. "Now, let's celebrate you comin' home, asswad, and get shit-faced drunk, telling stories about back in the day."

Gigi bounces on her stool, sending shock waves through my system from the way her ass is rubbing on my cock. "Fuck yeah. That's the best idea I've heard tonight."

"Gigi doesn't want to hear about all that boring shit, Morris," I hiss, because he's trying to start trouble.

It's what he's best at after all. If shit's going down, Morris is smack-dab in the middle, stirring the pot, making sure the shit stays moving.

"I very much want to hear about the *good old days,* baby. Hush your mouth." Gigi throws a wink at me over her shoulder.

"I could spend all night telling Pike stories."

"Don't you have a woman to satisfy?" I raise an eyebrow.

Morris shakes his head, grabbing the beer as soon as the redheaded prospect sets the bottle in front of him. "She's passed out. Figurin' the session we just had, she'll be out for a couple of hours if she even wakes up at all."

"You're a dirty old man, Morris." Gigi grips my knee like she's going to keep me quiet.

"He's old, all right," I mutter, reaching for my beer with the hand that isn't locked around her waist because nothing is going to make me let go of her.

"I think this calls for tequila," Gigi says to Morris, scooting backward, knowing exactly what she's doing because she's always thinking ahead.

"My kinda girl." Morris smirks.

"Maybe we should just go to bed." I want her out of the common room because the real shit hasn't even begun. The night's young, and the guys aren't as shit-faced as she thinks.

"No, Pike. We're not going anywhere until *we* catch up with Morris here. So, settle in, cowboy, and get comfortable."

Morris is laughing so hard, he's almost falling off his stool. "I can see why you like this one so much, kid. She's mouthy and bares those kitten claws."

"Morris, baby," Gigi replies, laying her hand on his arm. "I'm not a kitten, sweetheart."

Morris tips his head toward her, grinning like I've never seen the man grin before. "See, mouthy as fuck."

I look toward the ceiling, cursing under my breath. The long night just became longer because once these two get going, there's no stopping them until someone's passed out.

"Three tequilas," Gigi tells the prospect as he walks by, delivering a handful of beers to the guys at the other end of the bar.

"Long-ass fucking night," I whisper, pulling on my beer, swallowing down the bitter liquid along with the sour taste this entire evening is leaving in my mouth.

"Have a fucking sense of humor, Pike. Did you lose your balls somewhere around Orlando?"

Gigi chuckles, turning her head so her lips are so close to mine, I could silence her with a kiss. "Let me have a little fun, Pike. I know you have a past. Hell, so do I. I don't know a lot about you, and I want to hear what Morris has to say. Don't shit on my parade. Ya dig?"

"I dig." That's not the end of the conversation even if she wants it to be. "Just remember whatever he says —" I jut my chin toward him "—is probably bullshit."

"I never bullshit," Morris interrupts, staring at me over the lip of his beer bottle. "Well, almost never."

"If you learn something you don't like tonight, you

tuck that shit away and forget about it. I'm not the same punk kid I was when I lived here, surrounded by these men, five years ago. You dig?"

"I dig." Her eyes sparkle and drop to my mouth, and she pulls the corner of her bottom lip between her teeth, making me want to haul her ass into the back room and slide something else between those beautiful lips. "Now, Morris," she says, turning away from me quickly because she knows exactly what's on my mind. "Start at the beginning. How did Pike end up living with the Disciples? Didn't know you guys welcomed anyone into your world."

Morris snaps his fingers at the prospect who's still fumbling around behind the bar and hasn't delivered the tequila Gigi ordered. "We don't usually take in strays."

I roll my eyes because I know he's going to lay the shit on way thicker than it really went down. The reality of the situation is much more boring than he's going to tell her. He's going to glorify the entire thing, probably saying he rescued me from the side of the road like a wounded animal.

"We were pulling this job up in Jacksonville," he starts, at least getting that part right, but I know it's about to go sideways. "Some crazy-ass shit went down, guns came out."

"For fucking real?" Gigi gasps.

"For real, kid. Then this dumbass—" he ticks his chin toward me "—decides he's going to jump in front of one of the bullets, because his slow Tennessee ass can't move fast enough to get the fuck down."

Gigi turns, looking at me with wide eyes. "The scar on your shoulder?"

I nod, gritting my teeth because one of the fuckers shot me, not giving a fuck that I was an innocent bystander in the entire thing. I was filling my tank with gas, minding my own business, when they decided to open fire. I didn't have a chance to duck before I took one in the upper right shoulder.

"When shit died down, Pike was still standing there, holding his arm, glaring at me like it was my fault he was bleeding. We had words, and the fucking punk didn't care that I had a gun in my hand because he kept barking at me about how I put a hole in his body." Morris laughs, running his fingers through the tip of his goatee. He pauses when the kid finally sets down three tequila shots but is still moving like he has lead in his shoes. "About fucking time," Morris barks, shooing the guy away when he lingers a little too long. "What are we drinking to, kids?"

Gigi hands me a shot but doesn't give me her eyes. "To new friends and old times," she tells him, lifting her shot in the air. They clink glasses as I watch Gigi throw back the tequila like she's been doing it for years. "Now, finish the story. What happened after he had words with you?"

"I figured the kid had a pair of balls on him so freaking big he could be something to us. So, I had two choices."

"What were they?" she asks, not giving him a chance to finish.

"I could end his life right there, or bring his sorry,

bleeding ass back here to get patched up and figure out what to do with his mouthy ass afterward."

"Aww," she coos. "You totally rescued him."

"He fucking shot me." I scowl.

Morris places his hand on his chest, trying his best to look innocent. "I did not shoot your ass, kid. Wasn't my bullet you jumped in front of that night."

"Don't mind him." Gigi jerks her thumb at me, and I tighten my hold around her waist, reminding her these men aren't playthings.

Morris may not have been the one who shot me, but someone in this room fucking did. They didn't give two shits that I was innocent with piss-poor timing, filling my tank when they decided to play cops and robbers at the gas station in a seedy part of town.

There isn't a man in this room who hasn't drawn blood from another human being without so much as a backward glance at the carnage they inflicted or the death they left in their wake. They give zero fucks about human life. Their world revolves around money, drugs, pussy, and the brotherhood—and not in that order either.

"And..." She leans forward, hanging on his every word.

"So, this kid..." He laughs, shaking his head like he doesn't even believe what he's about to say. "He's yelling at me, poking me in the shoulder while I've got my gun in one hand like I'm just going to stand here and take his shit. I didn't know what to do, so I punched him right where he got hit, sending his ass to the floor in a flurry of curse words that would make the devil himself blush."

"You fucking punched him in his injured shoulder?"

Morris shrugs. "The kid wouldn't shut up about how I shot him. Figured I'd give him something to be angry with me about, plus, I needed him to shut the fuck up for a few minutes so I could get his ass into the back of the van."

"Did you know you were going to keep him?" she asks.

"What the fuck?" I hiss, shaking my head. "I wasn't a puppy, Gigi."

"Shut up," she tells me. "Morris and I are talking."

"Three more tequilas," I tell the prospect, figuring the only way I'm going to get her to stop talking to Morris is to get her so shit-faced drunk, she'll pass the fuck out.

"Welcome to the party, Pike," Gigi teases, wiggling her ass right against my dick.

I flatten my palm against her stomach, moving my mouth near her ear. "Be careful, darlin'. I'm not above throwing you over my shoulder and hauling your ass into my room and putting something in that sassy little mouth of yours."

"Is that a promise or a threat?" she asks with a wicked gleam in her eyes.

"Both."

I've never been more serious in my life.

"Such a big talker," she teases.

I do the only thing I can. Moving quickly, I throw

her over my shoulder like a sack of potatoes and march toward my old room.

"Put me down!" she screeches. "Help!"

No one pays any attention to her pleas for help. I even get a few high fives as I carry her ass to the back, ready to do exactly what I promised.

19

GIGI

He has one hand on my ass, only moving the damn thing when he smacks the hands of the other assholes in the room.

I wiggle, trying like hell to get out of his hold and off his shoulder, but that only causes him to tighten his grip around my leg.

"You're not getting out of this one, darlin'," he drawls, stalking on heavy feet, making my tits smack against his back with every step.

"You're an asshole."

"Speaking of asshole," he says, running a finger along the crease of my ass as we finally make it to the hallway.

I stiffen, squeezing my ass cheeks together as tightly as possible. "Don't you fucking dare!" I screech, lifting my head and catching sight of all the guys in the compound, laughing and watching us with total amusement. I give the biker assholes my middle finger, scowling at them for reveling in the spectacle Pike is putting on, even though I know I'm not helping it. "You're not touching my ass!"

"I promise you'll love it." His hand massages my cheeks, but I have them on lockdown, just like they're going to stay. "I'll make you want it always."

That's the problem. I know if Pike does it, I'll love the hell out of it. There hasn't been anything he's done to my body that I didn't want more of, craving it since the second I ran for coffee and never went back. He's skilled and generous, unlike anyone I've been with before…although my list is super-short and kind of embarrassing.

I reach down, trying to get my hands on his ass so I can pinch him hard enough that maybe I'll be able to break free. "The only thing I want is for you to put me down and let me finish my drink," I grit out, stretching as far as I can, but it's no use. His body is too long for my short everything even to get near anything worth pinching.

"You're done drinking," he says like he's the boss, which is laughable.

I go limp, knowing there's no use. I'm going nowhere except where Pike is taking me. "Where the fuck is your room? Another county?"

Pike laughs, making my body shake with his. "We're almost there, baby. You in a hurry to have my cock in you?"

A door opens, and Pike comes to a dead stop. "Calling it a night?" a man asks, and I crane my neck, trying to see, but damn my size.

"Takin' my woman to bed. Won't be back out until the mornin'."

"Morris put your shit back out and cleaned. Should feel like home for you, kid. You enjoy yourself."

I growl. "Hello, wanna help me here?"

The man laughs, moving around Pike, and crouches down to my level. "Looks like you're doing just fine, sweetheart," Tiny says.

"You're all fuckers," I hiss, which only gets me a small laugh and a headshake from Tiny as he goes back to standing on the other side of Pike and away from me.

"You got your hands full with this one, son. I hope you know what you're doing."

"Just reminding her who she belongs to, Tiny. You have a good night," Pike says.

Who she belongs to? Ugh. My father says shit like that all the time about my mother. Come to think of it, every man in my family says macho bullshit like that, and I roll my eyes every time.

Pike starts moving and I lift my head, catching Tiny's smile, the first one I've seen him crack since I met him tonight. Badass MC biker president or not, he gets a middle finger too before Pike turns a corner, opens a door, and we're suddenly in darkness.

"Will you put me down now?"

"Nope," he replies as he switches on the light, making everything in the tiny space visible. "Well, fuck."

I press my hands to his lower back, lifting my head up farther than before, and try to take in the sparse room covered with all things Pike. There are posters and artwork lining the walls, a twin bed along a black-painted wall, some furniture that had to be secondhand, and not one goddamn window for any type of natural light. "Is this a closet?"

My closet at my parents' place is twice as big as his *bedroom*. I couldn't imagine living in here on a daily basis without going a little mad from the lack of sunlight and the fact that it's the size of a prison cell.

"It has everything we need, babe." He finally relaxes his hold on my leg, allowing me to slide down his front, relishing the way his hardness feels against my body.

When my feet touch the floor, Pike's hands are on my hips and his eyes are on mine. He's so beautiful like this. Hair wild, his blue-green eyes burning with need, and those lips begging for mine. "Pike." I'm trying to kill a little time because now that we're alone, I know there's no turning back.

Pike shakes his head. "Been thinking about this since you left me," he says, and my breath catches in my throat. "Been thinking about the softness of your skin…" He runs his finger along the top edge of my jean shorts and across the sensitive skin on my stomach.

Goose bumps form everywhere, scattering across my flesh like they're reaching for his touch. "Pike," I say again, but my voice is needy. Even I can hear the way his touch affects me, and I'm sure it isn't lost on him either.

"Tell me to stop, and I will," he says, licking his lips, and my gaze drops to his mouth, remembering all the ways he brought me pleasure. He bends his neck, bringing those lips to my mouth, whispering, "I need you, darlin'."

I'm a goner. It's easier to pretend I hate him when he's not about to kiss me, staring at me like he's been in a desert without water and I'm the oasis.

"Kiss me," I whisper, staring into his eyes, losing myself a little more.

I barely get the words out before his lips crash down on mine, his hand sliding to my ass and pulling me flush against him. In the last fifteen months, I haven't forgotten how he tasted or the velvety softness of his tongue, no matter how hard I tried.

I slide my hands up his arms, tangling my fingers in his hair, holding him to me like he's my lifeline. My knees weaken as his tongue sweeps into my mouth, giving me exactly what I've craved and wanted since Daytona.

Pike turns, slamming the door behind us, but I don't even flinch at the noise because I'm too lost in the way he's kissing me to care about anything else around us. The world could crumble, and I wouldn't move from this spot, away from his body, away from his lips.

His hands are on my ass, lifting me in the air. I wrap my legs around his waist like they were always meant to be there as he walks us backward.

The kiss deepens, becoming more demanding as his hands move to my back, sliding up my tank top, finding my bra strap. I'm in his lap, his cock to my pussy, separated only by our clothes as he sits on the bed, working quickly to unclasp my bra.

I pull back, gasping for air as I stare at the handsome man underneath me. "Did you bring protection?" I whisper.

Pike nods as he grabs the bottom of my tank top, and I lift my hands because I want this more than anything right now.

"You knew I'd sleep with you?" I ask through the material as the cool air hits my skin and the bra goes with the shirt, both thrown to the floor behind me.

"I hoped," he says. His hungry eyes travel across my skin for a moment before he pulls my head back down, pressing his lips to mine.

I move my hands to his sides, reaching under the thin T-shirt, wanting and needing his warmth and hardness.

I've touched myself hundreds of times since I last was in his arms, trying to recreate the feeling only he'd given me. I'd failed miserably. Nothing could replicate the way he touched me, how he kissed me, or the way he made me melt into his body.

As I lift his shirt, our mouths separate and I lean back, taking in his ink and the lines of his taut stomach and firm shoulders. I only get a glimpse before Pike flips me, putting me on my back, and crawls between my legs, settling in like he's always meant to be there.

The sense of shame and uncertainty I had every time I was with Erik isn't there with Pike. I have no doubts he likes what he sees and loves everything he feels. I'm not ashamed of my nudity, and any worries I had about my inexperience were wiped away after our time together in Daytona.

Pike lifts up on one arm, staring down at me like I'm a goddess. "Dreamed about having you under me again, darlin'."

I run my fingers through the coarse hair of his beard, staring up at the man I know is about to give me so much pleasure, I'm not sure I'll ever recover. "Me too," I confess, because there's no reason to pretend otherwise.

He runs his hand down my neck, along my collarbone, over the swell of my breast. My eyes drift closed, and I sigh, letting every sensation wash over me, memorizing each touch in case I never feel them again.

Warmth covers my nipple, and I open my eyes, peering down my body and finding Pike with his mouth attached. A small moan escapes my lips as our eyes lock, and the pleasure his tongue's delivering shoots straight between my legs, making me squirm.

Without moving his mouth, Pike shuffles over, resting his front to my side. His hand is at my shorts, working the button and zipper quickly, and I lift my ass because I want nothing more than to feel whatever he's about to give.

My shorts and the fancy lace undies I wore just in case this would happen are thrown to the end of the bed, discarded without even a glance. He moves his hand to my mound, cupping my pussy, making the ache turn into a burning throb.

"More, Pike," I beg. My insides are like a raging inferno, and only his fingers can extinguish the flame.

He doesn't tease me or make me beg any more than I already have as he slides his fingers between my legs, and I rock into his touch.

"Greedy," he murmurs against my breast, and I can't argue with him.

I'm greedy as hell when it comes to him. I'm even needier, which should make me worry, but I want an orgasm so badly, I don't bother to think too much.

My knees fall to the bed as his fingers slide back and forth, capturing my wetness. I lift my ass, wanting more than he's giving, growing increasingly impatient with each pass of his fingers.

He slides one finger slowly inside, filling me, but it's not enough. I want more. I need more. I want the delicious ache of being filled, stuffed, owned. I arch my back, pushing my bottom toward his hand, letting him know I want more than he's giving.

I don't have to wait long before he adds another finger, stretching me more than I've been stretched since the last time I was in his bed.

Pike is exceptional at finger-fucking. Like, the best of the best. Or at least, the best I've ever had. He knows how to work every spot, sending me soaring over the edge faster than I ever have before.

My fingers fist the soft blanket, squeezing until my knuckles turn white as if it'll help the orgasm I want so badly to come easier.

"My girl wants this," Pike whispers against my skin, eyes moving to my face with a smile.

I seal my eyes shut, pushing my nipple against his lips, hoping he'll get the hint. He doesn't. He keeps staring, fingers working in and out of me, his thumb brushing against my clit with not enough pressure to have me singing the high notes, praising his work, and for the waves to rock my body.

"My girl needs this," he says, pressing the pad of his thumb flat against my clit.

I inch my bottom upward, rolling my hips, trying to get his thumb to move in the way I need to give me the damn orgasm.

"Enough with the *my girl* stuff and put your mouth to better use."

Pike's smile widens, and he slides down my body, fingers still inside me, thumb not giving me what I want. He settles his shoulders between my legs and pushes my legs farther apart. "Been waiting forever to taste you."

"For fuck's sake," I groan, bucking against his fingers because they've stopped although they're still inside me. "You have two seconds to put your..."

Heaven. That's what it feels like when Pike swipes his tongue over my clit, rolling the tip around to trace the outside.

"Fuck yeah..." I drop my head back, closing my eyes and letting the sensations wash over me.

The warmth of his mouth.

The wetness of his lips.

The hardness of his fingers.

It all works together in perfect harmony and is everything I remember.

He curls his fingers, rubbing my G-spot as he seals his lips around my cunt in the most perfect way. "God, yes, right there."

The goose bumps from earlier return as every fiber of my being seems to be standing at attention, wanting this as badly as I do.

I open one eye, staring down my body again and

loving the sight. There's nothing sexier than Pike nestled between my legs, eating like he's a starved man, fucking me like it's his sole purpose in life, and me…lying back and taking it all in.

Pike is right. I am a greedy lover. I won't apologize for it either. I'd lie here all night with him like this, orgasm after orgasm crashing over me if Pike would let that happen. But then again, I don't know of any man who is that giving.

My toes curl and my legs strain, trying to make the orgasm quicker. "Don't stop!"

His mouth is gone, and I groan my frustration. "Let it happen, darlin'. Don't force it."

I raise up on my elbow, glaring at the man whose lips are glistening from all his hard work. "Hey, Dr. Ruth, can you get back to suckin' and fuckin' without so much talk?"

"She's bossy too," he whispers, smiling up at me, mumbling something else to himself before his lips are back on my clit.

I collapse back onto the bed, trying to relax and let it happen naturally, because Pike's right…it's always better when it isn't forced.

Within seconds, my toes curl again, but this time, I don't strain, chasing it. His fingers move faster, his lips suck harder, tongue flicking against my flesh as my muscles tighten on their own and all the breath in my lungs vanishes.

"Yes! Yes! Yes!" I scream, wrapping my fingers around the blanket again as my body shakes out of control. "Fuck yes!"

Pike doesn't slow. He doesn't allow the orgasm to wane. He pulls me from one orgasm straight into another, leaving me gasping for air and limp.

I'm in so much fucking trouble, and this time, there's no way out.

20

PIKE

"What's your name, honey?" a woman leans on the bar next to me, ass sticking out like she's looking for attention. Attention I won't be giving her beyond answering her question.

"Pike."

"You new around here?" she drawls, pushing her tits forward with the arm that's tucked under her chest.

"Nope."

"I've never seen you."

"Midge, leave the kid alone," Tiny says, stalking past us and around the bar. "He's an old-timer, but he's been gone for a while. He's not a brother, but a friend, and completely off-limits."

She snarls, but by the time he looks at her, her face is neutral. "I was just saying hello and introducing myself." She smiles at Tiny and straightens, allowing her tits and everything else to go back to normal, thanks to gravity. "I'm Morris's old lady."

"No shit?"

Morris never seemed like the type to settle down, especially not with someone so close to his own age.

"He doesn't know it yet, but I will be." She winks.

I hate to tell the lady, but Morris isn't settling down for no one. I don't care if she was a *Playboy* centerfold, the man couldn't stick to one pussy if his life depended on it. He is all about variety and excess, rarely dipping his wick in the same well twice.

"Get lost, Midge. We got shit to talk about, and you have work to do." Tiny glares down at the small woman with so many wrinkles, she looks like she was taken out of the dryer after staying in there too long.

"Yes, sir, big man," she says, throwing me a smile before stalking off with a sway of her hips.

Tiny glances toward the ceiling and sighs. "She ain't nothing but fucking trouble."

"Why keep her around?"

"She ain't got anywhere else to go, and she's a damn fine maid too."

"You finally hired someone to clean?" I look around the place, noticing it's not any neater than the last time I was here.

The floor is dirty, my boots stick to the tile in some spots, old alcohol acting like glue. Beer bottles are everywhere, but it's been a long night and the guys were celebrating my return, even if most of them didn't give two shits. They'd use any excuse to have a party.

"She cleans for beer and cock."

My eyebrows go up. "Interesting arrangement."

Tiny grabs a beer from the cooler, holds it out to me,

and I take it before he grabs another one. "Where's the girl?"

I twist the top and take a swig, needing something to quench the thirst Gigi caused because the girl is insatiable. "Sleeping."

Tiny grins as he lifts the beer to his lips. "I like her."

Again, I raise my eyebrows. Tiny doesn't like many people. Most of the time, I never thought he liked me. "You do?"

He nods. "She's a good fit for you. Unlike that other skank… What was her name?"

"Which one?" I laugh a little, but there's truth in what I'm saying.

I may not have been a brother or a prospect, but I had just as much pussy in my bed as every guy in this place. Somehow, the men here let me take advantage of all the perks without risking my life or requiring the oath bullshit they all swore to one another.

"What are you doing up?" I ask him because it's almost morning, but I haven't slept a wink.

"I'm not up. I'm headed to bed, but I had a few loose ends to tie up." He leans against the bar across from me, taking another swig of his beer. "I have eyes and ears out all over the state. No one's looking for you or the girl. Hopefully in a few days, you two can get back to your lives without looking over your shoulder."

"I'm sorry about this, Tiny. If I would've known James…"

Tiny waves me off. "If you're in any kind of shit, I want you calling me. If you need help, pick up the goddamn phone. I thought we made this clear to you when we saw you in Daytona. You may not live here anymore, but you'll always be part of our family."

"I don't know what I did to deserve any of this." I grip the neck of the bottle, swiping my thumb down the glass. "I don't see you taking in any other strays."

Tiny laughs. "You're a good kid. If I had a son, I'd want him to be just like you, Pike. Instead, I got a daughter because I've done bad shit in my life and the big guy found a way to pay me back. You needed help and had a pair of balls and a mouth back then." He laughs louder, shaking his head. "Hell, ya still do. I thought I'd convince you to be one of us, to join the brotherhood, but when I knew it was hopeless, I couldn't just toss your ass out into the street."

"You really could've. My parents didn't give two fucks what happened to me, and they're my own blood, Tiny. You have no duty to help me or even protect us right now."

Tiny's laugh dies and he moves closer, leaning into my space. "Family is more than blood, kid. Shit goes down in your life and you need backup, you call me. Now, you have James in your life and his people, which is good, but I'll always be here for you."

"James seems decent."

Tiny's laughter is back. "He's an asshole. One of the biggest fucking dicks I've ever met, but he's solid. When he speaks, it's the truth coming out of his lips. Shit went down years ago between us, but we made our peace. And when I need help, something I can't call on the guys to do, I call James and his guys."

"I don't want to know."

Tiny nods. "Trust me, you don't, but if that girl is his family, James will pull you into the fold."

"I work for her dad."

Tiny's eyes widen. "My man's fucking the boss's kid? You got a bigger set of balls on you than I thought."

"Or I'm dumb as a fuckin' brick. It's debatable at this point." I crack a smile, trying to make light of the situation, but none of it's funny. "And her life may be in danger because of that very fact. I'm pretty sure her father wants to rip my dick off and shove it down my throat, but we gotta make it out of here in one piece for that to happen."

"I'll make sure you live," Tiny promises, and I believe he'll do everything in his power to keep us alive.

"Thanks, T."

"Now, as a father to daughters, let me give you a little advice."

"I'm listening."

"Treat her good and make her happy. A father has many weapons, and if the guy is a douche and treats her like shit, he doesn't need to bring out the big guns to drive them apart. But if the guy is good and makes her happy, in bed and out, not even a nuclear weapon or her father's unhappiness can make her leave you. You make it right with her, her father will fall in line."

I shrug. "He's pretty pissed, and if I didn't know better, I'd think he was part of an MC too. He's friendly, but I know there's more to him than meets the eye."

"City was never in an MC," Tiny says.

"City?" I ask because that's not a name I know him by.

Tiny raises his hands. "Joe Gallo, dumbass."

I tick my chin toward Tiny. "How the hell do you know Joe?"

"He did a tat of mine back in the day, and I know all about him and that family from working with James and Thomas. He's solid. Never been in an MC, but he has been around the biking world for years. He keeps to himself. Dedicated to his family and isn't afraid to go to any length to protect them."

"Yep. That's him."

"I wish you fuckin' luck with that one," he says before he tips his head back, polishing off the rest of his beer.

"Thanks for the encouragement," I grumble because I know the shit hasn't even started. Once we step foot outside this compound, the danger gone, a new risk awaits, and it'll be directed only at me.

"Get some shut-eye. You look like shit."

I run my fingers down my beard, smiling at the old bastard. "Still lookin' better than you," I tease him as I climb off the stool and toss the rest of my beer in the trash as I walk toward the hallway.

When I open my door, Gigi's passed out, blankets half off her body, breasts sticking out, and taking up the entire twin bed like she's slept there her whole life.

I undress, pulling her over to one side, careful not to let her fall before I climb in next to her and tug her against my body. Her skin smells of sex and vanilla as I nuzzle my face into her neck, tightening my arms around her.

"Pike," she whispers.

"Shh, darlin'. Go back to sleep," I whisper back.

She turns in my arms, lying flat on her back, and blinks up at me. "Where were you?"

"Just talkin' with Tiny."

"Is everything okay?" She fights back a yawn but loses, covering her mouth with her hand. She closes her eyes, turning again and burrowing her face in my chest then throwing her leg over my hip.

"Everything's good." My fingers find her spine, tracing the straight line down her skin. "Don't worry. We're safe."

"Are you sad coming back here?"

"No. It's like going home again, although a fucked-up home, after being gone for a while. I'm comfortable here, but I worry about you being in a place like this."

She laughs against my skin. "Clearly you've never been in a frat house."

"Can't say that I have."

"The guys are bigger and scarier, but there is just as much drinking and naked bodies at a frat party as there was here tonight."

"How many frat parties have you been to?"

"A lot," she whispers. "Too many to remember."

I tighten my arms around her, and I don't like hearing about her in a place with so many drinks or naked people, but I know we both lived lives before we met. The thought of another man touching her makes my stomach knot.

"No more though, yeah?" I ask, letting my jealousy shine a little.

She laughs softly. "There's no time for frat parties. I

figure this is like the last big hurrah, being at the compound. I'm going to use the time to party my ass off because adulting is going to suck and it's forever."

"You party as much as you want while we're here, but I'm going to be with you every step of the way. So, don't get any crazy ideas."

She pulls her head back, staring up at me with a smile. "What do you consider a crazy idea?"

"You're here with me and only in my bed. No one else."

Her smile grows wider. "Would you be jealous?"

I sigh, figuring I have to lay shit out because she's testing me. "Darlin', we both have pasts, but we're living in the now. I don't know if I have one hour or one hundred years, but whatever time I got, I want you where you are right now."

She blinks a few times, staring at me like I'm speaking a foreign language she can't understand. "I'm down with the now, but what makes you think you want to spend one hundred years with me where I am?"

"We got something special."

"Orgasms don't make a relationship." She rolls her eyes.

"They don't hurt either." I smirk. "But I've also been around enough wrong women to know when I've found the right one."

"Pike," she says softly, reaching her hand up between us and resting her fingers on my beard. "I'm not as… experienced as you."

"Really?" I say even though I knew that fact the first time she was in my bed. It's not hard to tell the differ-ence. I knew back then Gigi Gallo wasn't an easy girl and didn't give her body away to just anyone. Why she decided to offer herself up to me in Daytona, I'll never know, nor do I give a fuck. It happened, and I haven't stopped thanking my dumbass luck for being in the right place at the right time since then.

She pulls at the hairs near my chin, toying with the tips. "I've only had a few boyfriends, and those relationships were complete disasters. How do I know we won't be the same?"

I press my lips to her forehead, wishing we could stay here, this way, forever. "There's no way to tell if we'll work out, but that doesn't mean I don't want to do whatever I can to hold on to whatever this is. All I can promise is that I'll treat you good, be loyal to you always, and give you as many orgasms as you want."

"As many as I want?" she whispers into my neck, fingers still playing with my beard.

"As many as you want," I repeat.

"I never had one with someone else before you," she confesses. Her voice is so soft and quiet, I almost don't hear her.

The statement doesn't shock me. So many women never get off with their partner, and half the time, the guys don't even try. They think that by getting theirs, they did enough, and if it doesn't happen for the chick, it isn't their fucking problem. I've never been that way. Can't even begin to understand that way of thinking.

"But you did with me, yeah?"

"Every time."

"That has to count for something. What if you don't

stay with me, and no guy ever gets you off again?" It's a lie, but one I can use to my advantage since she has very little experience, and all of it before me was absolute shit.

"I do have a vibrator, so it's not like I'd never come again."

"I got a hand too, but it doesn't mean I'd be happy jacking off for the rest of my life."

She tips her head back, a smile back on her face. "Can I watch?"

My eyebrows draw together as I stare back at her. "Watch what?"

"You know." She waggles her eyebrows. "Watch you jack off. It would be the hottest thing ever."

"You going to give me that ass?" I ask, waggling my eyebrows just like she did. "Because that would be the hottest thing ever."

Her nose scrunches. "Um, no."

"A little more tequila and I bet you'd say yes."

She lets out a loud huff and flattens her lips. "You let me watch you jack off and give me enough tequila, and I'll think about giving you my ass."

I roll her to her back, and I'm on top of her quickly. "See, darlin'. We work well together. Communication and negotiation are important in every relationship."

"You just want my ass, Pike."

"I want all of you, Gigi." I slide between her legs. "But right now, I want that sweet cunt squeezing my cock until we both pass out."

"That I can do," she promises.

21

GIGI

The compound is massive. Not just the main building—everything is supersized. The ten-foot-high walls around the perimeter seem excessive, but I wouldn't be shocked if there was a moat on the other side of the gate either.

"Don't get any ideas, girl," cautions one of the men who's been following me around like he's my shadow.

I pull my hand back, letting the dusty green curtains fall back into place, and scrunch my nose. "Where would I go? Seriously, it's like Fort Knox out there."

The guy pulls a toothpick from his lips, sliding the same hand through his blond hair. "You look crafty and as if you'd claw your way over that wall like a superhero or some shit."

The double doors leading into a room that's set up like something you'd see in a corporate office creak, and the men file out, but there's no Pike, Morris, or Tiny. The looks on the men's faces don't give me much solace that this shit is over and we can finally go home. They called an emergency meeting an hour ago, telling me I wasn't allowed to attend even though my life was on the line and anything they said in there could either save me or end shit in a bad way.

To say I was pissed was an understatement. Even though I am a girl, I never have been treated like one by my family. We are all equals. It doesn't matter what you have between your legs, your opinion and thoughts count for something and are always taken into consideration.

The Disciples don't feel the same way. There is a macho hierarchy where the women cook, fuck, and suck dick, but beyond that, they aren't needed or wanted.

Thank God Pike didn't pick up on that shit when he lived here. He has enough of an attitude; I couldn't take the sexism on top of the rest of him.

The men scatter in opposite directions, pulling their guns from their waistbands as they walk. *Great.* Whatever they talked about has them on edge, because I haven't seen weapons out in the open in such numbers except for on television.

"What do you think's happening?" I ask Mr. Toothpick because he's the only one who's bothered to talk to me today besides Pike.

He shrugs. "My ass is out here with you, so I'm not in the know."

"They didn't clue you in?"

"They clue me in when they want me to be clued in."

The man talks in riddles, and he wouldn't be half

bad-looking if he cut his long hair and trimmed his beard so it wasn't so scraggly.

"Gigi." Morris's voice booms through the open space, drawing my gaze. "Get your ass in here."

I smile at Toothpick. "Guess I'm going to be clued in before you," I taunt him because it's the only form of entertainment I have, and I'm feeling bitchy.

He snarls, waving me off. "Lucky you," he mutters and slides the toothpick back between his lips.

Morris is standing in the doorway, leaning against the frame, eyes on me like my ass is moving too slow for him. "You out for a stroll?" he asks, confirming I am, in fact, moving too slow. But I have one speed, and it's sloth.

"The scenery lacks a certain charm." I smile, looking up at the big guy I've grown fond of in the short time I've been at the compound.

I can understand why Pike liked him even if he thought the guy shot him. I'm not sure I'd ever get over everything that happened, like him punching Pike in his injured shoulder, but men are cut from a different cloth like that.

"I'll make sure to call HGTV and see if we can get a makeover," Morris jokes, following me through the double doors.

Tiny's at the far end of the table, Pike next to him, both men staring at me as Morris closes the doors behind us. "Is everything okay?" I ask, walking slower than before because the looks on their faces say shit is far from okay.

Pike pulls out the chair next to him, and Tiny

motions for me to sit. I do it quick, like my ass is suddenly on fire and only the chair can put out the flames.

Pike throws his arm around the back, turning his head to face me. I give him a timid smile. "What happened?"

As Pike opens his mouth, ready to tell me what I want to know, Tiny clears his throat. "There was an attempted hit on Pike's father last night."

I gasp, because this shit is far too real. His mother is dead, and his father was in hiding, just like us. But somehow, it sounds like he didn't come out unscathed.

Tiny leans back, eyeing me. "As far as we can tell, he's alive."

"That's good, right?" I ask, swallowing the lump that's back in my throat.

"DiSantis isn't taking his time. The next twenty-four hours will tell us if Pike or you are a target. So far, there's been no movement toward either of you. I spoke to James this morning, and he said it's quiet over there. He's had his boys sitting outside your apartments, parked outside Inked, and ears everywhere in that shithole town listening for chatter."

"And?"

Tiny drags his hand down his face, maybe not used to being questioned about anything. He probably lays shit out and people just take what he has to say and soak it in. But I'm not built that way. I question everything, and just when the person thinks they're done, I want to know more.

"We're ready in case they come here, looking for either of you."

"You really think they're here?"

Tiny shrugs. "Don't know. I'm sending out some guys to see if there's anyone new around, asking too many questions. The next few hours are critical."

"And if they hear nothing, can we go?"

"If we hear nothing, James and I will make the call on if your ass can walk outside those walls tonight."

"Okay," I whisper, knowing there's no point in arguing about who gets to determine our fate.

"DiSantis isn't a fool. I'm sure he did his homework, and if he's after Pike, he figured he'd come here for cover from the hell storm he's raining down."

"I can do another day standing on my head." I lean back into Pike's arm that's still flung across the back of my chair. I stare at Tiny, looking to him for some comfort.

"Just lie low. Maybe stay in Pike's room as much as possible. If shit goes down, I'd rather you be in a room with no windows than out there." He jerks his head toward the door. "I'm sure you can find ways to keep yourselves occupied." He winks.

I let out a nervous laugh. "Nothing gets me hotter than knowing I may be taking my last breath."

Tiny swipes his hand across his lips, muttering obscenities. "Take a nap, play Scrabble or some shit, but keep yourselves out of sight."

"Scrabble?" I scrunch my nose. "Poker maybe." I tap my chin, thinking of ways to entertain ourselves.

"Strip poker works too." I turn to Pike, who's pale as a ghost. "You okay, baby?"

He gives me a small smile, hiding whatever passes across his eyes. "I'm great, darlin'."

His answer comes too easy, and I wonder what I'm not being told. Maybe he's in shock, mourning the loss of his mother and the possible death of his father.

"Now, you two get gone. I have shit to do, and the sooner this is over, the better," Tiny announces, pushing back from the table and climbing to his feet.

"You know you're going to miss me," I tell Tiny, standing and craning my neck to look up at him.

"Kid, the next time I see your face, I expect it to be under happier circumstances."

"Me too, Tiny. Me too."

Pike's on his feet, arm around my shoulders like he needs to be physically touching me at all times. I turn my head, looking at his face, soaking him in. "Why don't we grab a bottle of Jack before we head back?"

If the day goes to shit, I'm going to need something hard to chase away the fear that's settled into my bones. I've been good at keeping it under wraps. I've pretended to be sleeping, when half the time, I'm paralyzed by fear, waiting for the bad guys to come crashing through the doors, ready to take us out.

"I think we should stay clearheaded," Pike says, moving me toward the doorway right behind Tiny. "If something happens and I'm shit-faced..."

"We'll stay sober." I reach up and touch his hand that's closed around my shoulder.

Tiny puts out his hand, stopping us from walking to

Pike's room. "Here." He pulls a gun from his waistband and holds it in front of us. "Take this. If you don't need it, great. If you do, at least you have it. You remember how to shoot it?"

"I'll never forget," Pike says as he wraps his hand around the handle, holding it like he's done it a million times.

"Shit goes south, you shoot at anything coming your way."

Pike nods at Tiny, and I'm feeling a little left out again. "Do I get a gun?"

Tiny's eyes twinkle, but his expression doesn't change. "Absolutely not."

"This is bullshit."

"As is life," Tiny teases.

Pike moves one hand to the small of my back, the other one still holding the gun. "Come on. Let's let the guys do their shit so we can get out of here sooner rather than later."

"Fine, but I'm grabbing the Jack." I stalk away from him and push past Morris before Pike has a chance to usher me toward his room.

"Fuckin' women," Morris mutters loud enough for me to hear even though my legs are moving faster than before. "Now she's Jackie Joyner-Kersee."

I don't know who Jackie is, but she has to be badass if he thinks I'm anything like her. I'm so not chill right now as I stride across to the bar, throwing myself over the top, and reaching underneath to find a bottle of Jack. Once I have it in hand, I slide back down, turning to face the three of them, all of whom are staring at me with a look of amusement.

"Good luck," Morris says to Pike, slapping him on the back as I throw them a quick glance before striding down the hallway, cracking the top of the bottle open.

"You comin'?" I call out when Pike's not right behind me, hanging on me like he was a few minutes ago.

Tiny and Morris laugh their asses off, but I don't turn around to see if Pike's following me or not. I'm cranky and starting to go a little stir-crazy, missing the sunshine on my skin. All I can hope for now is that today's our last day in captivity and we walk out of here breathing.

Half a bottle of Jack and four hours later, I'm sitting on the edge of Pike's bed, wrapped in a blanket and nothing more. He's naked, pacing near the door like he's a caged animal, gun on the dresser.

"You okay?" I ask him, watching the muscles of his body flex and relax with each step.

His body is long, sleek, and sculpted. His legs are longer than his torso, all brought together with the most spectacular ass I've ever seen on a man.

"Just thinking."

I lean back, still staring at his nakedness because I can. "About?"

"How my family has fallen to shit because of the stupid, greedy things my father's done. But then there's you—" he motions a hand toward me "—and that part of my life feels like it's finally falling into place."

"I'm sorry about your mom and dad."

I can't imagine something happening to mine. I wouldn't even be able to get out of bed, let alone form coherent thoughts. My world revolves around my family. Always has, and I can't imagine that ever changing. I didn't even leave the state to attend college because I wanted to be close enough to go home whenever I missed everybody. Which ended up being more often than I'd expected.

Pike shakes his head. "I feel like I should be crying or at least be sadder than I am. They're my parents after all. They brought me into this world, but Gigi, they weren't good to me. There wasn't a day that went by where I didn't feel like I was a burden to them. Do you know how it is to be a little kid, playing with your old-ass toy truck that is falling apart, knowing you're not wanted." He looks at me, and I shake my head. "Of course, you don't. You have the Gallos. They love you. They worship the ground you walk on and would do anything for you if you asked."

"I'm sorry."

Those are the only words I have because I know I was lucky the day I was born. I could've very easily been born into a shit-ass family where I was just another mouth to feed. But I wasn't. I hit the proverbial jackpot. Not only do I have amazing parents, but my aunts and uncles are the bomb too.

"I'd give my left nut to have something good like that in my life."

I'm on my feet, walking toward him. "I wouldn't like that because I'm kind of partial to your left nut." I'm using humor because it's the only thing I can do. "Your right one just doesn't do it for me."

Pike grabs me as the blanket I have wrapped around myself falls to the floor. "You're such an asshole." He laughs, holding me tightly, skin against skin.

"But you love me."

"I do," he replies, running his fingers down my spine. "More than I have anyone in a long time."

"Pike." I'm breathless, wondering if he meant to say that, wondering if he'll take them back. "Is it a little too soon to say those words?"

He peers down at me, a swirl of emotion in his eyes. "I didn't just meet you, darlin'. After you left, I dreamed of no one but you. When I saw you walk into Inked, I couldn't believe my goddamn eyes. We've only spent two weeks together in total, but I feel like I've known you since the day you walked up to me and asked me for my number—and let me say, you never gave me yours."

"Well…" I don't know what to say to all that. If I were honest, I've thought about Pike a lot since the day I walked out the door for that nonexistent cup of coffee.

"You're young. Maybe you're not ready to say how you feel, but I've lived enough to know when there's something good in my life and something I don't want to let go of again."

"Um," I mumble, my vision blurring because this beautiful man, one who doesn't always share his feelings, is spilling his guts like water over Niagara Falls.

"I'll give you all the time in the world to figure out if

it's how you feel too, but until then, you're my girl and only my girl. You're mine, Gigi Gallo."

My stomach flutters at the way he says those words and at the intensity in his gaze. I've heard my father utter those words a thousand times to my mother, and every time, I'd roll my eyes. But now I understand how it made her feel. I understand why those words made her smile and go all gooey in the knees, because in this moment, I am finding it difficult to stand.

"Okay," I whisper.

"Okay?" He raises an eyebrow.

I nod. "I'm yours." I brush my hand across the beautiful back dimples he has just above his ass. "But as long as we're staking claims, you're mine too, Pike Moore. No other women are in your bed or on the back of your bike. If we're doing this, we're doing it right."

Pike's sadness from earlier is gone, replaced by a big, toothy smile. He slides his hand up my back, cupping my neck. "In the shittiest week of my life, you've somehow found a way to make me the happiest man alive."

I don't get a chance to reply and tell him I feel the same before his lips crash down on mine, stealing my words and my breath.

22

PIKE

My eyes fly open as a cold hand covers my mouth. "Pike," Morris tries to whisper, but being quiet has never been his thing. "Men are on the perimeter."

I blink up at him as I lift myself, letting his words slide over me, penetrating the haze I still have from the dream I was just in a minute ago.

Gigi shifts in my arms. "What's wrong?" She goes stiff as soon as she lays eyes on Morris, who's hovering above us.

"Get your asses up and be ready." Morris moves toward the door, but he's still staring at us, a worried look on his face. "Shit's about to go down."

Gigi rises next to me, holding the sheet over her chest. "Fuck. For real?" Her eyes are wide, and I can see the fear all over her face.

Morris doesn't answer as he disappears into the hallway. The only sounds are his heavy footsteps and those of his brothers moving around the compound as the door clicks behind him.

"Get dressed and go into my closet." I move my chin toward the door on the other side of the room. "Don't come out under any circumstances. And when I say any circumstances, I mean, don't come out until you hear me, Tiny, or Morris calling your name."

She scurries to her feet, gathering her clothes off the floor where I'd thrown them last night. "Don't come out under any circumstances," she repeats my words, pulling her shirt over her head and then moving for her pants. "Pike, what if…"

I shake my head, zipping my jeans. "No ifs. If you don't know the voice, don't come out. Stay quiet, and no matter what, don't cry. I don't want these fuckers finding you."

"Don't get yourself shot, okay? No jumping in front of bullets for me."

I stalk up to her, grabbing her neck and hauling her lips to mine. "Darlin', I'll do whatever it takes to get you back to your family and keep you breathing."

"I'd never be able to…"

I don't let her finish the statement before my mouth closes over hers, taking what I can get for what might be the last time. If shit goes south, which it could and probably will, I may never have another chance to kiss her beautiful mouth and feel her in my arms again.

I break away, even though I want to hold her like this forever and forget the shit that's going on outside this room.

"Go." I run my finger along her chin, memorizing every dip of her lips. "Get in the closet. Go all the way to the back and hide behind my things."

She nods, walking back slowly, dragging her hand down my arm until just our fingertips are touching. "Be safe and don't be a hero."

I've never wanted to be the hero, but I want to be hers. I'm not sure I've ever wanted to be anything more that in this very moment. No one would get by me and get to her. Not as long as I still have air in my lungs and the ability to move.

"Go, Gigi," I order her, pulling on my boots, gun by my side on the bed, my body facing the hallway.

A wave of emotion passes across her face as she opens the door to the closet and steps inside. I lift my chin at her, and she gives me a pained smile before finally closing the door, disappearing into the darkness.

I grab the gun, but I stay on the edge of the bed, knowing whoever comes through that door is going to get one of my bullets. I won't hesitate to pull the trigger, and the brothers here know better than to walk in here unannounced or without calling the all clear.

Gunfire rings through the building, sounding like fireworks on steroids and coming so fast it's like a hurricane of metal and fire.

A million thoughts cross through my mind as the shadow of boots passes by the door, heading toward the main room where the majority of the bullets are flying.

These guys, the ones I thought of like family, are hauling ass toward the gunfire, shielding us from their spray.

We're the intended targets, but they're willing to put their lives on the line so we can breathe another day. They live for shit like this. They crave danger, not giving a fuck if they live or die as long as they enjoy every minute of the time they're here, walking this earth.

I hold my breath, knowing someone's going to come through the door if anyone has survived. I pray—something I haven't done since I was living with my grandmother—hoping like hell we get out of here unscathed. Not just us, but the men putting their lives on the line as I sit in the dark, protecting my girl and waiting for hell to come to me.

I've lived through a hail of bullets before, but I had never been the intended target. I've been shot, and I sure as fuck am not looking forward to feeling the hot metal slice through my skin again. But I also want to live, having more to live for than ever before.

My father's sins were following me. His curse was the only thing he gave me besides his name. But after tonight, after the gunfire ends, no matter which side comes out on top, his time in my life will end as well.

The shouts of the men I know are barely audible over the gunfire as it grows louder, coming close to us. I prepare myself, lifting the gun toward the door, poised to shoot anyone who enters. My hand doesn't shake, even though I've never shot a man before. I've held a gun hundreds of times growing up in Tennessee, but never have I been more prepared to use it to kill another person than I am right now.

My body stiffens as a door slams nearby. Clearly, someone's searching and got through the front line. I lift my other hand, gripping my forearm to steady the gun because if I shoot, I sure as fuck ain't missing.

"Keep lookin'!" a man yells. "I know he's here."

He is me, and I'm thankful they haven't said anything about Gigi. I'm their intended target and not the scared girl hiding in my closet probably losing her shit but following my orders nonetheless.

A single shot rings out in the hallway, sounding more like a firework popping and echoing through the tiny corridor. The knob on my door turns, illuminating my room with just enough light to see the outline of a man. I squeeze the trigger, not hesitating to fire as he lifts his arm, ready to take me out too. But my shot is quicker, and the man falls backward, a clean shot right in his head.

"Don't shoot," another man says, but my ears are still ringing from the shot I just fired. "Pike." I can't see him because he hasn't shown his face, probably not wanting the same fate as the dead bastard on the dirty-ass floor.

The gun's still pointed at the door, my hand not as steady as it was, but I'll take out any other bastard that tries to walk inside. I keep my mouth shut, not knowing who's calling my name or their intentions.

"It's Morris. Don't shoot," he says. "They're gone. All dead but a few already out the door and running for the hills."

"They're gone?" I ask, not moving a muscle because I can't.

"Just this one cocksucker got by us, but you handled his ass. Three more made it out, but men are after them, making sure they don't get wherever they're going."

"Morris?" I ask because my mind is hazy and all I

can see is the puddle of blood oozing out of the man's body.

"Yeah, kid. It's me. Put the gun down. The shit's over." He's still hiding, taking no chances with me.

I don't blame him. It's not every day a man takes the life of another. Morris knows I've never done it and how it changes a man.

My hand drops as I take my finger off the trigger, but I'm not ready to put it down. It's like the metal has fused to my hand, becoming one with me. I'm in shock. I know it. I know my body is trying to catch up with what my mind already knows. I shot a man. I took a life.

"Is it down?"

"Yeah," I call back to Morris. "Come in."

He steps over the man's body, flipping the switch on the wall and bathing the room in light. "Nice shot," he says as soon as his eyes land on the man with a bullet clean through his forehead. "I always knew you had it in you."

"Can I come out?" Gigi says from the closet, no doubt hearing our voices but unable to wait for the all clear. The girl only has so much patience to follow orders, which is maddening, but at least she stayed in there long enough to keep her ass alive.

"Come out, girl," Morris tells her before I can. "It's over."

I'm on my feet and at my closet before she has a chance to see the dead guy on the floor. I grab her face, keeping her eyes on me. "You okay, baby?"

She nods, eyes glistening as she stares up at me. "I'm okay," she whispers, but her voice wavers. "When I heard the shot go off…" Her lip quivers, and her voice breaks, not finishing the statement.

"I'm fine. We're fine." I hold her gaze, trying to keep my shit together so I can convince her that what I'm saying is true.

"Yo!" Morris yells, making Gigi jump. "We got a body over here."

Gigi tries to look around me, but I hold her face, forcing her to look at me and nowhere else. "Don't look. You don't want to have that burned on your brain."

"Did you do it?" she asks, her voice whisper-soft, the quiver still on her lips.

I nod, rubbing my thumb across her cheek. "It was him or us, and I wasn't about to end what we have. I told you I'd do anything to protect you, and I did what I needed to do."

"You killed a man."

I nod again because I did. I pulled that trigger without an ounce of hesitation, thinking of him as the enemy and not a human being. I didn't give a fuck if he had a wife and kids. He wanted to kill us, and for that alone, he deserved the bullet he got.

The tears in her eyes build and fall when she blinks. "You protected me?" she whispers as her hands find my sides, gripping me like she needs to touch me to stay upright.

"I'll always protect you." I know my words are true. "I told you that, darlin'."

Boots are behind me, shadows moving around the room as the guys bend down, hauling the dead guy from the doorway. "Take him outside with the others," Morris says. "We'll deal with them together. And get Midge in here to help clean up this mess." There are a few grunts of understanding, followed by Morris's shadow growing in size on the wall behind Gigi. "I'll give you two some time to talk and some privacy."

I nod, not turning around because I'm not taking my eyes off my girl. She needs me. More than she needed me before this shit went down. She heard too much, knew too much, and that shit would mess with her head.

When I peer over my shoulder, there's only a small amount of blood visible near the doorway. The majority of the guy's brains and blood landed in the hallway just outside my door and out of sight.

I reach down, lifting Gigi into my arms, carrying her toward the bed. Her head moves to my shoulder, arms around my neck as I cradle her tightly, wishing she'd never had to experience this. I brought this to her door. My father brought this to mine.

"We're safe now." I sit on the edge of the bed, resting her ass in my lap, still holding her close. "No one's going to hurt you."

"I've never been so scared in my life, Pike." Her fingers toy with the hair on the back of my neck, sending a shock wave of feelings through my system. "Not just for me, but for you. I was so worried that…"

"Shh, baby. It's over. Stop thinking about it. I'm breathing. You're breathing. There's nothing else that matters right now."

"What about the guys?"

"I don't know what happened out there, and I'm not ready to find out. Tiny will call for us when he's ready to tell us what we need to know and what he wants to tell." I brush my lips across her forehead, needing to feel her softness and be reminded of all the good there is in life to replace the bad I've just done. "All that matters is you're okay."

"Do you think they'll come back?" she whispers, toying with the collar of my T-shirt, grazing my skin with her fingernails.

"I don't know if there'll be anyone to come back. If any of them made it out, the others went after them on foot. They don't have much of a chance on all this land with the Disciples on the hunt."

"I guess that's a good thing."

"It's a good thing for us, but not for them."

We're both thankful to be alive. I may have lived within these compound walls for years, but we'd never been attacked and I'd never been in what sounded like a battle zone. My body trembles slightly as the adrenaline that has been coursing through me starts to wear off.

"Do you think we'll ever get to go home?"

I run my hand up her back and nuzzle my face in her neck, needing her smell, her softness to keep me grounded. "We will, darlin'. DiSantis isn't stupid enough to lose all his men trying to kill someone who doesn't know dick about his business. I don't know how many came here tonight, but based on the sounds, I'd say he lost too many to try to come after me again."

"Kid?" Tiny calls, knocking on my door but not entering the room. "You two decent?"

Gigi laughs, and the sound is like angels singing,

making all the shit that happened seem like it was part of a distant past.

"Yeah, Tiny. We're good."

The door creaks, and Tiny sticks his head in the room. "Just talked to James."

"Oh shit," Gigi whispers, and her laughter dies. "We may have survived the gun battle, but now we have to figure out how to make it through my family."

"He's on his way with a few of her uncles and her father. They'll be here in a few hours. Get your shit together. You two are heading back."

I gawk at Tiny as he wipes his bloodied hand with a towel. "But what about DiSantis?"

Tiny shrugs with a smile. "Fucker's dead. Someone went after him tonight before the hit went down. Took a blade across his neck just before lights-out. He ain't gonna bother you again."

I let out a heavy breath like a weight has been lifted off my back that I didn't know was there. "That's it? He's dead. It's over?" I repeat like the words haven't sunk in.

"Yup. Dead as a fucking doornail. You have three hours before the guys get here to collect you two."

He starts to close the door, but I have shit to say and not a lot of time to say it. "Tiny," I call out, causing him to stop. "Thank you for tonight and everything."

Tiny nods, still wiping the blood because there're so many dead bodies out there, I'm sure there's blood on everything. "You are family, kid, and we take care of our own. I meant what I said earlier, you need backup or safe haven, you come here. Nowhere else."

I nod. "Nowhere else."

"Now get some rest. You made it through one hit squad, but you're about to be in front of another. I have a feeling you're going to get an earful on the way back."

"I won't let them say anything to you." Gigi gazes up at me from my lap.

"You're cute, darlin'. If they want to lay into me, let them. I can take it. It's not like they're going to be shooting bullets at me. I can handle a little angry talk. Let them get it off their chests, and I'll take it like a man. They're probably worried out of their minds."

"A little angry talk?" she says, laughing with every word. "I know you're used to badass bikers, but these are Gallo men. They may not wear patches or ride a hog, but I'm telling you now, they're just as fuckin' scary. A little angry talk." She bursts into a fit of giggles, knowing her family way better than I do. "We're going to get our asses chewed out for a living, and you're going to wish you were lying in that heap of bodies outside."

"Come on. We're alive. How bad can they honestly be?"

23

GIGI

I SLAM BACK TWO SHOTS OF JACK AS MORRIS YELLS THAT two cars are approaching. The same two cars that are carrying my family. The same two cars that not only carry my family, but men so pissed off, I'm pretty sure they broke every speed record to get here.

I know what awaits me. I've seen my dad and Uncle James angry before, but it was never pointed at me. I figure if I am going to make it through the long-ass drive home, I need a little liquor to make me more agreeable and less likely to argue back.

"You ready?" Pike asks at my side, holding out his hand to me.

"I don't think I'll ever be ready." I try to smile, but it's impossible knowing my dad is nearby, probably foaming at the mouth.

"It won't be that bad," he says with a straight face because he only knows my dad and uncles as the chill guys they can be sometimes and not the raving lunatics they can be when someone in the family is in danger.

"I'll remind you that you said that." I grab the bottle of Jack and try to pour myself another drink before Pike takes it from my hands.

"This won't make things better."

I try to pull the bottle out of his grip, but it won't budge as we play tug-of-war. "I beg to differ."

"Get your asses moving," Morris yells out, standing at the open door of the building, glancing back at us as we're locked around the bottle of Jack.

"Fuckin' fine." I let go, knowing it's a lost cause and we're out of time.

"The girl lives, sees death, but the attitude never leaves," Morris mutters, glancing up at the dark sky and shaking his head.

I walk away from Pike, stalking toward Morris, the guy I've grown fond of over the last few days. "Thanks for everything, big guy."

He blushes as he tips his head down to look at me. "Don't be a stranger, kid. Make sure to keep that boy in line, ya hear?"

I laugh, nodding at him as I wrap my arm around his middle. "I promise to make sure he walks the straight and narrow."

Morris's arm is around me immediately, holding me tightly. "Maybe I'll come visit. I could use another piece."

"I'd love that."

"You two done?" Tiny says, stalking by the doorway, heading toward the headlights.

I release Morris and practically run up to Tiny, hurling myself against him. He stumbles back like he's in shock and not used to being hugged. "Thank you for everything, Tiny."

Tiny pats my back but doesn't give me the rib-crushing embrace Morris just did. "Anytime, girl. Now, give me a minute with the boy."

I stare up at him, craning my neck all the way back to meet his eyes. "Can you make sure they don't kill Pike?"

"Can't promise anything when it comes to James," he says, amusement lighting up his face.

"It was worth a shot." I shrug and pop up on my toes to just reach his cheek.

Tiny doesn't move as I kiss his cheek and then step away. He looks a little shell-shocked, which is funny because he's so big and burly, but my little kiss seems to have knocked the badass right out of him and left him speechless.

Two cars pull in, gravel flying from the speed and hurling in all directions as they slam on the brakes. We're like deer, frozen in the headlights.

I was scared as hell in the closet, listening to the screams and gunfire going off everywhere. You'd think facing my family would be nothing after that, but nope. I'm just as scared as I was a few hours ago.

"Just stay calm," Morris calls out as Pike walks up next to me.

"You ready for this?" I ask, looking over at him, ignoring the sound of the car doors opening and boots hitting gravel.

"I don't know," he says before his eyes go to where my family stands.

I turn my head slowly, soaking in my uncle James, who looks like he's about ready to tear a man's jugular clean through his neck. My uncle Thomas, who looks just as pissed and no less scary. And then there's my daddy and Bear, looking like caged animals, shifting slightly like they're unable to stand still or all their fury would cause them to combust.

"Hey," I call out, putting on a smile and trying to act like our asses didn't almost get shot tonight. "I missed you guys." I slowly move in their direction, gaze going between all four men, trying to see if I could make their badass exteriors crack.

My dad rushes toward me, putting his eyes on no one and nothing but me. My slow walk turns into a full-on run until we're close enough that I leap into his arms, and he catches me like he used to when I was a little girl.

"I love you, Daddy." I feel like a kid again and finally safe in my father's arms.

"Baby girl," he whispers, holding my head with one hand and squeezing my body with his other arm. "I've never been so scared in all my fucking life and never more thankful than I am right now."

I bury my face in his neck, holding on to him like I don't think I've ever held him before. "I'm sorry," I whisper. "I'm sorry I had you worried."

"We'll talk about it in the car," he says.

Oh goodie.

Car talks have never been my favorite. I'm like a trapped animal and a captive audience with no escape or talking my way out of whatever my dad wants to put down. I freaking hate every minute of the car chats.

They are the most sucktastic things ever because they are so effective at breaking me.

"Joe," Pike says, walking up behind me, but my daddy's body goes stiff underneath me.

"Get your ass in the car with James and Thomas. I want to talk to my *daughter* alone."

Goodie times two.

"Yes, sir," Pike says without even arguing.

He probably knows it's a lost cause. There isn't any arguing with a Gallo man on a good day, but in a moment like this and with the anger on my dad's face, there is no way in hell Pike or I would win that argument.

My feet are back on the ground as Pike turns his back and is walking toward James and Thomas where they chat with Tiny and Morris.

"Let's get out of here," Bear says, giving me a wink instead of saying anything else.

I'm sure he wants all the details, but he isn't going to ask about shit when my dad's in a mood. And I'm pretty damn sure my dad's mood isn't going away anytime soon either.

"Daddy, can't Pike come with us, please?" I pitch my thumb over my shoulder toward the five guys.

"I want to talk to you alone, and James wants to debrief Pike." My father shakes his head. "They know the way home."

I hang my head, dragging my feet through the gravel as I make my way toward the car. I know I'm going to get my ass chewed out, but I'll live. It won't be the first time my father has read me the riot act about something.

But Pike may not be so lucky.

I turn toward Pike as I open the car door, giving him a small wave and pained smile when our eyes lock. He waves back, tipping his chin like shit is cool, but he's freaking clueless.

I don't know much about his dad and know even less about his entire family. But what he's about to deal with will, no doubt, be nothing he's prepared for or expects.

"We're out!" my dad yells across the parking lot, not bothering to wait for a response before he's climbing in the passenger seat.

"This should be fun." Bear catches my eye in the rearview mirror, always trying to make light of heavy shit.

No other words are spoken as Bear revs the engine, taking off the same way they came in…fast. I twist my fingers, staring out the window at the endless trees flying by in a blur as we exit the compound.

Maybe my dad is too pissed to even talk. Maybe he's too happy I'm alive to rip me a new asshole. Anything is possible. How can he be mad when we didn't do anything wrong, nor did we do anything to cause the clusterfuck of chaos that landed at our feet?

The silence is killing me. I figure maybe this is an instance where I've got to rip the Band-Aid off quickly and get it over with. Waiting just makes it worse, and I can't sit here in silence for the next two hours. "So…"

"Don't *so* me, little girl," Dad says.

I widen my eyes at his clipped tone. "Okay," I whisper, slouching down in the seat and crossing my arms over my chest.

"You could've been killed." He turns in his seat so he can look at me. "You almost were..."

"But I wasn't."

His eyes harden. "Were there bullets flying within fifty feet of you?"

I shrug. Now, I'm pissed. And when I'm pissed, I dig my heels in and turn on the smartass. "I didn't have my tape measure."

He surges forward like he's going to leap over the seat and wrap his hands around my neck, choking the life right out of me. His eyes aren't hard anymore; his glare is blazing hot. "What did you just say? Say it again."

"Dad, you're being a little crazy and unreasonable. Where's my big, badass father?"

"Your big, badass father is dealing with a lot of feelings after men just tried to bust into an MC compound, raining down fire, in an attempt to take out my kid and end her life."

"They weren't trying to kill me," I say softly because I know he's about at his wits' end and he doesn't need my shit.

"I know. They were trying to kill Pike, who—" he pauses, twisting his lips up, and I know what he's about to say before the words spill from his mouth "—you didn't tell me was actually your boyfriend!"

He yells those words, the sound echoing through the car like a bomb blast. "He's not my boyfriend, Daddy."

I keep up with the Daddy bit because it's always worked in the past and usually helps to defuse his anger. This isn't the first time he's been pissed at me, but it is the most pissed he's ever been that I can remember.

Bear shakes his head, muttering something under his breath, and he catches my eye in the mirror. I don't know what he's trying to tell me, but I know instantly I fucked up.

"That's right," Dad says, nodding his head, eyebrows drawn down, and his top lip curling like he's smelled the biggest pile of shit. "He's not a boyfriend. He's a guy you fucked."

Uh oh. This isn't good. Damn. I can't backpedal my way out of this one. There're no more secrets at this point, and I lied right to my dad's face about Pike when Aunt Izzy confronted me at Inked.

I don't move. It's as if my ass is glued to the seat, and every muscle in my body locks up as if I'm paralyzed. The only thing I can do is stare at my father with wide eyes and say, "I'm sorry."

He tips his head back, staring at the ceiling of the car. "She's sorry." His shoulders rise and fall. "No big deal, Dad. I met a guy at Bike Week and slept with him even though he could've raped me and left my ass for dead."

"I'm grown and I was careful."

"Adults die too, Giovanna. How many times did I tell you under no circumstances were you allowed in Daytona during Bike Week?"

"It was a mistake. We went for spring break."

"And did you tell me you were going to Daytona for spring break?"

"Did you tell your parents everything when you were twenty?" I pause, returning his hard stare because I'm sick and tired of being treated like a little kid. "Oh, wait. No, you freakin' didn't. You were out riding your bike, bangin' broads without giving any fucks."

He turns his head like he didn't quite hear me. "You want to repeat that shit for me?"

"No."

He grinds his teeth, and I wince at the sound. "I didn't fucking think so," he growls.

"She finally says something smart," Bear mutters.

"When we get back, I forbid you to see him again."

He forbids me? I raise an eyebrow, ready to dig the hole I've already dug a little deeper. "So, you firing him or me? 'Cause other than that, I don't know how I'm not supposed to see him. Care to explain, Daddy?"

My father slides a hand down his face before his fingers crumple into a fist near his chin. "Did the bullets scramble your brains or some shit?"

"Nope." I shake my head. "I'm seeing clearer than I have in a long time."

"The way your mouth is talking, I'd say you're still in shock."

"Not in shock. I'm feeling more alive than ever. So, who's leaving?"

"Izzy won't fire him, and you're not going anywhere. You two can work together without dating."

"Okay." I nod, thinking over my next words carefully. "So, the guy who was just ready to take a bullet for me, the guy who put his body in the way, hiding me so he'd die instead of me..." I close my eyes, remembering the way my body shook when the door to Pike's room opened and I didn't know which person had died. "I'm just supposed to tell him to kick rocks because my *father*, who's also his *boss*, doesn't want me to see him again." I open my eyes and roll them because I know it'll piss off my dad something fierce. "Hey, Pike, thanks for almost dying for me and being willing to throw yourself in front of a bullet, but my *father* doesn't think you're good enough."

"I didn't say he wasn't a good person."

I cross my arms again, lifting one shoulder, staring my father straight in the eye. "Just not good enough for me, right?"

My father's entire face scrunches up like he's about to shit a brick and it's painful as fuck. "His life is dangerous, Gigi. Look at all the shit you've been through in a couple days of him being in your life."

"It's not trouble he brought to his door. It was *his* father's fault, and if it weren't for the men in Pike's past, he'd probably be dead and maybe me too." I pause and our eyes are locked in a silent tug-of-war, but I don't give him a chance to talk because I'm not done making my point. "Didn't something happen to Mom when you two were dating? Wasn't she almost..."

"It was different," he says quickly.

"Shit happens, Dad. Life happens. No matter how hard you try to protect someone, you can't stop the bad from getting through all the time. Pike's innocent in this, and the decision of if we're going to see each other again falls to Pike and me. And frankly—" I swallow because if he hasn't leaped over the seat yet, my next words may be the nail in the coffin "—it's none of your business."

He blinks like I've slapped him, and his mouth moves but nothing comes out.

"I'm not trying to be mean, and if I am, I'm sorry. But imagine if Grandma or Grandpa said you couldn't see Mom anymore."

"I love your mother."

"Maybe I love Pike."

My father laughs. "You just met the kid."

"How long after you met Mom did you know you had feelings for her? Real feelings..."

"Well..." He looks at Bear because Bear was there in the beginning, and I have zero doubt he'll call my dad on his shit if he tries to lie. "Honestly, I don't remember a time when I didn't love your mom."

"Then why does it matter that I just met him?" I use air quotes on the last three words because we both know I didn't just meet him, but I have had fifteen months to think about him and the way he makes me feel.

"I..." He pauses, staring at me like he doesn't know what to say and hates to tell me I'm right.

"The man would've died for me tonight, Daddy. How many guys would do that? Let me tell you. Not many. Guys my age are a bunch of pansy-asses who cry when they get a paper cut. Chivalry is fucking dead. Pike would've taken that bullet and died with a smile on his face knowing I was going to live to breathe another day."

"I..." he says again, but I don't let him finish before I go on because I have shit to get off my chest.

"Here's this guy with a mother who's dead because his father is an asshole. The same father who treated him like shit as a little kid and a mother who wasn't much better. For growing up the way he did, he turned out to be a freaking great guy. He's envious of me, you know. He sees how close we all are, how much we love each other, and he knows exactly what he missed out on growing up and even now. So whatever misconceived notions you have about Pike, you may as well forget them all until you get to know the real man underneath."

"She's kind of telling you how it is, City." Bear glances at him with a slight shrug. "Pike's not too far off from the man you were at that age. You had a good family behind you, but you weren't a choirboy."

My father glares at Bear. "You're not helping. Whose side are you on?"

"Don't ask me to pick a side because I'll always pick the girl."

My smile's so big, my cheeks hurt. This is why I love my uncle Bear. He can totally call my dad out on his shit, reminding him of the man he is and used to be. It doesn't hurt that he's always willing to have my back. Always. It doesn't matter that we're not blood; he's been in my life since the day I was born and is just as much my uncle as any of my father's brothers.

"It's a fucking conspiracy," my father mutters, turning around to face the windshield.

"Just give him a chance, Dad. Give me a chance to live my own life and find my own happiness."

"I don't like it."

"I never asked if you did."

24

PIKE

"Three large black coffees."

"Would you like sugar, sir?"

"I said black," James barks out the driver's window, arm slung over the door, looking chill as fuck but sounding like he's wound so tight, he could break at any moment.

"Black means no cream, but it doesn't mean no sugar," the woman on the other end of the drive-thru tries to explain, but James is in no mood.

"No cream. No sugar. Just coffee."

"Iced or hot?" she asks.

James looks at Thomas like he can't get over this shit, and Thomas laughs at James's misery. "Hot," he growls out the window, practically foaming at the mouth.

"Please pull around, sir."

"What the fuck happened to ordering a simple cup of coffee?"

Thomas shrugs. "Life's moving fast, old man."

"Get the fuck out of here with that old man shit."

Thomas glances down, staring at his phone. "Well, this should get interesting."

"What?" James asks as he inches the car forward in the long line.

"Mom's requiring Pike to be at today's family dinner."

"She what?" I ask, shocked and a little scared.

"Joe isn't going to be happy about that," James states the fucking obvious.

From the moment our eyes met at the compound, I knew Joe hated me now. I'm not even sure hate is a strong enough word for all the things he's feeling toward me. I can't blame the guy. I'd fucking hate me too.

"I'd give my left nut to be in that car with them." Thomas laughs. "Gigi's more like Izzy than Suzy. She's probably reading him the riot act."

"Maybe one of them isn't going to make it back alive," James jokes, sliding up to the drive-thru window, trying not to make eye contact with the lady behind the voice.

Seconds later, Thomas's phone rings, and Joe's voice comes through the car speakers. "Do you believe this shit?"

"You know Ma."

"Why on God's green earth would she want him there?"

James turns to me, shrugging and rolling his eyes while the guys talk about me like I'm not overhearing the entire conversation.

"You know Ma is always the peacemaker and sticks her nose in everyone's business."

"This is my kid," Joe says.

"And you're her kid," Thomas reminds him. "I think that trumps your thinking."

"Does she realize Gigi could've died?"

"I'm sure she does. Our wives told her everything, Joe," James tells him, and I know there're no secrets left in this family. "You know they can't keep a secret, and Ma could pull the truth out of anyone, especially them."

"Fuck," Joe hisses. "Drop Pike off at my house, and he can ride with us."

"Do I get a say in this?" I ask from the back seat, wishing I could get out and run, but it's impossible without a door in the back of this Challenger.

Thomas turns, glaring at me to shut the fuck up but without actually saying the words. He doesn't need to either. I get the message loud and clear.

"We'll drop him off and go. We'll only have a few hours to sleep before we have to be there," James says. "She doesn't care that we've crossed the state and come back in the same day."

"You know how she is… There's never a good reason to cancel a dinner. Bullets. Near-death experiences. Hell, not even a hurricane would stop her," Thomas tells them.

I tip my head back, staring out the back window at the sky painted with pinks and purples as the sun starts to rise over the horizon.

All I want to do is talk to Gigi and crawl into bed, leaving all the bad shit behind. But I have a feeling I don't get a choice in whether I attend family dinner since the big men in the front seat aren't finding a reason I can't go. The fact that Joe wants me at his house and is going to drive me there himself seals the deal.

"We're grabbing a quick cup of coffee, but we'll be at your place a few minutes after you," James says, handing the money over to the woman.

"I'll be there waiting," Joe says before disconnecting the call.

"Well, that wasn't so bad," Thomas says, turning his head to stare at me as I lift mine, forgetting the beautiful sunrise because although that wasn't so bad, it wasn't good either.

I laugh. "So bad? I'm pretty sure the man wants to kill me."

"Here's your *hot* and *black* coffees," the woman says, holding three cups in her hands, waiting for James to take them.

He hands one to me, then to Thomas, and takes the final one for himself. He doesn't say anything else to the woman. He's had a shit night like the rest of us and doesn't want to get into another argument over something as simple as a cup of coffee.

"That man," James says, placing his coffee in the cupholder before he rolls the car forward, "is a devoted father. He'd lay down his life for his family. Just like we would in his shoes."

"I would've taken a bullet tonight to save Gigi."

"We know that, kid. Hell, even Joe knows that. He knows everything that went down at the compound.

Trust me, he's thankful that you helped get her out of there alive, but the man's out of his mind right now. Joe doesn't scare easily, but he's been a raving lunatic the last few days. He'll come around. Just give him some time and space to let him get his head on straight."

I rest the Styrofoam on my knee, letting his words settle deep. "Then maybe you should just drop me off at my place. Give everyone some space without me around, crowding shit."

Thomas shakes his head. "Ma wants you at her house, you'll be at her house."

I close my eyes, trying to picture the mother of these rough and tough men. She must be a powerful force if, even at their age, she's still the boss.

"And if Joe walks around there all broody and moody, she'll set his ass straight if she likes you."

"Why don't you two hate me?" I ask, lifting my head and prying the lid off the coffee.

Thomas laughs and shakes his head. "We've been in shit just as big as you were last night. You didn't cause what came at you, but we played a role in the hell we brought to our door. Our women were almost casualties too. We know how things easily spin out of control. That's life, kid."

"Hell, Izzy's been knee-deep in our bullshit so many times," James says, gunning the engine as soon as he's on the highway with nothing but open road before us. "But that was shit we brought on ourselves or she put into motion. Life happens. Shit happens. We rolled with it, and so did you. The family, including Joe, will get over what happened. And if you're lucky, they'll welcome you into the fold if that's what you're looking for."

"I want Gigi in my life." I figured I'd lay shit out for her uncles since they are here and I'm not going anywhere. "She's the best thing to ever happen to me. But the family…" I pause, wondering how to explain the shit I've been through and the lack of familial support I'd grown up with. "That isn't something I'm used to dealing with."

"I didn't grow up Gallo," James says, looking at me in the rearview mirror for a moment, "but they treat me as if I did. From the moment I stepped foot in her mother's house, I was welcomed as part of the family. Doesn't matter how you were raised, kid. Once you're in, you're one of them. One of us. Win over Ma Gallo and Suzy too, and you're in the fold."

"Gigi's mother is going to hate me." I'm never the guy a girl brings home to meet her mother.

Thomas laughs, smacking his leg. "You're just like Joe, and Suzy's crazy about that man. Suzy may seem straitlaced, but don't let her fool you. She'll take to you like glue if she sees her daughter's happy. You'll remind her of the man she fell in love with. The guy with the chip on his shoulder who's head over heels for a girl."

All of this is out of my comfort zone and territory I haven't ridden through before. I've never dealt with an entire family. I never gave a shit if people liked me, especially not a woman's parents. But this is different. I have to win over countless people, starting with her mother and then her grandmother before I could get everyone on board.

"You looked death in the eye last night and came out alive," James says. "Facing our family will seem like a cakewalk."

"Yeah," I mutter, staring into the blackness of the coffee, not believing a goddamn word. Sure, I was scared when the gunfight was going on and the door to my old room opened, but I knew how to respond. Family…isn't something I'm used to.

"Just relax. We'll be at Joe's soon."

"Oh goodie," I mumble and sip my coffee.

Thomas and James laugh, clearly getting a kick out of my misery and knowing full well shit isn't going to be as easy as they make it out to be.

An hour later, I'm climbing out of the back of James's car, and I catch sight of Gigi on the front porch, hugging a blond woman tightly. I assume it's her mother because that's the only thing that makes sense, but there's very little resemblance between the two.

Joe's next to them, glaring at me like I'm the enemy, and not over the shit that went down, or the fact that he probably knows everything about what happened between Gigi and me in Daytona. Well, not everything because I'd be a dead man, but he knows enough that he has to want to at least break my legs.

"Pike!" Gigi yells as soon as she sees me. She moves away from her mother, running down the front steps, across the driveway, and leaps into my arms. "I was so worried about you." She holds me tightly, locking her hands behind my neck and staring up at me. "I thought maybe my uncles would leave you somewhere on the side of the road."

"I'm fine, darlin'." I push the hair away from her eyes, needing to see her face. "Your uncles were nice."

I didn't say they were friendly because, under the circumstances, it wasn't like hanging out with my buddies, but they weren't assholes either. They laid shit out for me, telling me how it is and how to get in everyone's good graces.

She smiles up at me. "They were nice?"

I nod. "They weren't mean."

"Huh. That's shocking." Her smile widens. "I want you to meet my mother."

"I'm sure she hates me, Gigi. Maybe I should just go back to my place."

Gigi shakes her head, tightening her hold around me. "Not happening, big guy. My mother is a cream puff. She's going to go bananas for you."

"Bananas?"

"Yeah." She smiles again but bigger this time. "My mom is sweet where my dad's rough. She's going to love you as much as I do."

I glance toward her parents. They're in a heated conversation. Her mother's eyes are on me, but her father's only paying attention to his woman. She slaps Joe's chest, eyes raking over me as a smile spreads across her face. She looks harmless. A mess of blond hair, fair skin, and a tiny little figure. Gigi gets her size from her mother, but everything else about her is all her daddy.

"I want to kiss you so badly right now." I rest my forehead on hers, trying to control myself because her father could very well end me right here.

"We'll sneak away once things settle down. Maybe at

my grandmother's, we'll go for a walk or something. But for now, my mother's waiting, and I think her patience has just about worn out."

"Lead the way, darlin'."

She releases her grip on me and grabs my hand, pulling me toward the front porch as soon as her feet touch the ground. Joe ticks his chin toward Thomas and James before James peels out of the driveway like his ass is on fire.

Suzy, Gigi's mother, doesn't even glance toward the noise. Her eyes are locked on me, soaking me in, probably thinking the worst.

"So, you're Pike," she says with a small smile.

"Ma'am," I reply, squeezing Gigi's hand because this is almost as terrifying as the gun pointed at my head.

Her mother comes down the stairs, meeting us at the bottom. "Thank you for keeping my baby safe."

"Um, you're welcome." I nod because I don't know what else to say and I wasn't expecting those words or her kindness.

"Now, don't freak out. I know you're a badass biker and all, but this mama bear wants to give you a hug."

Gigi snorts as her father starts cursing. "Told ya," Gigi says, describing her mother perfectly.

"Hush it," Suzy tells her and holds out her arms for me.

I pause, gazing down at my girl, but she's smiling and jerking her chin toward her mama. "You better do what she says. She isn't as sweet as she seems, especially if you don't do what she asks."

"Seems to be a theme in this family." I let go of Gigi's hand and move into her mother's waiting arms.

Suzy's hug isn't soft. Her hold is pretty damn firm, especially for her size. "I can hear you two," Suzy says with a small chuckle. "I can also understand why my daughter likes you." Suzy pulls back, gazing up at me, eyes sweeping across my face. "You're just like her daddy."

My eyes go to Joe, who's now pacing on the porch, brooding about the fact that I'm being welcomed and still looking like he's ready to leap over the railing and murder me at any moment. "I don't know about that."

Suzy takes a step back, hands still on my arms, gazing up at me. "Sweetie, if you don't see the similarities between you and her daddy, you must be blind. Her first love was her father, and now my baby has found a man who's the spitting image of him." Joe's eyes are on me as she speaks, and his cursing gets louder. "Don't mind him. He has a lot of trouble dealing with his children growing up and sprouting wings."

"I do not." Joe stalks down the stairs, heading right toward us. "I have a problem with my daughter falling for a guy who's—"

"Exactly like you?" Suzy interrupts him.

Joe grunts. "I wouldn't go that far, sugar."

"He's a biker, has tattoos, piercings too. Probably a lady-killer with a chip on his shoulder and bossy as all hell."

"Yep." Gigi smiles.

"So, tell me, dear husband, how are you two different?" Suzy crosses her arms in front of her chest, staring at her husband, waiting for his response.

Joe waves his hand in my direction, and his eyebrows draw down. "He's…"

"What?" Suzy taps her foot, looking a little annoyed at this point, and the sweetness has all but disappeared.

"Shorter." Joe shrugs.

Suzy grabs his arm, plastering her body against his. "That's the best you can come up with, sweetheart?"

"Sugar…"

Suzy shakes her head. "Whatever you're feeling right now doesn't matter. Look at your daughter." She tips her head toward Gigi. "She's happy, Joe."

"Well…" Joe's eyes go to his daughter then to me before going back to his wife. "I won't say I'm happy about any of this."

"Would you ever be happy with any man she'd bring home? I remember you didn't like the other two either."

"They were spineless shits," he says quickly.

"And Pike is not."

"He's just so…so…"

"Like you," Suzy says with a smile, winking at her husband.

Gigi chuckles at my side, tangling her fingers with mine as she tugs me toward the front door, leaving her parents standing at the bottom of the steps. "We're going in. We've had a long night and could use a nap before Grandma's."

"Pike can take the couch in my office. Separate rooms," Joe says, "if you want Pike to live another day."

"You're cute, Dad." Gigi laughs as we walk into the

house. "Don't listen to him," she tells me. "He's a bit overdramatic."

"But he's right, and this is his house, darlin'. If he wants my ass to sleep on the porch, that's where I'll sleep. We're under his roof, and he gets to set the rules."

"Fine." She rolls her eyes. "I'll show you where his office is."

"Thank you. Now, tell me about your grandma. I've had enough surprises this week to last me a lifetime."

Gigi nods her head down a hallway, and I follow her as she starts to walk. "She's fierce."

"Great," I mutter because the fierceness in this family has already been off the charts.

"She's tough too."

"Even better."

"But..." Gigi stops outside a closed door and leans against the wall, tangling her fingers with mine. "If you win her over, you have an ally for life. It doesn't hurt that she's the boss of everyone, including her sons."

"So, you're saying I have to win her heart?"

"You have to win her mind." Gigi smiles.

I've got this one in the bag. Winning over the ladies has never been a problem. I'm sure another fierce and tough Gallo won't be too hard...

25

PIKE

WITH THE WAY GIGI DESCRIBED HER GRANDMA, AND based on the size of her children, I expected the woman to be tall, sizable, and downright scary.

"Baby, I was so worried about you," her grandmother says, wrapping her arms around Gigi and squeezing her tightly.

"I'm fine, *Nonna*. Pike made sure of it."

Gigi's already working the woman, trying to put in a good word for me because, like she said, she's the boss. The ride over here was tense. I sat in the back of the SUV with Gigi, getting an icy glare from Joe in the rearview mirror as her two sisters chatted in the seats between us.

Her grandmother's eyes are on me as she embraces her granddaughter in the driveway. "This is the boy I've been hearing about?"

Gigi pulls away, glancing over her shoulder at me, a smile on her lips. "Yep, but don't believe anything *he*—" she dips her head toward her father who's stalking by and ignoring us all "—says. You know how Daddy has a tendency to fly off the handle and overreact."

Her grandmother laughs with a slow shake of her head. "He's just worried about you, and sometimes his emotions get the better of him. Cut him some slack, sweetheart. Your daddy will come around, but you have to give him some time to adjust to the reality that you're no longer a little girl, but this beautiful and confident woman who's standing here today."

I smile because I already like this woman. She gives sound advice, and it doesn't sound like there's an ounce of judgment in her voice.

"I guess." Gigi shrugs and steps to the side, turning toward me. "But he should've come to this realization the day I graduated from high school."

I haven't moved a step. I'm too engrossed in their conversation, the way they look at each other and like each other. One taller and younger, one shorter and older, but of the same blood with the same eyes and mannerisms.

"You never stop being a parent, Giovanna. There's no off-switch once your children sprout their wings and fly away from the nest. We always worry. Always want the best for them. When they hurt, so do we. He's just doing what he thinks is best for you, even if he may be totally off base. Forcing something on him that he's not ready to face won't make changing his heart and mind any easier. Just give him time, and he'll come around and see the light. What's your mother say?"

I turn toward the SUV where Gigi's mother is on bended knee, speaking with the two younger girls. I can't imagine what it had to be like growing up a Gallo. Sure, they were all up in each other's business, which could be annoying, but there is so much love between them that the good had to outweigh the bad.

Gigi sighs. "Mom seems to be cool about Pike. She says he's the spitting image of Daddy."

I catch her grandmother's eye as she laughs. "Oh, that had to go over big with your father."

"Can you talk to him for me?" Gigi begs. "Please. You're the only one who can talk sense into him sometimes."

The woman's laughter grows louder. "Child, when it comes to a man loving his children, there's no talking sense into him. You have to give him time and make him see the light." Her grandmother's eyes rake up and down my body before landing back on my face. "So, you're the one causing all the fuss?"

"Ma'am." I dip my head, giving her a playful smile because my lady-killer smirk doesn't feel right. "I've heard so many great things about you."

"All lies, I'm sure." She waves her hand through the air and steps closer, squinting up at me as she cranes her neck. "Well, aren't you a looker?"

The smile on my face only gets bigger, because Grandma may be old, but she's a tiger. "You aren't so bad-looking yourself." I throw her a wink.

"And a charmer." She laughs. "You've caused quite a commotion in a family that's seen serenity for a long time."

"I'm sorry." My voice goes up as I speak, making it

seem like I'm asking a question when I'm making a statement.

"Don't be." She shakes her head. "You're both alive and well. Life has a way of reminding everyone of the preciousness of everything. Sometimes we need to have things shaken up a little to bring everything back into focus. Now, let me get a better look at you." She lifts her hands and wiggles her fingers.

Gigi ticks her head toward her grandmother, widening her eyes when I don't move right away. I take a few steps, closing the space between us as the woman stares up at me like she's trying to see something that isn't there.

"Quite handsome," she says, and she takes me by surprise when she wraps her arms around me, embracing me like she did Gigi. "Strong too."

I laugh, biting my lip to stop myself from saying something inappropriate. "Thank you." Again, the words come out like a question as the woman's hands splay across my back.

"Hush, child. Let an old woman enjoy herself for a minute."

Gigi shrugs, throwing her hands upward as she giggles silently behind her grandmother.

"Oh boy." Suzy walks by us with her two daughters in tow, taking in the hug. "Welcome to the lion's den, Pike. I hope you're ready for what you're about to walk into," she calls out, not bothering to look back at us.

My body stiffens at her words. I've never met anyone's family. Especially not all at once. I knew half the people inside, already working with them for a few days or riding with them back and forth from the Disciples' compound. But there were a few who were still a mystery to me. I've had the Gallos in small doses, but this is going to be supersized and in my face.

"Don't listen to her. We're as good as they come. Now, wrap your arms around me, and give Grandma a hug."

All the worry I have vanishes, and it's replaced by the goodness of the woman wrapped around me and her granddaughter, who is beaming at me like I walk on water. I do as I'm told, holding the woman tightly in my arms.

"Much better. Now," the woman whispers near my ear. "I'll give my blessing because I see depth in those eyes, but if you hurt my granddaughter, you won't have to worry about her father, Pike. I'll find you first and make you wish you'd never been born."

There's the fierceness I'd been warned about. The toughness I'd been told to expect. "Yes, ma'am."

"Grandma," she tells me like I'm already one of the family.

"Grandma," I repeat, glancing down and taking in her beauty, wondering what she looked like when she was younger. Is Gigi the spitting image of the hellion in my arms?

"Now, my sauce needs stirring, and there are more than a few curious women inside looking forward to laying eyes on you." She takes a step back and puts her hands on my chest, groping me through my T-shirt. "They're excited, while their husbands are not."

I tip my head back, drawing in a breath. "You're really selling me on walking through that door."

The woman laughs. "What lies on the other side of that door is all the goodness I brought into my life. I created it—not alone, mind you—and there's no better group of people on this earth. Once you're in, you're in forever. See this chip?" She touches my shoulder, drawing my attention downward. "Don't let it falter, but keep that shit in check and mind your elders."

"I know my place, ma'am." Her eyes narrow, and I immediately know my mistake. "Grandma."

"Not such a quick learner, but you'll get there," she teases and takes a step back. "I heard you almost took a bullet for my granddaughter."

"He was willing to die for me, *Nonna*." Gigi steps forward and tucks herself under my arm.

"I was only doing what was right, darlin'."

Her grandmother smiles at her, eyes moving between us, taking us in as a couple. "My granddaughter needs someone who's strong both in mind and body. She's not a weakling and will never be controlled, but if a man's willing to take a bullet for her, just like her daddy would under the same circumstances, she's not going to let that pass without snapping up the goodness and keeping it close."

"It's not like that, Grandma. I liked Pike before this all happened."

I glance down, eyes wide because I don't want to talk to her grandmother about our time in Daytona. I didn't want anyone to know, but it seems there are very few secrets in this family.

"I've heard all about spring break. I remember your aunt Izzy causing some chaos there a while back. Trouble seems to run in our blood along with our affinity for badass, bossy men."

Well, there it is. Grandma knows all about everything and everyone.

"Now, if we don't get our asses inside, the sauce will burn, and you know how much Grandpa hates when his meal is shot to hell. We wouldn't want your aunt Fran fixin' the meal in my absence, would we?"

Gigi looks up at me. "Aunt Fran is Bear's wife, and she's not the best cook."

Grandma starts toward the door, and we follow. "You're being nice. She's the world's worst cook, but she has a good heart and a nosy spirit about her."

When the front door opens, there are so many eyes on me, I almost trip over the top step. There's not a man in the bunch. Four women I've never seen before are gawking at me like I'm an exotic animal on display and only there for their amusement. The grandmother laughs, shaking her head as she walks past them, disappearing into the back of the house.

Gigi grips my side, still tucked under my arm. "Pike, this is my aunt Max," she points at a very beautiful, tall, and lanky black woman. "She's Uncle Anthony's wife."

"Girl, get it straight. He's my husband," Max corrects her and takes a step toward us, staring up at me. "You're causing a lot of trouble around here."

"I never meant to..."

Max waves me off. "Don't say it. It's been far too quiet around here for far too long. We needed a little excitement." Then she turns her eyes toward her niece. "You did well with this one." She angles her head at me, talking like I'm not standing right in front of them. "I can't wait to see your dad lose his shit."

Great. Not only am I here to be gawked at, but they're all banking on me pissing off her father for nothing more than sheer entertainment. The last thing I want to do is make Joe mad. It doesn't mean I'm going anywhere, but I don't want the man gunning for me my entire life.

"He already lost it, Auntie."

The two women laugh.

My gaze moves to the three ladies still staring at me, covering their mouths and whispering to one another. I catch a few words here and there. The only words I can make out are *fresh meat.*

"Your daddy was the biggest badass I knew, sweetheart, but his heart is even bigger. Give him time. He'll come around."

Gigi rolls her eyes. "I don't think you understand the depths of his..."

"Love?" Max finishes her statement. "He's not angry, Gigi. He's mourning the loss of his baby. I can understand how he feels. Every day, I see the misery in Anthony's eyes as Tamara grows up and pulls away."

Gigi gasps. "Oh my God. Where's Tam? I haven't talked to her since before all hell broke loose."

So, this is Tamara's mother. The cousin Gigi had gone to Daytona with after lying to their parents, and the same Tamara Gigi had a conversation with on the phone about my cock.

"She's in hiding." Max laughs. "Anthony knows about Daytona."

Gigi's eyes widen. "I'm sorry we lied."

"Eh." Max shrugs. "You two were just blowing off steam, but I wish you'd been honest about where you were going and what you were doing."

"Dad and Uncle Anthony wouldn't have let us go."

"You're a grown-ass woman, Giovanna. Your fathers can't tell you how to live your lives forever."

"Then why's Tamara hiding from her dad?"

Max laughs. "I didn't raise a stupid child. A strong one, for sure, but not stupid."

"Enough chitchat," a small, older woman says, pushing by Max and getting the evil eye. "I need to get my hands on this boy."

"Auntie Fran, go easy on him," Gigi says as the woman plasters her body against me, resting her head on my chest.

"Shh. Don't ruin this for me, girl. When you're my age, there're very few thrills left in life."

I stare down at the woman, staying still as she feels me up like she's blind and trying to figure out the dips and curves, memorizing my body.

"Bear's wife." Gigi shrugs because Fran isn't stopping the attention she's giving to my muscles.

"Don't ruin this for me," Fran says again, her fingers digging into my pecs. "God, to be young again."

I laugh because what the fuck else am I supposed to do with this small, older woman hanging on my body? Talk about awkward. But then, there's been no real normal around me in days. This is just another experience with this family, and I can't say it's a bad one either.

"If I were ten years younger…"

"He'd break you, Fran," a redhead says from behind her, and all the women giggle.

Fran's hands move to my arms, holding tight and squeezing until her fingernails practically dig into my skin. "No, he wouldn't. I have the biggest baddie of them all, and I'd say I broke him." She nuzzles her face deeper into my chest. "I think I could handle this kid."

"Um." I hold out my arms. I'm not going to hug the woman draped across me like I'm a blanket and she's in need of heat. I'm already treading in deep water, and any movement, even if it's innocent, could send me spiraling to the depths on my ass.

When Fran doesn't unstick herself, Gigi starts talking, ignoring my new body ornament. She points toward the pretty redhead. "This is my aunt Angel. She's Thomas's wife."

"It's nice to meet you," she says with a friendly smile.

"You too." I smile back, wishing I could at least shake her hand, but there's Fran.

She moves her hand toward a woman with long wavy brown hair and big, beautiful eyes. "This is Mia." Gigi steps closer, looming over Fran but having zero effect. "She's a doctor and my uncle Mike's wife."

I'm impressed. Mike doesn't seem like the type of guy who'd marry a doctor. I'd read all about him, knew about his career as a fighter before giving it all up for love. Looking at her, I can understand why he walked away from the ring.

"It's a pleasure to meet you." I tip my head because it's all I can do with Fran still twisted around me like I'm her new favorite accessory.

Gigi's grandmother appears in the hallway, shaking her head as soon as she sees Fran. "Give the boy some space, ladies. He's not here for your entertainment. Especially you, Fran."

"I'm not moving," Fran says, latching on tighter, and I wonder if I'm going to have to pry the woman off my body.

"Fran?"

My gaze moves across the room to Bear, who's staring at Fran, arms crossed over his chest and jaw set tight. "You have thirty seconds to let that boy go, or…"

Fran doesn't budge, and she doesn't even look in his direction. "Or you'll what?" She looks up at me with a playful smirk and a quick wink, looking like she's loving every minute of hanging on me and antagonizing the big guy.

"You're not going to be able to sit comfortably for a week."

"You promise?" she teases, finally turning her head away from my body.

"Woman, you have ten seconds to let go of that boy and get your ass over here…"

"He's such a big talker," she says, looking up at me and not paying any more attention to her husband. "He's all bark and no bite."

"You want teeth, baby?"

She continues to ignore him. "I should really trade him in for a newer model."

She barely gets the words out before his arm is around her waist and then her body's in the air, landing on his shoulder. "Woman, I think you need me to remind you of who this fine ass," he says with a smack right on her behind for everyone to see, "belongs to."

The move reminds me of the way I hauled Gigi out of the bar area at the compound in front of all the guys. I gave zero fucks if I pissed her off, but I had a hell of a time doing it. Just like Bear is having while Fran grabs at his ass like a woman starved for cock.

"Sorry about that," Gigi says, "Fran can be a…"

"No worries. I think she's great. Everyone is so far."

"Well, you know my uncles, but let's see how they are after all the shit that went down. You ready to face them?"

I nod, but I want to say hell to the fucking no, I'm not ready. The ladies are always easier. The men, not so much. This group of moody and broody guys knows all about my past, the last week, and that I slept with their niece. "I'm ready."

26

GIGI

"That wasn't so bad, was it?" I ask Pike as we walk toward the line of trees in the backyard.

"Compared to what?" He looks over his shoulder like he's checking to see if anyone is following us.

"It could've been worse." I shrug, gazing up and into his beautiful blue-green eyes.

"There's still time."

I wave him off because if they were going to cause a scene, they would've done it already. "They like to put on a big show, but they're all pussycats."

Ten years ago, they maybe would've chased Pike out of here, but they've become more chill with age. Plus, they know the harder they try to drive him away, the more I'll run toward him.

"Why don't you say that to their faces?"

I curl my fingers around his hand as he brushes some hair away from my shoulder. "Do you like them, at least?"

"Who? Your family?"

I nod.

"They're like a small army, but yeah. You were a lucky kid to have so many people surrounding you as you grew up. I never had anyone except my grandmother who I could count on and who gave a shit about me."

"I care about you now." I curl into his side as we stand in the shade and out of view of all the nosy Gallos who are probably plastered to the back windows, trying to keep an eye on us.

He pulls our hands in front of us as his face grows serious. "Now that everything's over, I wouldn't blame you if you want to go back to the way things were."

"The way things were?" I ask, confused and a little dumbfounded.

"Yeah," he says like we're talking about the weather and not about *us*. "We went through some scary, heavy shit together. We didn't know if we were going to make it another day, and sometimes that affects how we think. Now that we're alive and no one's coming after us, maybe we should take a step back and make sure this is what we both want."

I jerk my head like he physically struck me. "You want to break up?" I take a step back, tearing my hands from his. "You're saying that shit now? You've met my family, saved my life, and were willing to take a bullet for me, and now you're saying you want to break up and not be together anymore?"

Pike steps forward, reaching for me, but I move quickly, evading his touch. "I didn't mean it that way. Be reasonable, Gigi. Think about it."

My eyes widen. "Be reasonable?"

"Um, yeah."

"I can't believe after everything we've been through, you're saying this shit to me now."

"I don't regret anything. I would still take a bullet for you or do anything necessary to keep you safe."

I fold my arms in front of me, cocking one shoulder upward, and raise an eyebrow. "But now that the bad shit has passed, you don't want to date me?"

"I don't want you to have any regrets," he says softly, closing the space between us, but I don't allow him near enough to touch me. "You're young. You have your whole life ahead of you. You have a perfect family who wants only good shit for you. What the hell do you want with an older guy who has baggage and commitment issues?"

"You have commitment issues?"

"Darlin', I never stay in one place longer than a few years. My parents fucked me up. I'm always searching for something bigger and better. Looking for that place I can call home and find out where I belong. I've been traveling around for almost ten years, and I still haven't found it."

I wave my arms around, trying my best not to sock him straight in the jaw. "What the fuck was this last week?" My hand flies toward the house. "You just spent an hour charming my family, building the foundation that's necessary to be welcomed into the fold. Now, you're saying you don't have a place, and you want to up and run away like a pussy."

"I'm not being a pussy, Gigi. I'm giving you a

chance to think about if this is what you want. The shit we went through the last few days can fuck with your head and make it hard to think. We were living in the moment, hoping to have more, but now it's over. Shit's gonna settle, and I don't want you to look back and regret the time you spent with me before you up and marry some guy worthy of you."

I scrunch my nose because compared to any pile of horseshit I've ever smelled before, this was far worse. "You've got to be shitting me right now! Why the fuck did you come here if you felt this way?"

"It's not like I had any choice in this," he yells back, throwing his hand toward my grandmother's house. "But I like you, Gigi. Hell, I love you. I'm truly, madly, deeply in fucking love with you, and I don't want to be another mistake in your life. You deserve more than a guy who's good at ink, with a fucked-up family, and not much to offer other than how I feel."

I inhale and slowly exhale, letting all his words seep in. I know this man loves me. He's said those words before. Sure, we were probably about to die, but the possibility of not taking another breath doesn't make a man say shit he isn't feeling.

"Have I ever asked you for anything?"

"No," he says.

"Have I ever forced you to do anything you didn't want to do?"

"No."

"Ever asked you about your bank account and what you could bring to our relationship besides yourself?"

"No."

"You're right, Pike. I'm a lucky girl to be surrounded by all this." I tick my head toward my grandparents' house. "But I could give two shits about money or anything else. My parents taught me about the real important things in life. They taught me about loyalty, love, and most of all, family. I don't care if I'm piss-poor as long as I have someone with me who'll love me and do everything in his power to keep on loving me."

He tips his head back, staring up at the trees. "I'm not a saint. When I look at you—" he glances back down at me "—I see everything that's pure. I see an untouched soul who's had a life of good. And in the short time I've known you, I've brought you a whole lot of bad. I don't want that for you. I don't want you to have a moment's sadness in your life. I never want to see the look on your face I saw the night in my room after I shot that guy. I don't want to know I'm the one who put that look on your face."

"Are you done yet?" I ask, tapping my foot and giving him a dirty look because I'm barely keeping my shit under control.

He nods, not adding more fuel to the wildfire he's already started. I stalk up to him, pressing my fingers into his chest, letting my fingernails dig into the skin underneath his black T-shirt.

"Now it's my turn to talk and for you to shut the fuck up."

He throws up his hands. "I won't…"

I dig a little harder. "My turn, Pike." I glare up at him, and the corners of his lips twitch. "You didn't bring the bad into my life. That was your father's sin, not yours. Stop blaming yourself for shit you couldn't control." He nods, but I keep going because I'm not giving him a second to argue. "As for the look on my face, I didn't care that the bastard who wanted to kill you was lying on that floor, blood oozing from his body."

He scowls. "You didn't?"

I shake my head, twisting my lips. "I kept looking at him, imagining what would've happened if your gun hadn't gone off first. How that could've been you lying on that floor, bleeding everywhere, having taken your last breath." I lean forward, dropping my hand and resting my forehead where I've just poked the hell out of him. "It would've killed me seeing you like that. Do you know how close you came to dying?"

His arms wrap around me, one hand flattening on my back. "But I didn't die, Gigi. We lived. We're standing here, under the sun, listening to the birds sing, just as alive as we were last week when things were normal and you were never in danger."

I slide my fingers under his shirt, running my hands along the soft skin at his sides. "We're standing here because you made sure I lived to see another day. If it weren't for you, I could be dead right now."

He shakes his head. "If it weren't for me, you never would've been in that situation."

"Shut up, Pike." I listen to the slow, steady beat of his heart underneath his shirt. "I've never told another man besides my father that I loved him. I've had a few boyfriends, not many, but they never got the words from me."

"Never?" he asks as I tip my head up, seeing the shock all over his face.

"Never. You know why?"

"Why, darlin'?" he asks softly.

"Because they never got me. All they cared about was getting in my pants. Even Erik, my last boyfriend, I never saw a forever with. He was nice and all, but he didn't have what it takes to be with me for the long haul. My father and uncles would've chewed him up and spat him out. Hell, if someone would've come after us, I'm pretty sure Erik would've hurled me in front of a bullet to save his own ass."

Pike's hands are on my shoulders, pushing me backward so he can look at me. "That's what I'm talking about. You haven't had any good relationships in your life, babe. You can't compare what we have to those guys…and I use that term loosely. Every man you're with should be willing to die for you because you're his girl. You need to explore, sow those oats, before you decide you want a nobody like me in your bed every night."

"Pike, do you really love me?" I whisper, gazing up at him, my nails starting to press into his skin because he's beginning to piss me off again.

"I do," he says quickly.

"Then can you just shut the fuck up and see where this goes? I'm not ready to walk away. I don't want to date someone else, I don't want to find out what good and bad is out there because I've already found something good, someone good, and I don't want to let go because even if I find someone out there who'll love me, they'll never be you."

His hands cup my face, and I melt into his touch, wanting more, always wanting more. "I've never wanted anyone as badly as I want you. I've never felt so at peace with someone as I do you. I've never been surrounded by so much love as I have been with your family, even if they don't like me."

"They like you." I wish he'd shut up and kiss me already, but he doesn't.

"They're tolerating me, hoping I go away."

"Not everyone in that house grew up the way I did. They have pasts and skeletons in their closets too. It didn't change the way my family feels about them. The Gallos judge people on who they are, not what they did or how they grew up. All that matters is that we love one another. The men in my family are protective and overbearing, a little like you, and I know they'll love you and welcome you with open arms when they realize how good we are together."

"Gigi…"

"Pike, just kiss me already. And so help me God, if you try to break my heart again, I'm going to knee you so hard in the balls, you won't be able to sleep with another woman for months."

Pike smirks. "I kind of like my balls, babe."

"Me too." I smile. "Now, you better kiss me, or I'm going to leap into your arms and cause a scene that'll have my dad out here so fast…"

I don't get the rest of the words out before his mouth

crashes down on mine, stealing away the threat I was ready to carry out if necessary.

My hands slide behind his neck as I plaster my body to his, kissing him with all the force I can muster on my tiptoes. I've been waiting hours for a moment alone to feel his lips on mine, tongue sliding inside my mouth, giving me his small moans and the warmth of his body.

"Don't you ever threaten to leave me again," I murmur into his mouth, needing him to say the words.

"Never again," he whispers, pulling back and gazing down at me. "You're mine now, darlin', and I hope you understand what that means."

"I'm hoping it means a lot of dirty shit." I wink, pulling his head down because his lips are looking lonely.

"Gigi. Pike. Dinner," Nonna yells from somewhere in the distance. "Get your bodies untangled and get your asses in here."

Pike rests his forehead against mine, trying to catch his breath as we both gasp for air. "We better go." I know Grandma's still watching and isn't going to go anywhere until we "untangle" ourselves and start marching our asses toward the house. "But we're finishing what we started as soon as we get home."

"Your place or mine?" he asks, waggling his eyebrows with a playful smirk.

"I don't have a bed."

"Darlin', I only need a wall."

Oh. My. God. Fuck yes!

27

PIKE

"Give me ten minutes, and then come over. I'll leave the front door unlocked because I have a surprise for you."

I can't stop the smile on my face as I lean forward, brushing my lips across hers and squeezing her ass. "What kind of surprise, darlin'?"

She bats her eyelashes, smirking. "What kind of surprise would it be if I told you?"

"You're a tease."

She giggles when my fingers find the bottom edge of her jean shorts and my lips slide down to her neck. "Hey," she says, pushing against my chest. "If you don't stop doing that, I won't be able to let you out of my sight, and the entire night will be ruined."

"If I fucked you right now, it would ruin the night?"

She lets out a loud huff. "Well, no, but I want this time to be special."

"Baby, every time with you is special," I murmur against her skin before running my tongue from her ear to her collarbone. "I don't know if I can wait ten minutes."

She tries to wiggle out of my hold, but I grip her thighs, wanting to sink between them even though we're outside. "You waited fifteen months, I think you'll survive another ten minutes," she says, pushing against my chest again. "Please, Pike."

I loosen my grip, allowing her to put space between us. "Well, since you said please. But get your surprise and come to my place. I have a bed."

"And walls too." She winks.

"Walls too, darlin'."

"Okay, I still need ten minutes. I'll grab the surprise and be over."

"Perfect." I try to grab her again, wanting to taste her lips or skin, but she isn't having any of it.

She backs away, shaking her head. "No touching."

I raise an eyebrow. "I hope that isn't part of the surprise because touching is required for what I have in mind."

"There will be touching," she says, still moving toward her front door. "But not until I say so."

"Not until you say so?" My mouth falls open, but I'm totally playing. I know this girl, and she doesn't play hard to get. I also know just the right buttons to push to have her begging for more than my touch.

There's a wicked gleam in her eyes. "Of course. I'm the boss."

"Naturally," I tease, but she is.

I learned today that every woman in her family is the boss too. It doesn't matter how big or tough the man is, his wife has the final say in how things go down. I loved their strength and that their husbands didn't care as long as their women were happy.

"Now, go." She shoos me with one hand and takes her keys out of her back pocket with the other. "I'll be quick."

I throw up my hands and turn toward my door. "I'm going. I'm going."

"Catch ya in ten," she says before disappearing into her apartment.

I step inside my place, flipping on the light and kicking off my boots, thankful as fuck to finally be home and still breathing. I wasn't sure I'd make it back, and after a long-ass day of travel and Gigi's family, I'm happy as shit for a little peace and quiet.

I strip off my clothes as I walk toward the bathroom, needing a shower and a reset after all the bullshit that went down the last few days. I don't waste too much time under the spray because my girl's coming over with a surprise that I'm hoping includes very little clothing and a whole lot of fucking.

After a quick wash, I dry off, pulling on a pair of sweat pants and nothing else. I don't see the need when I don't plan on having clothing on my body for very long.

I glance at the clock, realizing it's been ten minutes, but Gigi's nowhere to be found. I press my ear against our adjoining wall but only hear silence. I wait another minute, pacing a path down my hallway, back and forth between my bedroom and living room.

"You comin'?" I text her because I've never been a patient man.

I take five trips up and down the hallway, turning my phone over in my hand, waiting for her reply, but I get no response.

I'm out the door, knocking on hers. "Gigi!" I yell because it's not like her to promise one thing and do another.

It isn't like she could lie down and accidentally fall asleep. The girl just moved in and doesn't have any furniture in her place.

I try the handle and it's unlocked, but I hesitate for a second because I also don't want to walk in and scare the hell out of her, getting myself kicked in the balls in the process.

"Gigi!" I yell again, pounding louder this time, and when there's no response, I open the door, figuring a kick in the balls is worth knowing she's okay.

My foot connects with something, and it skids across the floor, slamming into the wall. I look over, realizing it's her cell phone, and my heart immediately slams into my chest like a brick.

"Gigi!" I yell again, but I only get my echo back and not another sound.

I frantically look in each room of the tiny space, searching for my girl, but find nothing. My hands are sweating and my heart's beating double time as I push open the door to her bedroom, catching sight of a person's back.

A back that isn't Gigi's.

I lunge for the man, turning him around, laying eyes

on his mask-covered face. His eyes widen, the only part of his face that's visible before I rear back, hurling my fist through the air and connecting with his jaw.

"Pike!" Gigi screams, and I move my eyes toward her voice. She's in the corner, hands at her neck, huddled in a ball, and tears staining her cheeks.

I lay into the man who's staggering in front of me, whaling on him with my fists until he falls to the floor. I kick him in the ribs once, making sure he's out cold before I run to Gigi, kneeling in front of her. Her eyes are wide, and her cheeks are stained with tears.

"Are you okay?" I ask her, lifting her into my lap, checking over her body.

"I'm fine. He was hiding in here when I walked in," she says quickly, whimpering at the memory. "He… He…"

"Did he hurt you?"

She shakes her head and curls into my chest, gripping on to my T-shirt with her long fingers. "He put his hand over my mouth and hauled me back here, but he didn't have a chance to hurt me before you showed up."

"I'm so sorry, baby. I should've been here sooner."

"I'm okay," she whispers like she's trying to convince herself or maybe just me, but by the way she's shaking, I'd say she's anything but okay. "We have to call the police."

"I will in a minute." My priority is making sure she's okay before I let her out of my arms.

"No, Pike. I don't want him waking up and coming after you. My heart can't take any more," she whispers. "Please." She crawls out of my lap, staggering, but catching herself on my shoulder. "I have some packing tape we can use to tie him up."

"You're crafty," I tease because right now, we could use a little lightness in our fucked-up week.

"You have no idea." She smiles, wiping away the tears from her cheeks. "I'll grab the tape, and you check the guy." She's out of the room before I have a chance to rise to my feet.

"Let's see who you are, motherfucker." I hunch down next to the man's face, staring at the asshole who went after my girl.

Gigi's back, holding a roll of packing tape, eyes pinned on the lifeless body on the floor. "You didn't kill him, did you?"

I shake my head and laugh, reaching for the man's mask. "Darlin', I may be strong, but my punch didn't kill him."

"Thank God," she mumbles.

When I pull the mask from his face, I'm knocked backward, falling on my ass.

"What's wrong?"

I shake my head, blinking like my brain doesn't believe what my eyes are seeing. "It's my father."

Thank you for reading FLAME. I hope you loved Gigi and Pike as much as I do! **Their story continues in Burn, Men of Inked Heatwave #2.**

ARE YOU READY FOR MORE?
PREORDER YOUR COPY OF **BURN** NOW

It's going to be another ***wild*** ride…
menofinked.com/burn

Want to know when the next Men of Inked book releases?
Join my VIP newsletter or get a Text Notification sent directly to your phone. Text **GALLOS** to **24587**
**US Only…Sorry!

Want more Men of Inked?

There's two series with the Gallos and they're waiting to be devoured.

Want to read the ORIGINAL Men of Inked series and meet City, Anthony, Thomas, James, Mike, and more? Check out the Throttle Me and get to know the other side of the Gallo family. **One-click Throttle Me and read now—It's FREE!**

If you love James, Thomas, and men of ALFA Investigations. **Download your FREE copy of Sinful Intent here!** The series is sexy and suspenseful and filled with your favorite characters too!

Visit ***menofinked.com/books*** to learn more about Chelle Bliss books.

And don't forget to sign up for my newsletter to find out about new books and special members only goodies… *TAP HERE to sign up now!*

You can also join my Facebook group, *Chelle Bliss Books*, for exclusive giveaways and sneak peeks of future books.

Do you LOVE audiobooks?

Flame is NOW available in audiobook. Visit menofinked.com/flame for more information.

Plus, my entire audiobook collection is available on your favorite retailer or online local library.

Visit *menofinked.com/audio-bm* to see where you can get your next favorite listen. Plus, while you're there… listen to a FREE audiobook too!

Get a Text Audio Alert
Text **AUDIO** to **24587**
USA Only

Join my audio only newsletter and get the latest audiobook news and special giveaways!
Join here: menofinked.com/audionews

ABOUT THE AUTHOR

Chelle hails from the Midwest, but currently lives near the beach even though she hates sand. She's a full-time writer, time-waster extraordinaire, social media addict, coffee fiend, and ex history teacher.

She loves spending time with her two cats, alpha boyfriend, and chatting with readers. To learn more about Chelle, please visit menofinked.com or chellebliss.com.

Want special perks?
JOIN MY NEWSLETTER and get access to the Members Only section on my website. Special Discounts, Free eBooks, and so much more!

Get Text Notifications sent directly to your phone (US only)
➔ Text **GALLOS** to **24587**

JOIN MY PRIVATE GROUP

WHERE TO FOLLOW CHELLE:

WEBSITE | TWITTER | FACEBOOK | INSTAGRAM

Want to drop me a line?
authorchellebliss@gmail.com
menofinked.com

facebook.com/authorchellebliss1
bookbub.com/authors/chelle-bliss
instagram.com/authorchellebliss
twitter.com/ChelleBliss1

MEN OF INKED: HEATWAVE SERIES

Same Family. New Generation.

- Book 1 - Flame (Gigi)
- Book 2 - Burn (Gigi)

MEN OF INKED: SOUTHSIDE SERIES

Join the Chicago Gallo Family with their strong alphas, sassy women, and tons of fun.

- Book 1 - Maneuver (Lucio)
- Book 2 - Flow (Daphne)
- Book 3 - Hook (Angelo)
- Book 4 - Hustle (Vinnie)
- Book 5 - Love (Angelo)

MEN OF INKED SERIES

"One of the sexiest series of all-time" -Bookbub Reviewers

Download book 1 for FREE!

- Book 1 - Throttle Me (Joe aka City)
- Book 2 - Hook Me (Mike)
- Book 3 - Resist Me (Izzy)
- Book 4 - Uncover Me (Thomas)
- Book 5 - Without Me (Anthony)
- Book 6 - Honor Me (City)
- Book 7 - Worship Me (Izzy)

ALFA INVESTIGATIONS SERIES

Wickedly hot alphas with tons of heart pounding suspense!

- Book 1 - Sinful Intent (Morgan)
- Book 2 - Unlawful Desire (Frisco)
- Book 3 - Wicked Impulse (Bear)
- Book 4 - Guilty Sin (Ret)

SINGLE READS

- Mend
- Enshrine
- Misadventures of a City Girl
- Misadventures with a Speed Demon
- Rebound (Flash aka Sam)
- Top Bottom Switch (Ret)

NAILED DOWN SERIES

- Book 1 - Nailed Down
- Book 2 - Tied Down
- Book 3 - Kneel Down

TAKEOVER DUET

What happens when you sleep with your biggest enemy?

- Book 1 - Acquisition
- Book 2 - Merger

FILTHY SERIES

- Dirty Work

- Dirty Secret
- Dirty Defiance

LOVE AT LAST SERIES

- Book 1 - Untangle Me
- Book 2 - Kayden

BOX SETS & COLLECTIONS

- Men of Inked Volume 1
- Men of Inked Volume 2
- Love at Last Series
- ALFA Investigations Series
- Filthy Series
- Takeover Duet

View Chelle's entire collection of books at menofinked.com/books

To learn more about Chelle's books visit *menofinked.com* or *chellebliss.com*

ACKNOWLEDGMENTS

I always get to this part of the book and suddenly draw a blank. There's so many people who help bring a book to life and someday, when I have my shit together, I'll make a list along the way. But… that day isn't today.

First, to my beta group — thanks for being quicker than usual, although still not fast enough for my bitchy self. I know you ladies are waiting ever so patiently, not really but I'll go with that lie, for the continuation of Pike and Gigi. It's coming…Soon. I swear.

Lisa, my lovely editor, you're the best. You deal with my crazy shit on the daily. You have given up on trying to teach this old dog new tricks, which makes me happier than a pig in shit. Someday, I'll hand in a cleaner manuscript, but until then…just keep loving me like I love you.

Rosa, Julie, and Rose — thank you for proofing Flame and loving Gigi and Pike as much as I do. Your hard work and quick turn around helped make this entire project smooth as silk. You're the best type of humans.

Dylan Horsch and Aaron Rogers — thanks for the kickass photo and allowing me to have it for the cover of Flame. It's the perfect vision for Pike. You nailed his look and it's my most favorite cover ever.

Brian, my guy, thanks for putting up with my shit, because we know it's a lot, and giving me plenty of time to bring Pike and Gigi to life. You're my FLAME.

Who else am I missing? Probably dozens of people because I'm lame.

Bloggers and reviewers — You're all rockstars. Thank you for taking time out of your busy day to read Flame and help share the fabulousness of the Gallos with the world.

Printed in Great Britain
by Amazon